THE MYSTERY OF
THE GOLDEN GOBLET

A HARDLY BOYS ADVENTURE

By
TOM CHERONES

Tom

Port Hole Publications
Florence, Oregon

ISBN-13: 978-0-9827627-9-0
ISBN-10: 0-9827627-9-8
Copyright 2012 by Tom Cherones
All Rights Reserved
Published by Port Hole Publications, Florence, OR
Cover and interior images: Terry Dodson

A NOTE FROM THE AUTHOR

This book is a parody of *The Hardy Boys*, an adventure series for boys that began in 1927, ran through the 1930s and beyond, and even continues to be published today. Written under the pen name of Franklin W. Dixon, the series is actually the product of many authors, and was originated by Edward Stratemeyer.

I was a fan of the boys as a youngster. I moved on to Sherlock Holmes, Perry Mason, Nero Wolfe and other fictional detectives and have enjoyed reading mysteries all my life.

As an adult I have collected and reread many of the original Hardy Boys books and still enjoy them.

These heroes were 17-year-old boys. That worked when I was a kid but now I wanted my heroes to be more like me. Nero Wolf was fat. Perry Mason was a lawyer. The Hardy Boys were still the best, but my heroes should be my age. So, I invented the *Hardly* Boys, 70-year old men with the hearts and minds of teenage boys.

When my heroes are released from "cryogeriatric" captivity, they want to pick up where they left off more than 50 years before, to finish high school and be detectives like their still active 95-year-old dad. As 70 year-olds living among modern teenagers, they are the ultimate "fish out of water" in just about everything they do.

This book was a great deal of fun to write, as I created a couple of old guys still young at heart.

I had a lot of help from friends and family and I'd

like to thank a few of them for their contributions to my story: my wife, Carol Richards, for her help and encouragement; my friends Anne Gibbons, Bill Fitts, John Richards and Holly Azzari for their ideas and corrections.

I hope you enjoy the book and I recommend that you reread an old "Hardy Boys" or "Nancy Drew" book for the fun of it.

Tom Cherones
September 2012

CONTENTS

Coach Thomas took his stalwart quarterback Tom Hardly
aside to give desperate, last-ditch instructions.

CHAPTER I

The Speeding Sedan

The game was not going well. Baymoor High trailed the Greely eleven by six points late in the fourth quarter.

Coach Thomas took his stalwart quarterback Tom Hardly aside to give desperate, last-ditch instructions. The senior paid close attention to his coach as the other players awaited his return to the huddle. Whit Moore, the burly center, nearly prostrate from the activity of the close game, chatted breathlessly with Tom's younger brother, Billy.

This time-out on the field is undoubtedly a good time to introduce our boys.

Tom and Billy Hardly, along with their chum Whit Moore had only recently been released from captivity. They had been held at a secret location in suspended animation for more than fifty years by a group of evil scientists whose leader, Neils Wasserburg, they had sent to prison while helping their dad on a highly classified government case. Wasserburg had invented a process he called cryogeriatrics in which the subject was preserved in a near-frozen state, but while the mind was preserved unchanged, the body aged at almost the normal rate. The cryo container was designed to exercise their bodies to maintain muscle tone.

"We were human Popsicles," Whit liked to say.

Because of Wasserburg's diabolical device, when

the Hardly boys and Whit Moore were finally released from the cryogeriatric capsules, their bodies had aged more than fifty years. But, just as Wasserburg had planned, their minds remained the same as when they were placed into suspended animation. They were teenaged boys in the bodies of healthy seventy-year-old men.

"It was like that Mel Gibson movie," Miss Jane had said.

"Who," asked Tom, "is Mel Gibson?"

Even though more than forty years had passed since Neils Wasserburg had died, his dastardly schemes and evil plots had not been forgotten by the good citizens of Baymoor. When the three boys, as they still thought of themselves, returned to their hometown, they were accorded a hero's welcome, complete with a parade. Baymoor was proud of its native sons and the townspeople wanted the boys to know it.

Despite their chronological age, the Hardly boys decided to finish their senior year in high school so they could resume their lives where they had left off. Even though they had been back a few months, they were still in a fog about computers, cell phones, color TV, jet planes, and other aspects of life in the twenty-first century.

The boys' mother, Hazel Hardly, had preserved their vehicles and keepsakes from their many adventures, in a storage shed. She had been confident the boys would return one day and could not be persuaded to sell any of their gear or donate it to charity. "No," she had said time and again when someone pointed out how unlikely it was that her sons would ever be seen again, "they'll be back. I feel it in my bones."

When the boys did return, she took great pleasure in having what she called "opening day." She invited all the townsfolk to join the Hardly family at the storage unit where the boys' motorcycles, roadster, airplane, mahogany speedboat, commemorative plaques, and police commendations had been carefully preserved. Everyone who was able took advantage of the invitation. The Hardlys were well liked by the townspeople and a spontaneous round of applause broke out as the door was pulled open and Tom and Billy stepped into the unit.

"Wow!" exclaimed Tom when he saw his beloved biplane sitting there in perfect condition. "This is really swell, Mom!" The boys embraced their ninety-year-old mother in a double bear hug. "You are the best mom in the world," exclaimed Billy.

The beloved mother beamed as she pulled three fresh drivers' licenses from her pocket. "The police had these specially made for all you boys," she said. "They even waived the driving test, saying you had always been law-abiding, and they expected you had not lost your road savvy."

She handed the glossy licenses to Tom, Billy and Whit, who took them with eager gratefulness.

Tom and Billy, sons of the internationally famous detective DeVern Hardly, were quite respected in their own right as amateur detectives. DeVern Hardly had retired from the New York City Police Department many years before in order to open his own private detective agency in the small town of Baymoor on Welsley Bay, not far from New York City. In those days, the boys' mother, Hazel, could generally be found awaiting a phone call to let her know that her menfolk had once again escaped from the clutches of some dastardly villain and would soon be home. Sometimes she made pimento cheese sandwiches for the boys or a picnic lunch for them to share with their chums.

Miss Jane Hardly, DeVern's spinster sister, who lived with her brother and his wife, was often gruff and disapproving of the boys' proclivity for getting into danger, but she really loved them. She spent much of her time making pies and cookies or preparing their favorite meals.

Back on the football field, Tom returned quickly to the huddle with a trick play designed by Coach Thomas. With only seconds to go and the ball on their own 17-yard line, the Baymoor team had to make the play work. The stout center, Whit, snapped the ball to Tom, who lateralled to the left halfback, Billy, who then dropped back to throw a pass to Tom, who had eluded the entire Greely eleven and was lumbering down the field. Billy reared back and tossed the pigskin to the elusive quarterback for a touchdown. The crowd was in a frenzy as Marshall Johnson drove home the final point to seal the victory for the hometown squad.

Tom and Billy Hardly retired to the locker room to change into street clothes and head out with their friends to celebrate this unlikely football victory. Tom, seventy, was as dark complected as Billy, sixty-nine, was fair. Although they were no longer physically youngsters, the brothers were as eager as ever to follow in their famous father's footsteps as professional detectives. Their devoted mother still had hopes that they would attend college and become lawyers or doctors. The boys, however, were determined to continue solving mysteries, as they had before being captured and cryogeriatrically incarcerated by Wasserburg. They expected to help out their famous father, who was ninety-five, by taking on cases that he was unable to handle while he was away on important government assignments. Offers of work came to the Hardly home even when DeVern Hardly was away on far-flung missions.

As the brothers left the locker room, they yelled back to their friend Whit to hurry up. The portly lad finished off the bag of potato chips he had stashed in his locker as emergency rations, and hurried after his chums. Whit, seventy, was renowned throughout Baymoor for his hearty appetite. His fifty-year sleep in the cryogeriatric deep freeze had done nothing to take the edge off his seemingly insatiable desire for food.

Waiting to celebrate the team's rousing victory with the boys were Whit's sister, Anne, sixty-eight, and her friend Jessa Sheridan, sixty-nine. Tom was known to have special feelings for Jessa, and Billy often said that, for a girl, Anne was "OK." Jessa, who had had faith that Tom would return one day, had never married. Anne had married as a young woman but had been widowed several years ago.

When the boys caught their reflections in mirrors and windows, they were always shocked at their physical appearance. The faces looking back at them were of grown, even elderly, men. But in their own minds, they were still teenagers—and seeing their friends and former classmates had also been a shock. Anne and Jessa were still pretty and as sweet as they had been as young girls. But Anne's long hair, which she pulled back in a loose bun at the base of her neck, was more silver now than blond. Jessa's dark auburn hair, worn short and curly, was streaked with gray.

Whit pulled up to the Hardly house in his brightly colored jalopy and the exultant group hopped in the car for a trip to the drugstore for ice cream and malts. They were bumping along the coast road at a good clip when suddenly a large sedan, its horn honking loudly, passed them at such high speed that they were nearly blown off the road. As the car disappeared in the direction of town, the gang regained their composure.

Billy said, "We should turn those hooligans in to the police, I'll be bound."

"I got the license number," said Tom. "Let's stop at police headquarters and report this incident to Chief Langly before they kill someone."

At the police station, the group stood anxiously by while Chief Langly waited to learn the registration details on the dangerous vehicle. Seated at his massive wooden desk, the Chief was doodling on a sheet of paper, the phone held closely to his ear. Suddenly he sat up straight in his swivel chair. "What? What?!" The Chief's face turned ashen at the news he was receiving.

"I see." Without another word he hung up the phone.

"You folks are going to have to run along now," said the Chief, as he walked out of the room. "I'm getting too old for this stuff," muttered the forty-something officer.

The Hardlys and their friends left the police station and headed for the drugstore. They placed their orders and took them to a large booth in the corner where they settled in to enjoy their ice cream. They ate for a while in silence, each of them pondering the scene they had just witnessed at the police station.

When the girls left for the powder room, Tom mused aloud, "I wonder why the Chief wouldn't tell us what he learned about the owner of the speeding sedan?"

"What's the big secret anyway?" blustered Whit, who had just ordered his third banana split.

"I've never seen the Chief so closed-mouthed," said Billy. "I wish Dad were in town. I'll bet he could find out the answer."

Jessa and Anne returned to the table. "Let's get a few friends together and have a picnic tomorrow," suggested Jessa.

"It's Saturday, so no school for you boys," said Anne with a smile.

"That's a great idea," exulted Tom, "Let's just try to forget about the speeding sedan and enjoy the weekend."

The plan was made. The boys would bring their speedboats and the girls would pack a lunch. They agreed to meet at 10:00 a.m. at Rustler's Cove.

Saturday dawned bright and sunny with not a cloud in the sky. Rustler's Cove had been the site of many good times for the group in the past. A sandy beach was perfect as a landing spot for the mahogany boats.

Marco Remo arrived in his boat, the *Capri,* with Marshall Johnson and Marco's sister Sophia. Billy and Tom sped quickly to the beach in their boat, the *Flatfoot,* while Whit drove Anne and Jessa to the rendezvous in his yellow roadster.

Although Marco, Marshall, and Sophia were teenagers, they had enjoyed getting to know the three older guys and hearing tales of their exploits when they had been youngsters themselves. Marco was fond of saying that listening to Whit and the Hardly boys was better than watching the History Channel.

The teenagers had welcomed Anne and Jessa into their group. As Jessa, Anne, and Sophia spread out the repast, the boys went for a refreshing dip in Welsley Bay. Billy challenged the pals to a race to the channel buoy a few hundred yards away. Taking the dare to heart, the chums began the race in earnest. Tom teased his rotund cohort Whit, calling him a "whale with feet." Whit responded by taking the lead in the race for the buoy. In spite of his rotund body, Whit was a gifted swimmer and led for a few strokes until Tom and Billy sped by their fat friend to finish in a tie. Marco and Marshall quickly joined the other three.

"You guys are really something," Marco said as he caught his breath. "I hope I'm in such good shape when I'm your age."

As the boys clung to the bobbing buoy, a speeding

boat careened uncomfortably close, sending a large wash of salty water over their heads. The wayward craft was much larger than the boys' boats, its powerful twin engines roaring in unison as it passed the startled swimmers.

Whit exclaimed, "The man piloting that boat looks like the driver of the speeding sedan."

"You're right," agreed Billy. "And I think they splashed us on purpose. Let's keep an eye on that boat, see where it lands."

Tom was boosted up on the rim of the bobbing buoy for a better view of the speeding craft. "It's headed into the Lockjaw River's inlet," he proclaimed. "Let's go after them."

The boys swam quickly to their boats. "We'll take the *Flatfoot*," said Tom. He did not need to remind the others that it had proven in a recent race to be a superior watercraft to Marco's *Capri*.

The girls looked up in surprise as all five chums piled into the Hardly boys' boat. "It's the driver of the speeding sedan," Tom shouted to them. "Don't wait for us."

"What sedan?" asked a startled Sophia. "Where are they going? Aren't they coming back for lunch?"

Jessa was calmly gathering up the sandwiches, salad, fruit, and desserts that the girls had prepared for lunch and putting them back in the wicker baskets. With a small sigh Anne began helping her as she explained to Sophia about the sedan that had nearly run them off the road the day before.

"That's right," said Jessa. "I doubt the boys will be

back this afternoon." She carefully replaced the plaid thermos of lemonade in its slot in the largest basket. "When the Hardly boys and Whit are in hot pursuit of miscreants, they are not easily distracted," she explained to the puzzled Sophia. "And I'm certain Marco and Marshall will be equally enthusiastic.

"So I think," continued Jessa, as she closed up the last picnic basket, "we might as well save this lunch for another time. I hope they nab those spoilers!"

With Tom at the helm, the *Flatfoot* soon arrived at the mouth of the river. Tom knew to be careful as he and his adventurous chums headed into the Lockjaw River in search of the offending vessel.

"We'll find those ruffians soon," he declared. "That boat is just too big to go very far upriver."

Tom powered down the sturdy craft as the boys, two on each side of the boat, looked for their quarry. A startled covey of wood ducks skimmed over the boys' heads as Tom nimbly steered the boat in and out of hidden coves. A water snake slithered by the *Flatfoot,* rewarding the lads with a close look at its shiny skin, but the outlaw boat was nowhere in sight.

Finally, as the boys motored into the port of Baymoor, they spied the object of their search tied up at the pier. Tom moored his craft near the *Lizzie Borden.*

"What a strange name for a boat," Whit remarked.

"It sure is," said Marshall, as the others nodded agreement.

They had moored in the smarmiest section of Baymoor's famous waterfront.

"Let's have a look in that sleazy bar," said Marco.

"I'm loath to step into that dive," Tom replied.

"Egad, Tom," blurted Billy, "you're the oldest. Go on in." Billy continued with a hint of disdain in his voice, "The boys and I will keep watch out here."

Tom Hardly entered the riverside watering hole known as the Thirsty Eye. He stood for a moment in the smoky entryway, his eyes adjusting to the dim light. It was hard to make out details of the shadowy forms sitting on worn barstools and at tables strewn with peanut shells in the nautically themed bar.

As Tom peered at the clientele, he approached the bar. "What'll it be?" queried the barkeep, who had been out of sight restocking clean glasses beneath the bar.

Surprised by the man's sudden appearance, Tom was somewhat taken aback but quickly recovered his composure. "I'll have a sarsaparilla."

The bartender stared at Tom. "A root beer?"

Tom nodded.

"You want a shot of bourbon on the side, old man?"

"No," replied Tom. "I'm not old enough to drink."

"You're what?!" said the startled bartender. "You sure look old enough to me."

"I'm much younger than I look. Just get me a sarsaparilla, please."

The bartender eyed Tom scornfully. "One root beer coming up."

Tom accepted the bottle of root beer and asked if anyone had entered the establishment in the last fifteen minutes.

"You a local fella, ain't you," said the man behind the bar. "I seen you in church last Sunday."

Tom introduced himself. "And you are . . . ?"

"I'm Sonny Stufflebean," replied the man, "and ain't nobody come in here in o'er an hour, and ain't nobody left neither."

The elder Hardly brother saw Sonny's eyes shift quickly toward the stairway leading to the second floor. He's lying, thought Tom. "OK, Mr. Stufflebean, thanks," said Tom as he put a dime on the bar for his drink.

"That'll be two dollars," said Stufflebean. "You don't get out much, do ya?"

Tom was momentarily blinded by the sunlight as he returned to his friends outside. "The bartender's name is Sonny Stufflebean. He said no one has come into the bar within the last hour, but I'm sure he was lying. They're here," Tom continued, "but they're in hiding. We'd better see Chief Langly."

As the boys turned in the direction of the police station, they ran smack into Officer Harry Hunnicut who was patrolling the waterfront. "You boys lost?" said the burly officer. Tom, knowing that Hunnicut, a bit slow witted, would be no help in their search for the elusive boatmen, and aware of the policeman's proclivity for long-winded conversations, laughed and replied that they were on a picnic. The officer looked around slightly puzzled, then shrugged his massive shoulders. "Well, if you don't want to tell me what you're up to, I guess I'll just get on with my duties." He patted his sidearm as if to reassure himself that it was still there and walked on.

The Hardly boys and their friends headed quickly to the police station, where the desk sergeant was frowning over the crossword puzzle from that day's newspaper. "What's a six-letter word for 'toy orb?'" he asked when he saw Tom standing at his desk.

"Marble," answered the older Hardly boy. "But we're working on another puzzle. Is the Chief in?"

Sergeant Blith had met the Hardly boys several times, and he knew their father had helped the police department on numerous occasions. Suspecting that Chief Zack Langly would want to see them immediately, he knocked on the door and ushered the boys into the Chief's office.

With his back to the door, Langly stood stock-still, left arm raised above his head, a tattered flyswatter in his hand. A ceiling fan whirred softly. Suddenly, with a flick of the wrist, Chief Langly slapped the flyswatter down on the corner of his desk. "Got 'im!" Using the flyswatter to slide the carcass of the pesky insect onto a piece of newspaper, he crumpled the paper and tossed it into the trash can beside his desk. Only then did he turn to see who had entered the room.

"Hello, boys," he said. "Hot, isn't it?"

"Hot indeed," said Tom. "And we have some hot news to relay."

With only an occasional interruption from one of the others, Tom related the story of the speeding boat and the chums' search for the scoundrels in the Lockjaw River inlet. He recounted how they had found the *Lizzie Borden* tied up in a run-down part of town and how he had questioned the bartender and was certain he was lying. "The men from the boat were in the Thirsty Eye," asserted Tom. "I'm sure of it."

"And," Billy chimed in, "we think the helmsman was the same man who was driving the speeding sedan that nearly ran us off the road."

The blood drained from the Chief's usually florid face. The five chums glanced at each other in surprise as the Chief swallowed twice and then cleared his throat. "Boys," Zack Langly muttered as he eyed Tom and Billy Hardly, "I wish your dad were in town. I could use his help with this problem."

Sensing an opportunity to convince the Chief of their own considerable investigative abilities, Tom and Billy quickly seized the moment, pleading their case as competent detectives.

"I don't know," said the outmatched Chief. "This is a very dangerous situation."

All five boys were naturally intrigued by this admission. "Let us in on it, Chief," said Tom, the group's usual spokesperson. "We've been harassed twice by these hooligans."

The Chief's swivel chair squeaked as he leaned back, gazing upward, perhaps hoping to find the answer he sought in the cracked and patched ceiling. In a moment he sat up straight. He looked at Marco, Marshall, Whit, Billy, and Tom in turn, then nodded to himself. "All right. Sit down. I know I can trust you boys," said Zack Langly, "and I'll tell you a story."

The lads looked around the office but saw only two

chairs. They exchanged glances and continued to stand. The Chief, staring off into space as if trying to decide where to begin, didn't notice the boys' awkward situation. Leaning back in his chair once again, the Chief furrowed his brow and began his tale of stolen treasure.

"At the end of WWII—"

"We were just kids," said Tom. "Sorry, Chief. I didn't mean to interrupt."

The Chief acknowledged Tom's apology with a nod and began his story again: "At the end of WWII, the Nazis stole a golden goblet encrusted with jewels of all sorts: diamonds, sapphires, rubies, emeralds, and the occasional garnet." He paused, looking first at Tom then at Billy. "Your dad can tell you the story of how the stolen goblet was tracked down and taken back from the Nazis. What's important now is that the goblet is safely housed here in Baymoor. Has been since 1947, when Cyrus M. Rosenfeld bequeathed it to the Baymoor Museum. He moved away after graduating from high school. Made a fortune in aluminum wire and plastics, but he always had a soft spot in his heart for his hometown."

The Chief had the boys' full attention. "You said you encountered Officer Hunnicut down at the wharf. He has been assigned to keep an eye on Sonny Stufflebean and his skuzzy bar. There have been some suspicious characters in the neighborhood of the Thirsty Eye and we think Stufflebean may be fencing stolen property."

Billy interjected, "Pray tell, Chief, what more do

you know?"

The Chief looked at the boys without seeing them as he gathered his thoughts and resumed talking. "We think there might be a connection—"

"Chief! Chief!" Officer Hunnicut burst into the room without knocking. He stopped just inside the office, leaning forward, hands on his knees, and took in great gulps of air.

"Calm down, Hunnicut," Langly admonished. "Catch your breath, then tell me what's the problem."

"But, Chief," Hunnicut gasped. "They've taken it. The golden goblet is missing and they're gone in that boat!"

The Chief stood up quickly. As usual his gun belt was hanging on a scuffed wooden coat rack behind his desk. He reached for the belt, strapped it on, and was ready for action. "Boys," he admitted, "I need your help."

The five chums needed no urging to join the fray. "How can we help, Chief?" asked Tom.

"I'm gonna deputize you fellows," he said. "Since we don't have a police boat, I want you to take me in the *Flatfoot* for a look around."

"If you're waiting on us," replied Billy, "you're backing up."

The boys were quickly sworn in as Baymoor deputies and soon they were crowded into the *Flatfoot* along with the Chief and Officer Hunnicut. At the helm, Tom pushed the starter. Nothing happened. He tried again. Nothing. A quick examination revealed that the distributor cap had been stolen.

"Boys," said Langly, "that goblet has been in the safe keeping of the Baymoor Museum for more than fifty years. This is a real black eye for the town."

"We'll get the goblet back," said Tom Hardly resolutely.

But he had no idea what was about to transpire.

CHAPTER II

The Air Search

Fearing the loss of time, the Hardlys suggested that an air search might be helpful. Before they had been captured and cryogeriatrically preserved, Tom and Billy had saved the money they earned from their many exploits and bought a two-seater surplus Army Air Corps trainer. It was a beautiful blue and yellow Stearman biplane. Billy was still training to be a pilot; Tom had already earned his wings.

For two hours that Saturday afternoon, the stout fellows scoured the countryside, flying over water, then land and back again. They had no luck spotting either the sedan or the *Lizzie Borden.*

"I'll be dogged," exclaimed Billy as Tom turned the plane toward home and headed back to the Baymoor airdrome. As they were crossing Pirates Field, near the coast, shots rang out.

"Criminy!" yelled Billy leaning out of his seat. "There are holes in the wings!"

"Hang on!" Tom said as he pushed the throttle forward and made a controlled dive for the safety of the RTR Singleton Airport.

Once they were on the ground, Tom and Billy surveyed the damage. Several bullets had ripped through the fabric of the biplane's wings. Billy put a finger through one of the holes and whistled softly. "These guys mean business."

"You're right, Billy. Let's go into the airport office

and call Chief Langly."

When the Chief came on the line Tom lost no time in explaining what had happened. "We've been shot at," he said.

"I want you off the case right now," said Zack Langly. "You'll get killed. And then what would I tell your mother and father. And your aunt! She would strip the hide off me if I let any harm come to you boys."

"No sir," replied Tom, "we're in it now. We're going to get these villains and recover the goblet."

The Chief's arguments were to no avail. The boys were resolute. "Justice will out," said Billy.

When Chief Langly got off the phone with Tom he sat for a moment then shouted through the open door to Sergeant Blith. "Did you find me that phone number for DeVern Hardly?"

Blith appeared in the office with a Post-it note in his hand. "Yes sir. Here it is. Mr. Hardly is in the Grand Tetons. That's in Wyoming."

"I know where the Grand Tetons are," said Langly. "Just give me the number and close the door on your way out."

Chief Langly finally reached DeVern Hardly, who was working on a hush-hush government job out West. He told him about the missing goblet, about Tom's encounter with Sonny Stufflebean at the Thirsty Eye, and about how he had deputized Tom and Billy. Then he took a deep breath. "DeVern, here's the worst of it. Your boys went out in their plane this afternoon looking for those villains, and they were shot at! There were holes in the wings of the biplane. I am worried nearly to death. What would I say to Miss Jane if anything happened to them?"

DeVern Hardly spoke soothingly to the Chief. "Miss Jane does dote on those boys, Zack. But I wouldn't worry if I were you. They can take care of themselves. And in the unlikely event any harm did come to them, it's the bad guys she'd go after, not you." The Chief thought he heard DeVern Hardly chuckling as he hung up the phone.

"Those Hardlys," he muttered to himself. "You'd think DeVern might not want Tom and Billy to put themselves in harm's way again so soon after their return. Oh well, no one can say I didn't warn him. And, with those budget cuts, I can sure use the help."

Armed with the famous detective's approval, Chief Langly was emboldened to call at the house on Baker Street that evening.

Miss Jane opened the door. "Welcome Chief, come in," she said. "I've just made some fresh pastries." The Chief was known to have a sweet tooth. He walked back to the Hardlys' comfortable kitchen, where Miss Jane served him a slice of her justly famous blueberry pie and a large piece of chocolate cake.

"I'm here," he said, digging into the moist cake with his fork, "to see Tom and Billy."

"What are they up to now?" she asked. But she didn't wait for a reply. "I'll get them." She pushed open the kitchen door and called for her nephews. "Tom, Billy, the Chief is here to see you." She let the door swing shut behind her and went back to loading the dishwasher.

As Tom and Billy entered the room, Chief Langly stood up. "I talked to your dad today," he said. "He's given me permission to enlist your aid in retrieving the golden goblet."

The boys spoke in unison. "We're ready!"

"What do you need us to do?" asked Tom.

The Chief sat back down at the table and took another bite of cake. He looked thoughtful as he chewed. "What do you think about another air search?" asked the Chief.

"I think it might prove fruitful," Tom replied.

Billy nodded. "If we go to the early morning church service tomorrow, we can be up in the air by nine o'clock."

"Right you are," said Tom. "Enjoy the rest of your dessert, Chief. We've got homework to finish if we're to go chasing villains tomorrow. Going back to school after fifty years is harder than we thought it would be. At least they put us in the same class to avoid more disruptions."

"I told you so," said Jane Hardly over her shoulder. "I told you—"

"But you didn't tell us not to take our slide rules to class, did you?" said Billy.

"Slide rules?" exclaimed the Chief. "Slide rules!"

"You might have warned us about that, Miss Jane. How were we to know nobody uses slide rules anymore?" The memory of that day still rankled the younger Hardly boy. "We looked like idiots in math class."

"True," said the more easygoing Tom. "We did.

But our math teacher thought we were fat city. He had us demonstrate how a slide rule works to all his classes that day." Tom grinned at the Chief. "Billy did not think that was at all cool."

"You got that right," grumbled Billy.

"OK," said Tom, taking his brother by the arm and pulling him toward the hall. "Let's go take a look at our English homework."

The Chief was still chuckling as the Hardly boys climbed the stairs to their rooms.

Mrs. Hardly had kept the boys' rooms intact while they were missing. After a few weeks of belated reunion with their belongings, each boy had swapped out his 1940s bed, desk, and chair for more modern furniture. Tom, a bit handier than Billy with screwdriver and hammer, had selected Ikea furnishings. He quickly became adept at using the small but indispensible Allen wrench with which almost all Ikea purchases could be assembled. Billy, on the other hand, was an avid convert to the world of computers. He had bought an iMac and, having discovered the joys of "point and click" shopping, had spent one afternoon exploring online furniture stores and furnished his entire bedroom in a couple of hours of Internet shopping.

Most of the movie posters and sports memorabilia that had adorned the brothers' bedrooms were given away to Goodwill or simply discarded, but each boy had kept one or two favorites. Tom had kept a baseball signed by Mel Ott and a New York Giants pennant. He had been distraught to learn that his beloved Giants had moved to the West Coast in 1957. Billy had refused to give up his poster of *Rebel Without a Cause,* declaring that though he adored the twenty-first-century singer-songwriter Amy Lee, whom he had discovered while browsing the Internet, Natalie Wood had been his first love and would always hold a special place in his heart.

Learning just how much music had changed from the 1940s and early '50s to the twenty-first century had stunned Tom and Billy and their friend Whit. "We went to sleep to the sounds of the Andrews Sisters and Perry Como," Whit said, "and woke up to Lady Gaga and Usher." Though they retained a nostalgic fondness for big band music and what they were surprised to hear called "the oldies," all three boys quickly embraced the contemporary music scene to which their new high school friends introduced them.

Billy was fond of saying that he had fallen in love with Amy Lee at "first listen." "And then I saw her," he would add. "If she weren't too old for me, I would seriously consider trying to woo her away from her husband." One of Billy's bedroom walls was covered with posters of Amy Lee and her band Evanescence. Tom and Whit agreed with Billy that she was "lovely" but could not be brought to admit that she was "the most beautiful singer—face and voice—who ever lived."

Both Billy and Tom had quickly become Netflix fans, though Tom spent far less time than Billy watching movies and TV shows. "It's homework in a way," protested Billy when Tom scolded him for spending so much time in front of the computer screen viewing shows from his instant queue. "My assignment is to get caught up on what we missed the past fifty years—and Netflix is helping me accomplish that."

"Seems to me it's as much detriment as boon," Tom said. "You're not even getting the modern expressions right. 'She's got tissues' indeed."

"You thought it made sense," Billy countered. "And she *did* have tissues. She was crying."

"Whatever," said Tom with an exaggerated shrug.

Billy had thrown a pillow at him and the conversation had disintegrated into a brief wrestling match that ended abruptly when Miss Jane appeared in the doorway, arms akimbo and mouth pursed.

"You boys are old enough to know better than to roughhouse indoors. If you're going to play like that, go outside."

The brothers made their peace and went outside to play catch.

At 9:00 a.m. the Hardly boys clambered into their biplane and headed for the skies. The airport mechanic had repaired the bullet holes—no real damage had been done to the fabric-covered craft. Tom took the plane in wider and wider circles, swooping in and out of valleys and down low over boats in the rivers and ocean. The boys found no trace of the elusive crooks.

"Jiminy" said Billy. "I fear we'll never find these guys."

"Not to worry" opined Tom. "It's too early to concede defeat. I'm confident we'll soon snare these birds. We'll talk to the Chief tomorrow and devise a new plan. In the meantime, let's see if the girls are up for a picnic."

The boys returned to the airport a little before noon and collected Anne and Jessa. Anne walked out of her house with a large picnic basket. "We made more sandwiches," she said with a smile. "I hope this time we get to eat them."

"Great!" said the boys, looking a little sheepish. "The others are going to meet us at Rustler's Cove."

When the foursome arrived at the picnic spot, Marco, Marshall, and Sophia were already there. Soon their portly pal Whit drove up in his jalopy and tapped out a cheerful tattoo on his horn. "Time to eat," he said.

"It's always time to eat in your book," said his sister. "But this time I agree with you."

The girls set out the food and everyone dug in with gusto. As they were finishing their lunch, the *Lizzie Borden* came into view, headed for the Lockjaw River inlet.

"Damn," said the burly Marshall Johnson, "it's that boat!"

Looking askance at the foul expletive, the Hardlys cried in unison, "Good grief!"

"Let's go after them," said Billy. "They've got to be heading to the dock in Baymoor."

The group hastily packed up the remains of the picnic, piled into their cars, and headed into town. The rogue boat was nowhere to be found. Remembering his suspicions about the Thirsty Eye, Tom pulled up outside the disreputable-looking establishment. "Wait here," he said to the others. But a search of the Thirsty

Eye found only a sullen Sonny Stufflebean behind the dirty bar. "You want another root beer?" he sneered.

"Thanks for nothing," said Tom.

Back outside, Tom decided he and Billy would make another search through the skies of the Guernsey Coast. Whit agreed that he and Anne could give Jessa a ride home. The chums split up and the Hardly boys headed out to the Baymoor airdrome.

They flew up and down, in and out, but found no trace of the criminals, who seemed able to appear and disappear at will.

"There's a U.S. Army Air Corps training field over in Piscataway," said Billy. "Let's see if they can help us search for the *Lizzie Borden*."

"I think," said Tom, "it's called the Air Force now."

"All right," said Billy irritably. As the boys approached the field they could see several trainers in the air doing figure eights, loops, and Immelman turns.

"Those pilots are super," ventured Tom as he radioed for permission to land.

"They're OK," Billy retorted.

The Stearman rolled to a stop and Tom and Billy alighted. They were escorted to the commandant's office where they pled their case.

The commandant had never worked with DeVern Hardly or his doughty sons, but he was well aware of their reputation. He had heard the story of the boys' miraculous rescue and now he listened intently as they recounted the story of the missing goblet and the mysterious boat. "You're in luck, fellas," the commandant said. "We have some trainees needing to log flying hours who would love nothing better than to go looking for the *Lizzie Borden* for you." He took down the Hardlys' home phone number and promised to call if the *Lizzie Borden* was spotted.

The search continued for two full days, to no avail. The commandant telephoned Tom Hardly on Tuesday afternoon. "I'm sorry, Tom. My crews haven't seen anything suspicious, and there's been no sign of the *Lizzie Borden*. I've had to call off the search. I wish we had been able to help."

"OK, sir. We appreciate your assistance." Tom hung up the phone and explained the situation to his brother. Though disappointed, Tom and Billy were not despondent.

Shortly after Tom's conversation with the commandant, he and Billy were walking on the pier near the Thirsty Eye. "Would you look at that?!" exclaimed Billy, pointing to the bay. The *Lizzie Borden* could be seen heading out to sea. Where had she come from, where had she been, where was she going? The lads stood there agog for a moment and then leapt into action.

Tom and Billy went to a nearby diner which their buddy Whit had recommended. The diner's owner, George Castleberry, a friend of the Hardly family, was happy to let them use the phone in his tiny office at the back of the restaurant. He closed the door on his way out. Tom called the commandant at the air base. This time, he assured him, they were certain they had their quarry cold. Then he made a call to Chief Langly, who said he would notify the Coast Guard.

The boys ordered a malted and sat at the counter while they waited for the Chief to call back. "This time," exulted Billy, "we have those blackguards in the crosshairs."

"I believe you're right, Billy."

When the phone rang in Mr. Castleberry's office, Tom hopped off his stool and hurried to answer it. The Chief reported a complete lack of success on all fronts. Two planes quickly dispatched from the air base had found neither hide nor hair of the *Lizzie Borden*. The Coast Guard, on the scene lickety-split, had seen nothing out of the ordinary, just a single ship at anchor in Welsley Bay.

"No sign at all of the *Lizzie Borden*," said the Chief. "Not a trace. You and Billy probably just misread the name on the boat.

"But don't feel bad," he consoled. "Anybody can make a mistake."

Tom paid the bill and walked outside with Billy before reporting on his conversation with the Chief. Billy kicked at the pavement with the toe of his sneaker. "We didn't misread anything!" he exclaimed. "That was the *Lizzie Borden* we saw heading out to sea."

"I know," said his brother. "Don't worry, Billy. We're going to find that mystery boat and solve this case."

The Hardly boys returned home somewhat crestfallen. The smell of an apple pie fresh from the oven perked them up immensely. Their mother had prepared Lyonnaise potatoes, steak, and broccoli for dinner. Just as they were sitting down to this fabulous repast, DeVern Hardly appeared in the doorway. "Room for one more?" he asked.

"Dad!" cried the lads. "Boy are we glad to see you!"

"We'll talk after dinner," said DeVern as he took his seat at the head of the table.

Dinner conversation at the Hardly residence could range over a broad array of topics from professional sports to the latest Broadway play, from gardening to music to current events. Like his favorite fictional detective, however, DeVern Hardly thought business conversation should be banned from the dinner table. He never talked about his own work during meals, and dinner guests were politely, but firmly, discouraged from bringing up business matters while eating. "Business matters," DeVern said, "are not an aid to digestion."

That evening, conversation moved from a consideration of which pastries Miss Jane should enter in the upcoming county fair (her pies and cakes consistently won blue ribbons) to Hazel's decision to reupholster the living room furniture ("I want something bright and cheerful in there") to the boys' schoolwork and extracurricular activities.

"Your grades," said DeVern, taking another helping of broccoli, "are excellent. Not surprising, but nonetheless gratifying."

"We were just telling Chief Langly that going back to school is harder than we thought," replied Tom.

"You're not just whistling Dixie," chimed in Billy. "Even history class can be a bummer—sorry, Mom." Billy knew that his mother disapproved of slang. "History class can be frustrating. And I love history. But there are all these events and people and places that the other kids know about and we've never heard of. And it's not like they were *alive* when the things happened. I mean most of our buddies' *parents* weren't even born when the Vietnam War ended."

"Um hm," said Tom thoughtfully, "but Sophie and Marco and Izzy, all those kids, grew up hearing about Vietnam and the civil rights movement and the first woman on the Supreme Court and so on from their parents and grandparents. It's history for them, true, but it's history they've heard about all their lives—a sort of living history."

"Yeah, yeah," said Billy, shooing away the explanation with his hand, "but it puts us at a disadvantage."

"And Billy," said Tom, with a grin at the younger Hardly boy, "does not like to be at a disadvantage. But it's OK, little brother, you can run circles around all of them when it comes to the American Revolution and the Napoleonic Wars and—"

"All right, all right, you can give it a rest now," said Billy. "Not that you aren't right," he added. "I do reign supreme on eighteenth- and nineteenth-century history."

"I'm glad to hear it," said Mr. Hardly. "Keep up the good work." He turned his attention to Tom. "How are you doing with your jujitsu lessons?"

"Pretty well," Tom replied. "I do not say that I could take on a horde of bad guys, but I assert that I could hold my own against one or two."

"Well, I hope you won't have to find out," said Miss Jane with a sniff. "Fighting should always be the last recourse."

"But, Miss Jane," Tom said, with a wink at his mother, "don't you want me to be able to defend myself against an attacker? And what about Billy? I need to be able to protect my baby brother."

"Your 'baby brother' can take care of himself," retorted Billy. He held up his fists and began sparring with an invisible opponent. "I do just fine with my boxing equipment in the basement."

"Someday you're going to be glad that at least one of us has some martial arts moves."

"Says who?"

"Says me."

"All right, boys," chided Mrs. Hardly. "That's enough."

The family topped off the delicious dinner with a Jane Hardly signature apple pie and decaf coffee. Then the boys followed their dad into his office. "What's up, boys?" he asked, leaning back in his swivel chair and propping his feet on the desk.

The boys related their tale of woe to the famous detective. DeVern Hardly gave the lads his full attention, stopping them only occasionally to ask for clarification or for a missing detail. When they had finished, he set his chair upright and leaned forward, resting his forearms on the desk. "That was an excellent job of reporting, boys. Now I'm going to take you into my confidence on a matter of great importance and the utmost secrecy. I believe your story falls in line with the government case I'm working on. And I could use your help in rounding up these miscreants."

The boys were ecstatic. Dad had asked them for help on a government case. What could be more exciting?

"I must depart early tomorrow," he told his sons, "but I will leave my case file for you to review. You must promise me to be extra careful as you continue your pursuit of these villains. This is a truly dangerous assignment.

"The men and women we are pursuing will stop at nothing to achieve their goals. The two women, Lola and Inez Trafalgar, are sisters. They are as beautiful as they are dangerous. Someone who once knew them quite well nicknamed them 'the Black Widows.' When I tell you they are very proud of that epithet, you will get an inkling of their character.

"You'd better take your friend Whit into your confidence. That boy has an uncanny ability to be in the right place at the right time—just like his granddad. John Moore was a newspaper reporter at the turn of the twentieth century. Had more scoops than you could shake a stick at. 'Moore's luck' people called it, though I don't know how much of it was luck, how much was plain hard work, and how much was intuition. People used to say Moore could find the facts blindfolded on a cloudy night. Not a bad trait for a journalist." Mr.

Hardly stood up and walked from behind his desk. "Or a detective." With handshakes and pats on the backs, DeVern headed off to bed.

Tom and Billy had paid close attention to their world-famous dad. Now Tom picked up the case file, cryptically labeled #230691872-C. He began removing items from the file and setting them on the desk. The brothers found photos of some of the characters involved but recognized no one save the driver of the boat and auto. He was Clive Custard, a notorious gangster from England. The boys read page after page recounting details of Custard's numerous intercontinental exploits. They vowed to be careful if they caught up with this villain. After about an hour they put all the materials back in the file, placed it on their dad's desk, and headed off to bed.

When the boys awoke to a bright sunny day the next morning, DeVern Hardly had already left. He was headed to who knew where and back again.

At age ninety-four, DeVern Hardly had not lost his interest in fighting crime nor had he lost his love of the chase. "Ninety-five is the new fifty," he often said. He was still in surprisingly good physical condition, which his sister attributed to good genes and DeVern himself attributed to regular exercise, daily naps, and the goat serum he had flown in twice a year from Afghanistan. The serum was prepared in a village near the shared border of Uzbekistan, Kyrgyzstan, and Tajikistan. DeVern told anyone who asked that he had read about it in the *Wall Street Journal*, which was true. He *had* read about it in the *Journal,* but he had first learned about the goat serum in 1957 while working on a top secret mission for the U.S. government in Afghanistan.

Over tea one afternoon in a local goatherd's tent, DeVern Hardly had commented on the man's seemingly inexhaustible energy. "You arise at five—"

"Four," said the man.

The great detective bowed his head in assent. "Very well, Asa Haq. You arise at four. You ply your trade as a goatherd until dusk. Most nights you're translating documents for the CIA until midnight, and on nights when you're not translating, you're settling village disputes in your role as chief or playing with your numerous grandchildren. Your hair is as black as it was when you were twenty. Your eyes are bright, your skin clear." DeVern, sitting cross-legged on a rug, took a sip of his tea. "And your sexual prowess is legendary. What is your secret?"

"I will tell you," said Asa Haq with the hint of a smile, "because I will have no secrets from one who is like a brother to me."

Reflecting on the fate that had befallen Asa Haq's eldest brother, DeVern Hardly felt a frisson of disquiet. But Asa Haq had had myriad opportunities to rid himself of his American cohort had he wished to do so. And none of Asa Haq's other brothers had met an untimely end. The detective relaxed. "My ears await your words, my brother."

Asa Haq eyed his guest over the rim of his own cup. "Goat serum."

"Goat serum?"

"Two drams daily. I can arrange for you to test its

efficacy yourself."

DeVern Hardly had been taking a dose of goat serum every day since then.

Miss Jane had prepared a breakfast of griddlecakes and sausage, which the young sleuths ate with gusto.

The boys attended their classes as usual. But they were eager to get on with their investigation, so after school they corralled Marshall Johnson, Marco Remo, Whit Moore, and Isador Lipman and asked for their help. They were all excited to be in on the case. It was decided that Marshall and Marco would go out in the *Capri* and scout the bay while Whit and Izzy, as he was affectionately dubbed by his friends, would patrol the backwoods of Baymoor. Tom and Billy would try again to spot the suspects from the air.

The day wore on. The Hardly boys were getting tired of their fruitless search. Suddenly, Billy, sitting in the spotter's seat of the Stearman, yelled at his older brother, "I see something!"

"What is it?" Tom exclaimed.

"It's a speedboat," said Billy, "at three o'clock. I think it's the *Lizzie Borden*. Holy smokes, Tom! It's headed straight for that ship." As Billy watched, the bow of the ship opened and seemed to swallow the speedboat.

"The boat disappeared, Tom!" said an excited Billy. "The ship's bow opened up and the boat just glided on in. No wonder the *Lizzie Borden* couldn't be found. It wasn't in the bay."

Tom pointed the Stearman toward the Baymoor

airdrome. When they arrived, he asked Hoppie, the airport manager, who was a friend of the Hardly family, to service the plane. Then he and Billy were in their car and headed for the *Flatfoot* so they could investigate the boat-swallowing ship.

They hopped in their speedy boat and headed downriver for the open spaces of Welsley Bay. But as they crossed the breakwater, they were disappointed to see nothing at anchor in the bay.

The ghost ship was gone, along with any hope of quickly solving the case.

CHAPTER III

A Vision of Loveliness

The boys awoke early the next morning. Miss Jane was busy in the kitchen preparing a scrumptious breakfast of home fries and scrambled eggs. As the boys were finishing this hearty repast the phone rang. Tom answered the call. "The Chief is missing," declared Hunnicut.

"What?!" said Tom. "How? When?"

"I don't know any more about it," said Hunnicut. "His wife just called and said he never came home last night."

Tom hung up the phone and related the tale of woe to Billy. "We must do something," said Billy. "The Chief may be in grave danger."

The boys' mother was still in bed, so Tom told Miss Jane that Chief Langly was missing and he and Billy were on their way to the police station. "What about school?" exclaimed Miss Jane.

"The Chief's life may be in jeopardy," said Billy. "I think that's a good excuse for missing school."

"You be careful!" cried Miss Jane as Tom and Billy burst out of the house, hopped on their motorcycles, and sped into town. Police headquarters was a beehive of confusion. Officer Hunnicut, Patrolman Von Miles, and Sergeant Blith were all talking at once when Tom and Billy walked into the reception area. The three men turned toward the Hardly boys and simultaneously began to tell them about the

Chief's disappearance.

"Whoa!" said Billy. "Time's a-wasting. One at a time, please."

Tom nodded at the ranking officer. "Give us the lowdown, Hunnicut."

The Hardlys' presence seemed to calm Harry Hunnicut. He told them what little was known about the mystery of the missing Chief. "No one," he said, absentmindedly straightening his tie as he talked, "has seen the Chief since 6:17 last evening when he said he was headed out on an errand and then home to Cora. 'I'll see you boys at eight tomorrow morning.' Those were the last words I heard him say. He never got home." Officer Hunnicut paused as if collecting his thoughts.

"Go on," said Tom.

"His wife said he was so often late she wasn't worried, but when she woke this morning and he wasn't there she became concerned."

"Right," said Billy. "Let's see what we can discover."

Tom suggested that Hunnicut, Von Miles, and Blith return to their regular duties. "Billy and I will search the Chief's office for clues," said Tom. He suspected that the three Baymoor policemen were too distraught over the Chief's disappearance to be of any appreciable assistance in that search.

Billy sorted through the trashcan beside the Chief's desk, then on to the bookcase, but found nothing amiss. He shifted his attention to the Chief's desk top. The stack of papers all appeared to be in order. He lifted a

"Wanted" poster to take a closer look at the miscreant, and in doing so, uncovered an ashtray containing two lipstick-stained cigarette butts. The lipstick traces were of two different shades. Tom determined the smokes were of a Mexican brand.

"It's the Trafalgar sisters," said Billy.

"You're right!" said Tom. "The profile of them in Dad's file said they always smoke Records con Filtros." Tom reminded Billy what they had heard from their father about the Trafalgar sisters. "'They are as beautiful as they are dangerous.' Remember? That's how Dad described them. And he said they were called 'the Black Widows.' Do you think Lola and Inez Trafalgar could have lured Chief Langly into their web?"

"Dad said these people would stop at nothing to achieve their goals," said Billy.

"You're right," replied Tom, "Kidnapping a police officer probably wouldn't faze them for a minute. I think we have to assume that the Trafalgar sisters are in Baymoor and that they have the Chief."

The boys returned to the reception area and took their leave of Hunnicut and Blith. Patrolman Von Miles had returned to his beat. "We'll let you know if we learn anything about the Chief's whereabouts," said Tom as he and Billy left police headquarters.

A search of Baymoor seemed to be the first order of business. Both boys were expert motorcyclists and they decided to split up so as to cover more ground in their increasingly urgent search for Chief Langly. Billy would take the east side of Baymoor, which included the waterfront, while Tom would scour the western environs. The brothers agreed to meet at the Baymoor airdrome in an hour-and-a-half. Billy kick-started his trusty two-wheeler and sped off eastward. Tom headed in the opposite direction.

Billy dutifully searched every street and alleyway in the designated sector but found nothing to indicate the whereabouts of the Baymoor police official. As Billy motored through the squalid streets of the Baymoor waterfront he was aware of that element of Baymoor's population that was as seedy as the neighborhood's bars and hotels. Scruffy men with scraggly beards and stained peacoats lumbered along Front Street in search of mischief.

Meanwhile Tom cruised the wealthier neighborhoods of Baymoor: expensive homes on large lots with stately shade trees, tidy lawns, and colorful displays of fall flowers. He saw no sign of Chief Langly. He circled around one more block then headed for the airdrome so he wouldn't be late for the rendezvous with his brother. The Hardly boys had learned the importance of punctuality from their world-famous father, and they prided themselves on always being on time.

While waiting for Billy, Tom rolled the Hardly airplane out of its hangar and began the safety check he routinely performed before each flight. When Billy failed to appear at the appointed hour, Tom began to worry. Leaving the Stearman in Hoppie's care, Tom roared off on his bike in search of Billy. As Tom headed for the east side of Baymoor, his anxiety increased with every mile. He rolled into the downtrodden waterfront as the late afternoon fog was smothering Front Street. Tom drove past pier after pier looking for a sign of his brother.

Suddenly he stopped, the blood draining from his face. There on its side, next to an empty pier at the lonely end of Front Street, was Billy's motorcycle. His helmet lay on the ground beside it. There was no sign of Billy.

"This might be one of those times Dad was talking about," Tom said aloud.

Not long after the brothers had been freed from their cryogeriatric imprisonment, DeVern Hardly had offered to buy them cell phones. "I am not," he had said, "a fan of cell phones in restaurants or indeed most public places. I find their ubiquity annoying, even disturbing. But there are times," he had added with a smile, "when they are quite beneficial."

"There sure are, Mr. Hardly," Whit had chimed in. He had taken to the brave new world of gadgetry like a cat to cream and had already acquired a cell phone himself. "Just the other day, Anne and I were on our way to pick up pizza for supper when I remembered I'd forgotten to order breadsticks. I gave Anne my phone— the pizza place number is in my Favorites—and she phoned ahead so the whole order was waiting for us when we arrived."

"Mmmm," Mr. Hardly had murmured. "One man's critical concern is another man's trivial pursuit."

"Huh? That's one of your aphorisms, isn't it, Mr.H?"

"You might say so, Whit."

"Well, I think it would be outstanding if Tom and Billy had iPhones like mine. We could make video calls in FaceTime. Look at this." He had held the phone out to Tom.

"Get the dratted thing out of here," Tom had replied, shooing Whit away. "I appreciate your generosity, sir," he had said to his father, "but I don't believe I will need a cell phone."

Now, as Tom looked around for a telephone booth, he realized he hadn't seen one since he and Billy had returned to Baymoor. *Where the heck does Clark Kent change his clothes,* he wondered. *And of rather more urgency, how am I going to phone the police?* Turning down his dad's offer, he concluded, had been a mistake.

Spying an auto body shop nearby, he walked over and asked to use the phone. He put in a call to police headquarters then returned to the spot where he had found Billy's bike.

While he waited for Officer Hunnicut, Tom righted his sibling's fallen bike and began to search the area for clues. He made a spine-chilling discovery: two cigarette butts of Mexican origin with two different shades of lipstick were on the ground near the overturned motorbike. "The Black Widows!" he exclaimed aloud.

When Officer Hunnicut arrived, Tom filled him in quickly. "So you see," he concluded, "I'm certain it's the Trafalgar sisters. And they have the Chief and Billy. We've got to find them—and soon."

Hunnicut and the Baymoor constables searched high and low along Front Street and the entire waterfront district, to no avail. Sergeant Blith had enlisted the aid of the U.S. Coast Guard, but they turned up nothing after searching all the vessels along the Baymoor waterfront.

DeVern Hardly, in the Poconos on an important government case, was inaccessible. Responsibility for the search rested with the elder Hardly brother.

Night had fallen and further investigation into the disappearance of Chief Langly and Billy Hardly would have to wait until morning. When Tom arrived at 223 Baker Street, Miss Jane and his mother, Hazel, were in the kitchen. Tom broke the news about Billy as gently as he could and assured the women that he would begin his search anew at first light.

He made a few phone calls, enlisting the help of his stalwart friends. They all agreed that missing school was justified under the circumstances.

It seemed most likely to Tom that Billy and the Chief were being held in a watercraft or at least near the water's edge.

He was out of the house at sunup and met Whit, Marco, Marshall, and Isador at the boathouse on the Lockjaw River, where his boat, the *Flatfoot,* and Marco's *Capri* were housed.

"Do you have your cell phone, Whit?" asked Tom as his pudgy pal boarded the boat.

"Yep." Whit held up an iPhone encased in a bright yellow Otter Box; he had chosen yellow to match his roadster. "And except for a couple of dead spots, there's pretty good reception on the river. We might be better off texting instead of talking—"

"I don't know what testing is," said Tom.

"Not testing. *Text*-ing."

"OK. Texting. Nor," he added quickly, "do I want to learn about it at this particular time." Whit, who was rapidly becoming a technonerd, was always eager to explain what he had learned to the Hardly brothers. "If you can stay in touch with the fellas in the other boat, I don't really care how you do it," concluded Tom.

With that, Marco took Isador and Marshall and headed upriver while Tom and Whit motored toward the open sea. After three hours of searching along the river's edge, Marco reported no sign of Chief Langly or Billy. Tom and Whit poked in and out of coves and inlets of the Lockjaw River but found nothing of interest.

Finally, the *Flatfoot* stood out to sea. Tom and Whit were desperately hoping to find a clue to the whereabouts of the Chief and Billy.

As Tom steered his craft around Welsley Bay, a froth of flotsam off the port bow caught his attention. What the boys saw next chilled their hearts. Mixed with the assorted detritus, two Mexican cigarette butts with different colored lipstick floated by.

CHAPTER IV

An Undersea Dungeon

Billy Hardly woke from his chemically induced sleep to
the low roar of ventilating fans. He sat up slowly and
looked around. He seemed to be inside a metal cage.
Beyond the cage he could see that the walls of the
oddly shaped room were sweating. Water ran down in
rivulets onto the metal floor. He grabbed hold of the
door to the cage and tugged on it. It didn't budge. "I do
believe," he said aloud, "that I am in what Miss Jane
would call 'a pickle.' Yes. I am almost certainly in a
pickle."

As he took stock of his surroundings, he thought
he heard a low moan above the roar of the fans.
"Hello," he called softly. "Anyone there?"

Another moan was followed by a hoarse voice.
"Who's that?"

"Chief?" said Billy. "Is that you?"

"Hardly?"

"It's me, Billy Hardly, Chief." Billy peered
through the bars of his cell and realized that the Chief
was in another cell on the other side of the room.

"What are you doing here?" asked the Chief.
"Wherever *here* is. Where *are* we?"

"I don't know," said Billy. "I was on the dock
looking for you. The next thing I knew I woke up here."

"Something tells me we need to find a way out of
this predicament," opined Langly. "The sooner the
better."

"You bet," agreed Billy. "What do you know about all this?"

"Not much," said Langly. "Two women came into my office last evening and reported suspicious activity at a hotel on the waterfront. I said I'd stop by there on my way home. The next thing I knew I woke up here in this cell."

A door clanged in the distance and the Chief and Billy Hardly turned in the direction of the noise. Two women smoking Records con Filtros sauntered over to the cells. One had on dark red lipstick; the other, orange.

"It's the Trafalgar sisters, Chief!" exclaimed Billy. "The Black Widows!"

"Ah," said Inez, she of the red lipstick. "Our fame precedes us."

"Infamy is more like it," said Billy. "My dad told me about the two of you."

"DeVern Hardly," sneered Lola. "Someday—"

"Yes, yes," interrupted Inez, turning to look at her sister. "But not now, Lola, darling."

"How do you know who my dad is?" asked Billy.

"We know your story," said Lola. "And we know all about that snooping, meddling, sneaky—"

"Lola, that's enough!" snapped Inez. "Try to keep your attention on the matter at hand." Inez turned back toward Billy and the Chief. "All right, gentlemen, where is it?"

"Where's what?" asked Billy. He looked over at the Chief, who shrugged. "We don't know what you're talking about."

"We know," said Lola, aiming a well-manicured index finger at Billy, "that you have the goblet. The gold one encrusted with diamonds, sapphires, emeralds, rubies, and the occasional garnet."

"But we don't!" exclaimed Langly.

"*You* have it!" cried Billy, glaring at the two sisters.

The women were taken aback. They each lit another cigarette from a burning butt. "It's possible," said Inez slowly, "that they are telling the truth." She dropped the cigarette butt on the floor and ground it underfoot with her sharp-toed, high-heeled shoe. "Well, Clive will find out for sure."

"We have nothing to say to you or to Clive. Right, Billy?"

"You got that right, Chief."

Inez's thin smile held no hint of warmth. "I think," she said, glancing from the Chief to Billy and back again. "that you will be glad to talk to Clive. He is very persuasive."

"Where are we?" asked Billy.

"You needn't worry about that, sweetheart," said Inez, turning away and walking quickly to the door. "I don't believe you'll be here long enough to care."

"We'll be back," Lola said as she followed her sister out the door.

"I do not like the sound of that," muttered Billy.

The two captives compared notes. "Any idea where we are, Chief?"

"None," replied Langly. "It must be the basement of one of those old buildings off Front Street. It's odd though," continued the Chief, "the light bulb over my head is swaying as if the wind were blowing."

Billy looked up. The same thing was happening to the naked bulb in his own dank cell. "Chief!" Billy ejaculated. "We must be in the hold of a ship! The last thing I remember was being near the waterfront on Front Street. We must be getting under way," said Billy. "The light bulb is beginning to cast a bigger arc."

"I don't hear the sound of an engine," said the Chief quietly. "What the heck is going on here?"

"Maybe it's a sailboat," said Billy. "But where does the electricity come from? I don't hear a generator."

The mysterious vessel seemed to be gaining speed.

Back on board the *Flatfoot*, Tom and Whit stared at the two Mexican cigarette butts with different colored lipstick that had surfaced. A trail of bubbles led away from the debris.

Then Tom saw it: the snorkel of a submarine! The underwater machine began to pick up speed as the generators were activated and air was sucked into the engine compartment by the snorkel device. The boat was headed on a course of 108 degrees away from Welsley Bay toward the open sea.

Tom knew he couldn't follow the sub for long. He turned to his plump cohort. "We must alert the Coast Guard," he said.

Down below, the answer came to Billy and Chief Langly simultaneously: "It's a submarine," they cried. The caged prisoners had no way of knowing that at that very moment Billy's brother and the portly but intrepid Whit Moore were on their way to get help.

Tom steered his sturdy speedboat quickly toward the Baymoor Coast Guard Station. He was almost certain Billy was aboard the escaping submarine.

Tom leapt from the deck of the boat as it glided to a stop next to the cutter at the Coast Guard station. "Tie her up to the dock, Whit," said Tom. "Then join me on board the cutter."

Tom gave a shout to Lieutenant Shaeffer as he crossed over to the military boat. "I believe," he said breathlessly, "my brother has been abducted and is trapped aboard a submarine headed for the open sea. Chief Langly may be aboard as well."

The lieutenant had worked with DeVern Hardly on more than one occasion and had great respect for him. He knew the world-renowned detective trusted his sons implicitly and would expect the lieutenant to give them the same sort of cooperation he would have given Mr. Hardly. He was sure he could trust the lad's judgment. "Tell me all you can," the lieutenant requested.

"We saw debris that surfaced. It included the same kind of cigarette butts that Billy found at police headquarters and that I found near my brother's overturned motorcycle on the waterfront," reported Tom.

"Anything else?" asked Shaeffer as he gave orders to get the Coast Guard vessel under way.

"We traced the telltale bubbles heading out to sea long enough to determine the course was 108 degrees," said Tom.

Lieutenant Shaeffer pulled the chart of the area to the navigator's table.

"We were near the channel buoy when we saw the submarine leave," said Tom.

Shaeffer quickly drew a line on the chart. A course of 108 degrees would take the mysterious vessel directly to Blackbeard's Island, a desolate and barren patch of land responsible for many a shipwreck.

"Why would they go there?" asked Tom. "There's not a safe place to tie up a boat larger than a dingy."

"We'll have a look nevertheless," said the skipper. "It's only eleven nautical miles. Full speed ahead." The cutter began to move forward.

It was dark when the intrepid crew, along with those plucky lads, Tom and Whit, arrived at Blackbeard's Island. The cutter's powerful searchlights moved slowly across the island, dipping into every nook and cranny. There were no trees or shrubs, no sheds or buildings. Nothing but a few cormorants could be seen as the cutter circled the small island. It was completely deserted.

Meanwhile, belowdecks on the submarine all motion had ceased. "We're moored somewhere," observed Billy. "And the hatch must be open. I smell the distinct odor of land and seawater."

The door across from the cells opened and a shaft of light danced across the dripping bulkheads. A man with a neatly trimmed goatee walked toward the captives. He wore a white lab smock and was pulling on a pair of black plastic gloves. "Well, well, Chief

Langly, Mr. Hardly, we're happy to have you as our guests," he chortled.

"Not your guests. We're your prisoners," corrected Billy. "What do you want with us? Who are you?"

"*I* know who you are," put in the Chief. "He's the notorious Clive Custard," the Chief explained to Billy. "You remember when you and the others were run off the road by a reckless driver and I called for registration information?" Billy nodded. "I learned that the car is registered to Clive Custard.

"I don't know what he's doing here," continued the Chief, turning back to face their captor. "But I know he's up to no good."

"Silence," hissed Custard. "You'll know everything you need to know soon enough."

He turned to the open door and snapped his fingers. Two heavy-set men with bulging muscles that proclaimed their devotion to weight-lifting walked purposefully into the dank room, "Clive," said the larger of the two henchmen, with a nod toward the man with the goatee, "what now?"

"Open the cells, Manny. Gus, you cover them with your pistol."

The one called Manny unlocked Billy's cell. "Out you come, ol' man."

Billy glared at the ruffian but stepped out of the cell. Manny unlocked the second cage then took out a nasty-looking .45 and pointed it at the chief. Gus kept his gun pointed at Billy.

"Up the ladder, and don't try nothin'," Manny ordered, motioning the two captives toward the exit.

The hatch at the top of the ladder was standing open. Gus led the way. Chief Langly went after him followed by Billy and Clive. Manny brought up the rear.

As Chief Langly stepped through the open hatch he was greeted by more men with weapons. Lola and Inez Trafalgar were there, too, smoking their omnipresent Records con Filtros. A strange flickering light illuminated the space in which they stood.

As Billy's eyes became adjusted to the light he was astonished at what he saw. They were standing on the hull of a submarine. Billy and Chief Langly exchanged a look of real concern. The sub was inside a cavern as large as a domed football stadium, which was lit with torches along its rough walls.

There was no apparent entryway or exit. A ledge ran around the cavern about four feet above the water; below the ledge, the cave walls disappeared into the murky depths.

"Take our guests into the playroom," Clive chortled. Lola and Inez smiled knowingly at each other.

Gus and Manny pushed Billy and Chief Langly roughly toward a steel-barred enclosure on the ledge. As the cell door was locked behind them, the two captives heard Clive give an order to an unseen accomplice:

"Bring the surgical kit and the cauterizing iron."

CHAPTER V

A Needle in a Wet Haystack

At first light the next morning, the Coast Guard ordered an air search. The pilots flew a grid search of the entire area for several hundred square miles. Nothing suspicious was spotted, only freighters and fishing boats.

Lieutenant Shaeffer and Tom were baffled by the disappearance of the outlaws' submarine. Tom was certain that Billy and Chief Langly were being held aboard the underwater craft.

At that moment Billy and the Chief were peering through the bars of their cell in the undersea cavern. Their future did not seem bright. On the ledge that ran around the cavern, Inez and Lola Trafalgar paced back and forth, smoking incessantly and talking softly to each other. When the sisters' pacing brought them near the cell, the captives could make out an occasional word, but not enough to understand what the Black Widows might be plotting.

On the hull of the submarine Clive was talking to Gus and Manny, gesturing now and then in the direction of the cell and clearly giving the lackeys instructions. Suddenly, another man emerged from the submarine. He held a piece of paper in his hand and was waving it at Custard as he walked hurriedly toward him. Billy and the Chief watched Custard read the message then call to the Trafalgar sisters. "Captain Folsom is anxious for a report. We'll leave Manny and

Gus here and rendezvous with the *Citrus Maru*," he explained.

A flurry of activity ensued as the crew prepared for departure. Gus and Manny, stationed outside the cell, glared at the captives and muttered imprecations under their breath. Their jobs as bodyguards in the dank cavern did not seem to suit them.

Custard and the Black Widows cast one last lingering glare at the prisoners before making their way aboard the *Sneaky Fish*, the submarine's apt appellation. Gazing back impassively at their captors, Billy and the Chief watched them disappear belowdecks. The lines were cast off and the craft slipped beneath the murky waters and was gone.

"The odds are somewhat better now," Billy whispered to Chief Langley.

"You have a strange notion of 'better,'" was the muttered reply.

On board the *Sneaky Fish*, the Trafalgar sisters were in a heated discussion. "It doesn't make any sense," said Inez. "If they don't have the goblet, who does?"

"They only *say* they don't have it," said Lola. "Can we believe them?"

Clive waved his hands dismissively at the bickering sisters. "Stop it! I'm tired of your pointless squabbling. If they know, they'll talk when we return."

The *Sneaky Fish* eased its way out of the hidden cavern and headed toward the open sea, running along the surface. Within a few minutes she came alongside the *Citrus Maru*, which appeared to be an ordinary commercial freighter. But when a signal flashed from the submarine was answered by the freighter, the entire front of the huge ship opened. The *Sneaky Fish* motored into the gaping maw and disappeared. When the sub was inside and the bow was once again closed, the *Citrus Maru* looked like any other freighter at anchor in the bay. No wonder it hadn't attracted the attention of the Coast Guard spotters.

Clive and the Trafalgar sisters headed immediately for the captain's cabin to report on their latest activities. Captain Moses Folsom was a fearsome-looking man with dark bushy hair, heavy eyebrows, unkempt beard, and a long scar on the left side of his pallid face. A throwing knife in a black nylon sheath lay on his desk. As the trio approached, he pulled the knife out of the sheath and flipped it across the room. It sailed past Inez Trafalgar and stuck in the scarred and pitted paneling of the wall behind her.

Inez was outraged. "How dare you—"

"Close your blowhole, Inez," growled the captain. "The boss wants to know what's happening. Talk to me." Clive recounted the story of how the Chief and one of the Hardly boys had been captured and were being held in the underwater cavern. "They say they haven't got the goblet. And it may be true. I'll know if they're telling the truth after I have a 'talk' with them."

Folsom was not known for his good nature or his even temper. "We *must* find it!" he exploded. "Buttman wants that treasure." He walked over to retrieve the knife sticking in the wall. With a leer, he spat, "And you know what he's like when he doesn't get what he wants! Find out what the Chief and that old man know, then dispose of them. Now, go."

Folsom returned to his desk, took a whetstone from the center drawer, and began sharpening the knife. "Are you still here?" he asked, without looking up from his task.

Clive and the sisters backed through the door and headed to the *Sneaky Fish* with new resolve.

Back in the underwater cavern, Chief Langly and Billy Hardly hadn't wasted any time hatching a plot. They knew they had to overthrow their guards and escape from their dank dungeon or face almost certain torture and death. Billy suggested a plan that would lure the dim-witted thugs into the captives' cage. The ruse had worked in every Johnny Mack Brown and Durango Kid movie Billy had ever seen. He saw no reason it wouldn't work for him.

Chief Langly let out a shrill cry, held his stomach, and collapsed to the floor of the cell squirming in apparent agony. Billy ran to his side as Manny and Gus looked on. "You've got to help me!" cried Billy. "He's dying!"

The two guards exchanged a look. Neither man was blessed with inordinate brainpower and it seemed possible that Custard might blame them if one of the prisoners was dead when he got back. After a whispered consultation, Manny unlocked the cell door and he and Gus went in to attend to the fallen prisoner.

As soon as they reached him, the Chief sprang into action, knocking both of the slow-witted men to the ground. In no time Chief Langly and Billy had the upper hand. Weapons and keys were wrested from the embarrassed henchmen, and soon they were locked in the cell, while Billy and the Chief, now outside the cage, wondered what to do next.

They had taken the guards' cell phones, but no service was available inside the cavern. The two escapees walked around the narrow ledge that encircled the murky water, but saw no exit. The only way out was through the underwater tunnel that the *Sneaky Fish* had taken.

"The problem," said Billy, while he and the Chief sat on the ledge across from the cell they had so recently vacated, "is that we don't know where the tunnel is and we aren't equipped to breathe under water."

"You've got that right," muttered Langly.

Billy stared down into the saline depths. "Chief," he exclaimed, "look at the water!"

"What about it?" asked the Chief. "It's water."

"It's moving!" exulted Billy. "The tide is ebbing. We may be able to find the way out."

Sure enough, within a few minutes the receding water had revealed the top edge of the tunnel. "An air gap," cried Billy. "We've got to swim for it, Chief."

The Chief shook his head ruefully. "I should have known you'd come up with some harebrained scheme."

"If you've got a better idea," retorted Billy, "I am all ears."

"No," admitted the Chief. "You're right. We've got to swim for it."

Billy and Chief Langly removed their shoes and trousers and tied them in a bundle. Then they walked around the rim of the cavern to the spot closest to the barely visible tunnel.

But, just as they were about to jump into the water the submarine returned. Billy and the Chief moved quickly and crouched behind a rock outcropping, as the sub entered the cavern and began to surface.

The two refugees knew they had very little time. Once the hatch was open, Clive Custard would emerge from the sub and realize his prisoners had escaped. If they were going to try to swim to safety, they had to make their move now. If Custard ever got them into what he had so menacingly called "the playroom," they would almost certainly never get out alive.

Billy Hardly and the Baymoor chief of police decided to brave the treacherous waters rather than subject themselves to the ministrations of the evil Clive Custard.

Billy and the Chief leapt into the sea and swam toward the exit. There was a small air gap between the water and the cave ceiling, but the rough waters forced them against the rocks and sapped their energy. It seemed forever to Billy and the Chief, but after about a hundred yards they reached a narrow opening and scrambled up rough rocks to safety.

"We're on Blackbeard's Island!" gasped Billy, as he and the Chief got their bearings, breathing heavily and thanking their lucky stars for their escape from the dastardly ruffians.

When they had regained a little strength, they put on their wet trousers and shoes and began a vain search for some means of escape.

"This isn't any good," said Billy, surveying the bleak island.

"You're right," the Chief agreed. "Let's look for a place to hide."

They knew that a search would soon be mounted by Custard and his crew. The Chief found a small patch of bushes growing near one of the rocky outcroppings that dotted the island. "I think these bushes will shield us if they are looking for us from the submarine," the Chief suggested. "If they come looking for us on land . . ."

"We won't give up without a fight," declared Billy.

They dried the weapons they had taken from the guards and disposed themselves as comfortably as possible behind the bushes.

"Do cell phones work when they're wet?" queried Billy.

"Depends. But there's no signal out here anyway," replied the Chief. "I don't think we'll be able to 'phone home' with these."

"Why would we want to phone home? Wouldn't phoning the Coast Guard make more sense?" responded a puzzled Billy.

"Oh, right," said the Chief. "Of course you've never seen *ET*. Well, never mind. We can't use the phones in any case."

"I'm surprised we never knew about the underwater cavern," said Billy.

"It's barely visible even at low tide," said Chief Langly. "And this isn't a very welcoming island. The locals never come out here."

"Look!" said Billy, pointing toward the water where the snorkel of the *Sneaky Fish* could be seen rising from the depths. Soon the top portion of the sub was visible as it began circling the island. A man with binoculars could be seen on the tower.

"Stay still," whispered the Chief.

"You don't have to tell me twice," replied Billy.

From their vantage point behind the clump of bushes, the two men watched the submarine slowly make its way past the shore, while the man with the binoculars scanned the island. After the submarine completed its second circuit, the man on the tower went belowdecks and the submarine headed out to sea.

"Whew!" exclaimed Billy. "That's enough excitement to last me for a long time. Let's figure out how we're going to get off this rocky prison."

Billy and Chief Langly began looking around for something with which to build a signal fire, but found no wood or debris to use as fuel. The only living things on the barren rock known as Blackbeard's Island were nesting seabirds. Billy was watching a couple of the birds wheeling and turning in the air when he was suddenly struck with an idea. "Guano is organic and will burn!" Billy exclaimed.

"You're right," said the Chief. The men began scraping together a large pile of the seabirds' dried wastematter in preparation for lighting a signal fire. Chief Langly took apart three of the bullets from the weapons wrested from the hapless guards in the cavern. Billy tested several rocks to find two that would spark when hit together.

After about an hour, the two refugees were ready to light their fire. Billy sparked the gunpowder the Chief had extracted. The dried guano caught fire and smoke began wafting skyward.

"Now, my fellow castaway," said Billy, bowing toward the Chief, "we wait."

Hours later, a FedEx pilot flying over the island on the way to the Baymoor airport saw smoke from the barren rock. The pilot, who flew in daily, knew that something was amiss and radioed the airport tower at Bayport. A Coast Guard helicopter was soon dispatched to investigate.

The lady Coast Guard pilot located the source of the smoke and saw the two men waving at her. She quickly found a suitable landing spot and Billy and Chief Langly were taken on board. The pilot radioed ahead, and when she set down at the Coast Guard heliport in Baymoor, Tom Hardly, Officer Hunnicut, and Lieutenant Shaeffer were there to meet the rescued pair. As requested, Tom had brought a change of clothes and a dry pair of shoes for both men.

After the Chief and Billy related the story of their ordeal, the Coast Guard dispatched a team of frogmen and two cutters to the island. The underwater cavern was empty and no sign of life was found on the island itself. An air search team sent out to look for the *Sneaky Fish* at sea reported no success. Once again, the searchers saw nothing suspicious.

"I wish Dad were here," Tom lamented. "He'd know what to do."

"He's incommunicado," Billy reminded his brother.

"I know," said Tom, disconsolate.

Tom and Billy said their goodbyes and headed off with Officer Hunnicut, who had agreed to give them a ride to their house after he dropped the Chief off at headquarters.

When the boys got home, dinner was almost ready. As they headed upstairs to wash up, Tom said, "The thought occurs to me that we may want to reconsider Dad's offer of cell phones."

"The thought occurs to you?" Billy stopped on the stairs and gawked at his brother. "And to what do you attribute this astonishing about-face? I thought you wanted nothing to do with 'those dratted things.'"

"I know," Tom said somewhat sheepishly. "I may have been a tad hasty in not letting Whit show me how his phone works."

Billy grinned as he took the last few steps two at a time. "You were a wet rag, no foolin'. So, what caused this 'thought' to occur?"

"There were a couple of times while you and the Chief were missing when having a cell phone might have been advantageous." Tom paused at the door to his room. "Where do you suppose Clark Kent changes into his Superman garb?"

"What?!"

"Haven't you noticed that there are no phone booths in town?"

Billy considered the question. "You're right. I don't know what he does."

"Anyway," said Tom, "when Dad gets home, I think we should talk to him about getting phones."

"Roger dodger," replied Billy. "I didn't want to rattle your cage, but I've played around some with Whit's phone and was going to suggest we revisit the cell phone question." Suddenly Billy gave a leap and dunked an invisible basketball into an unseen basket. "Verizon on the horizon!"

Mrs. Hardly and Miss Jane had been cooking all afternoon and had a delicious dinner prepared for the returning sleuths. As a surprise they had invited Jessa Sheridan and Anne Moore to join them for dinner and hear stories of the boys' recent exploits. The lads and their friends enjoyed the repast enormously.

As Miss Jane was serving dessert, who should arrive on the scene but Whit Moore, who had a nose for the Hardly woman's pies. "I don't mind if I do," Whit replied when invited to join the group.

"What a surprise to see you," said Tom with a touch of sarcasm that was lost on Whit.

After dessert and coffee, they moved into the den to ponder the mystery of the golden goblet.

"We have more questions than answers," observed Tom, after several minutes of conversation.

"I have one more question," said Billy. "If the Custard gang didn't steal the golden goblet encrusted with diamonds, rubies, sapphires, emeralds, and the occasional garnet, who did?"

"That really is the sixty-four thousand dollar question," said Anne.

"Why sixty-four thousand dollars?" asked her brother. "That's a peculiar amount. Not," he added, "that I would spurn such a sum should someone offer it to me. But it does seem odd."

"It was the name of an old TV show," said Jessa quickly. Anne and her brother delighted in verbal sparring and could get into quite heated discussions. Though they enjoyed their battles of wit, the gentle Jessa was sometimes uncomfortable with their tart comments and humorous sarcasm. She much preferred for everyone to get along.

"OK," said Tom, intent on helping Jessa change the subject, "the point is that we want to solve this mystery but we don't know how. Who's got a suggestion?"

Whit thought something might be learned if he went in disguise and hung around the Thirsty Eye. "That Sonny Stufflebean is almost certainly messed up with the Custard crowd, and the dubious clientele at that bar of his might have information we can use."

The girls immediately raised objections, fearing for his safety, but Whit pooh-poohed their fears. "I can take care of myself," he boasted.

The Hardly boys thought his idea a good one and said they would hang around the waterfront just outside the bar. They too would be in disguise.

After school the next afternoon the three friends put their plan into action. Whit arrived first, wearing a navy peacoat, a black long-sleeved T-shirt, bell-bottom jeans, and a Greek fisherman's cap.

In addition to his long-standing fondness for food, the newly awakened Whit had discovered in himself an interest in twenty-first-century fashion. He had been amazed at the variety of clothing styles available and enjoyed experimenting with different looks. Though most of his clothes were on the casual side—T-shirts, what he persisted in calling tennis shoes, and dungarees—he had acquired one three-piece suit, some dress shirts, and several blazers. His sister teased him about his newfound fashion sense, saying he should start his own line of clothing for the "weight challenged." Whit merely laughed and continued to stock his closet.

He shuffled into the smoky bar and sidled up to Sonny Stufflebean, the bartender, who was wiping off one of the tables in the bar's small eating area.

"I'll have a diet cola," Whit said. "Make it a double."

Stufflebean stared at Whit. "Another underage geezer," he muttered to himself. He went back behind the bar and poured the drink then walked to the other end of the counter, all the while shaking his head.

Tom and Billy were outside the bar in search of clues that might lead them to the whereabouts of Billy's captors and perhaps even the golden goblet. The boys' father was renowned for his ability to disguise himself merely by changing his mannerisms and the way he walked. He might also don a brightly colored scarf and a dashing hat or change his hairstyle, but as he was wont to say, a truly effective change had to come from inside. Tom, too, was a master of disguise; he had the knack of "becoming" whatever character he wanted, with a minimum of costuming. For his investigation on the waterfront Tom wore a scraggly beard from his father's costume collection, and a gray wool beret. Head down, shoulders hunched forward, he slouched along, looking furtively from side to side.

Billy, who had not inherited what he called "the chameleon gene," sported a long blond wig covered by a disreputable looking felt hat. He had on a wrinkled duster coat over faded jeans and a red plaid shirt. He had finished off his disguise with a pair of scuffed and battered dress shoes.

As Tom shuffled along Front Street, he came to an alley and heard voices emanating from behind a loaded dumpster. Hearing the word "goblet" he paused to listen. "They're holed up in one of those warehouses up the coast near Waldport. If they don't have the goblet, they know where it is," growled one man.

"I think they want to cut us out altogether," said his cohort. "But that might be harder than they think."

"You're right about that," replied the first man. "Come on. Let's get out of here."

Tom turned around before the men left the alley and headed back the way he had come. He soon caught up with Billy, who had nothing to report. Tom quietly related the conversation he had overheard. "Let's get Whit and take the *Flatfoot* up the coast toward

Waldport, see what we can find."

The brothers picked up Whit from the tatty bar and told him the plan. At the boathouse where the *Flatfoot* was housed, the three chums shed their disguises. They nosed out of the Lockjaw River into the open sea and turned north, headed up the coast toward Waldport. As they cruised in and out of coves and inlets. Tom glanced skyward.

"We'd better head back before those storm clouds get any closer. If we're not home before it rains Miss Jane will give us the dickens," he laughed.

Miss Jane was inclined to predict death and destruction at every turn for her nephews. The boys knew, however, that her bark was worse than her bite. If they were lucky she might have one of her delicious pies cooling on the windowsill, for she was very fond of Tom and Billy despite her occasional sharp-tongued harangues. She also had a fondness for Whit Moore, whose love for good food she appreciated.

As the chums sped south toward Baymoor the sky darkened menacingly and the sea became rough. Soon large raindrops began pelting the boys as Tom turned an anxious eye toward the heavens.

"We'd better look for shelter or we're in for a drenching," he said.

Whit spotted a dock at what appeared to be an abandoned warehouse with a large overhanging roof near the mouth of a small river. Tom gunned the boat and headed for the spot Whit indicated. As lightning flashed all around them, Tom guided the boat to safety with expert skill.

"Boy this is some storm!" Billy ejaculated, while thunder boomed. As the rumbles subsided the boys heard footsteps above them in the warehouse. Soon voices could be heard and Whit put a finger to his lips, cautioning the others to be quiet. A sixth sense warned him that those above them were up to no good.

"This is a perfect spot, Blackie, for storing the goods," one of the men said.

"You bet it is, Rusty," replied Blackie. "Those Feds will never think to look here."

Tom Hardly turned up the volume on one of the highly sensitive listening devices the boys had recently acquired, and motioned for the others to do the same on theirs. The three boys listened in horror as they heard Blackie declare, "If that snoop DeVern Hardly shows up, we'll put a hundred pounds of concrete around his feet and drop him into sixty fathoms of the Atlantic—and that will be the end of him."

But this wasn't the biggest surprise they were in for.

CHAPTER VI

A Surprising Development

The boys motored into Baymoor resolved to reach the famous detective, who was somewhere in the Poconos on a big government case. "Moore's luck strikes again," said Whit as they tied up the *Flatfoot* in the boathouse.

"I'll say it does," said Tom, slapping his friend on the back. "Of all the docks in all the bay you picked the one with the bad guys in it."

"We've got to warn Dad of the danger posed by Blackie and Rusty," said a worried Billy Hardly. Tom agreed that every effort must be made to contact their famous dad.

Tom, Billy, and Whit headed to police headquarters to inform Chief Langly of the location of the warehouse and the conversation they'd overheard. "I'll call Bret Murphy of the state police," vowed Chief Langly. "He'll send a squad out to round up those thugs."

The boys had skipped lunch and the always-hungry Whit Moore begged for a lunch break. "Chief," said Tom, "we'll feed our starving chum while you're waiting for Trooper Murray to return your call. We'll be at JoJo's on Wylie Street." The hungry boys were finishing delicious helpings of fried clams and sweet potato fries when the police chief approached their table.

"Boys," said the deflated officer, "the state troopers found no one at the abandoned warehouse. The only indication that anyone had been there was an ashtray with two—"

"—lipstick-stained cigarette butts!" yelled Billy.

"The Black Widows," said Tom in a hushed voice. "And they're up to no good, I'll wager. It's imperative that we get word to Dad."

The boys knew their famous father was somewhere in the Poconos but they didn't know exactly where. They had tried phoning him, but some malfunction with DeVern Hardly's phone had prevented them from even leaving a message. The Chief and the boys agreed that Mr. Hardly needed to know about the overheard threats and the presence of the Black Widows as soon as possible, but they were stymied as to how to reach him.

"I have an idea," asserted Tom, "that just might work. We'll stop by the Quickee-Print and then head on out to the aerodrome."

At the print shop, Tom explained what he wanted. DeVern Hardly had once helped the shop's owner out of a serious predicament and he was glad to be able to assist DeVern's sons in any way he could. "I can have that for you within the hour," said the owner.

The job was ready in less than an hour and the boys headed to the airport.

Hoppie, the airport manager, helped the boys rig the blue and yellow biplane with the towing banner Tom had bought from Quickee-Print. The banner read: D H PHONE HOME. BLACK WIDOWS ABOUND. Hoppie cautioned the brothers about the additional drag the banner would cause, but he knew Tom was a careful pilot and wasn't overly concerned. The boys left

Baymoor and headed west toward the Poconos with their cryptic message.

As the brothers flew toward their destination, curious onlookers speculated about the puzzling message. "Must be about one of them new horror movies," opined one onlooker. Tom and Billy were interested in only one person reading the message, and he would know exactly what it meant.

They had left Baymoor with a full tank of fuel and had flown as long as they could, crisscrossing the Pennsylvania mountain range as low as they dared fly. Now they had to release the banner and return to earth to refuel for the trip home.

They headed for the small airport their friend Hoppie had recommended. He had made arrangements with the airport manager to ship home the banner and refuel their plane.

As they flew low over the airport, Tom pulled the lever to release the giant banner.

"Rats," Tom muttered, "it's jammed. I'm not sure we can get down safely with this banner attached."

"We're almost out of fuel," lamented Billy. "You've got to try to land with the cursed banner attached."

Tom radioed the small Pennsylvania airport and told the tower controller of their predicament. "I'll call the emergency crew to line the runway. Good luck. Take runway 27; the wind is ten miles per hour from the west." Tom lined up the sluggish craft with the runway and throttled back slightly for a hot landing, as the fire trucks pulled up to the runway.

"Hold on, Billy," Tom cautioned his younger brother. The experienced pilot put the struggling airplane down in a perfect landing and rolled to a stop on the runway. Several men in overalls swarmed over the crippled aircraft and detached the troublesome appendage. The boys taxied to the fuel truck and alit quickly, glad to be back on terra firma.

After filing a report with the local airport authorities, the boys took off for home. They wondered if their famous dad had received their message. When the boys returned to Baymoor that evening, Chief Langly and two men in suits were waiting at the airport.

"Your dad called," said Chief Langly, "and asked me to call these agents from the FBI and fill them in. It looks like we're in the middle of a government case here that involves more than just a missing goblet.

"This is Special Agent Lou Steele and Agent Ken Kraus. These men are with Special Projects in the Bureau," Langly said, nodding toward one man and then the other.

"We took the goblet," said Special Agent Steele.

Stunned amazement greeted this announcement. Then the Hardly boys exclaimed in chorus. "*You* stole the goblet?!"

"We didn't actually steal it," explained Steele. "We appropriated it for a special project. We're going to use it as bait. The big boss of the group we're after has a weak spot for jewels and gold. We hope to smoke him out in the open with this goblet and catch him red-handed."

"Do you know who the big boss is?" queried Tom.

"His name is George W. Buttman," Steele replied. "His appetites include wine, women, gemstones, and money. He's greedy and he's ruthless. He'll stop at nothing to get what he wants. His tentacles are long and varied, and he keeps his musclemen and cohorts in the dark about his plans. He has a huge organization— ships, airplanes, even a submarine."

Chief Langly and Billy looked at each other. "We know about the sub," allowed the Chief.

"DeVern Hardly has been working with us for months to get to Buttman. He has established an undercover persona at Buttman's resort in the Poconos, but hasn't obtained any information yet," reported Kraus. "It's a dangerous assignment," he added.

"What can we do to help?" asked Tom.

"Your dad said you'd be ready," Steele responded. "We have reason to believe Mr. Buttman will be going to the resort soon. We want you to take your girlfriends, book rooms at the Brownbrier Resort, and await his arrival."

Tom and Billy were taken aback and stared at each other for a moment. "A sleepover?" gasped Billy.

"It's for our country," asserted Tom. "We must do it."

"We'll have to call Jessa and Anne right away," said Billy. "Maybe Mom and Miss Jane should come along," he added.

"Too dangerous," said Tom. "We'll call Whit for backup."

When the boys got home, Miss Jane and Mrs. Hardly were waiting anxiously for news of the boys' day. They had prepared a grand dinner for the returning adventurers. "Is it okay if we invite some friends for dinner?" asked Tom. "We have to ask a favor."

"Of course, " said the women. "We'll eat in an hour."

Whit was out but Anne and Jessa were happy to be invited. They knew the Hardly women always set a good table. After dinner the boys asked all the ladies into the parlor.

"We have an assignment," said Tom, "which we must discuss with you."

"The FBI," said Billy nervously, looking at his mother and his aunt, "has asked us to help in Dad's government case."

"Well, I'm not surprised," averred Mrs. Hardly. "You boys have proven yourselves over and over again."

Jessa and Anne nodded in agreement.

"Yes," said Miss Jane, "but you run too many risks. And you—"

"Now, Jane," said Mrs. Hardly, trying to stem what she knew might be a long scold by her loving but sharp-tongued sister-in-law, "let's hear what the boys have to say."

"What they want us to do," said Tom with a glance at Billy, "is to go to the Brownbrier Resort in the Poconos and wait for George W. Buttman's arrival. Since Monday is an in-service day for the teachers, we don't have school. We can stay for several days if necessary."

He paused, took a deep breath, then said in a rush, "They want us to take Jessa and Anne with us and pose as two married couples."

This announcement was greeted by stunned silence. The girls stared at each other. Miss Jane, speechless for once, twisted the hem of her apron in her hands and looked from Tom to Billy and back again. After a few seconds Mom broke the silence. "Boys," she said, with a hint of a smile, "your father needs your assistance. You must do as he asks. I know these ladies will gladly help."

"Of course," said Jessa straight-faced. "You can count on us."

Anne nodded. "Anything for the good ol' U,S, of A.," she said with a wink.

Miss Jane nearly swooned. "This is just too awkward," she exclaimed and rushed off to the kitchen to finish cleaning up the supper dishes.

"Never mind her," said Mrs. Hardly. "When do you need to leave, Tom?"

"As soon as possible. I'll call now for reservations. I'd better get a room for Whit, too. Dad said we should keep Whit involved in the case. Never can tell when Moore's luck might come in handy."

Three rooms were available for the next evening, so the boys decided to leave in the morning. The girls went home to pack. When Tom finally reached Whit, he agreed to go and said he'd be glad to drive. Whit, Anne, and Jessa arrived early the next morning at the Baker

Street house. The boys were ready and they all piled into Whit's roadster.

Miss Jane and Mrs. Hardly had made a picnic lunch. Crustless tuna sandwiches, potato salad with pickle and carrots, and a thermos of lemonade were packed carefully in the picnic basket, which was loaded into the yellow roadster.

With hugs all around and a wave, the kids were off on their adventure. The weather cooperated, and Tom and Billy, who had volunteered for the rumble seat, were quite comfortable as they motored through the Pennsylvania countryside. They arrived at the Brownbrier Resort hotel just after 2:00 p.m.

Leaving his companions to stroll around the palatial lobby, Tom approached the marble counter running the width of the room.

"Are you checking in, sir?" The clerk at the reception desk was an attractive older woman with a dazzling smile.

"Indeed we are, ma'am," replied Tom.

"Do you have a reservation?"

"Hardly."

The clerk looked at Tom.

"Hardly?"

"That's right. Hardly."

"Very well, sir. Let me check and see if we have anything available." Tom could hear the ticketa-tick as her fingers flitted across the keyboard. "How many rooms will you need?"

"I reserved three rooms," said Tom.

"You reserved three rooms?"

Tom nodded.

"I thought you said you didn't have a reservation."

"No. I said I do have a reservation."

The clerk's smile wattage dimmed a bit. "I asked if you had a reservation and you said 'hardly.'"

"Right."

"There are not degrees of reservation, sir. You either have a reservation or you don't have a reservation. Scarcely having one is the same as not having one."

"I didn't say I scarcely had a reservation," said Tom. "You asked if I had a reservation and I said 'Hardly.'" Tom started chuckling then laughing outright. "I get it. You thought I meant I hadn't made a reservation."

The clerk's smile was definitely fading at the edges. "Just so, sir."

"That's my name."

"That's your name, sir?"

"Yes."

"What is your name, sir?"

"Hardly."

"I don't— Oh!" The clerk's smile returned in full force. "Your *name* is Hardly."

"Now we're both in orbit."

"Sir?"

"Uh, we dig it? Get it? Understand?"

"No, sir, I'm afraid I don't understand."

"That is what it means."

"What *what* means, sir?"

"In orbit. It means 'in the know.'"

The clerk nodded. "If you say so, Mr. Hardly."

"My mom is always admonishing us not to use slang," said Tom. "I guess that's one reason. Because expressions don't always stay the same from one generation to the next." He looked pensive. "Maybe sometimes they don't even mean the same thing at the same time in different places." Tom smiled at the woman. "My mom is a pretty smart cookie."

The clerk wished she had taken the day off. The old man was not unpleasant; in fact he was rather charming in an odd way, but she was finding the conversation wearing.

"I'm sure she is, Mr. Hardly. Now let's get you checked in." More typing followed and soon the woman was pushing a sheet of paper across the smooth marble surface. "If you'll just sign here and verify that all the information is correct."

Tom skimmed over the information then reached for the pen the clerk proffered and signed his name. "There you go."

The clerk retrieved the paper and handed three keycard envelopes to Tom. "Would you like two keys for each room?"

"That would be swell," Tom replied.

The clerk turned away to make the extra keys as Tom pulled out one of the keycards from an envelope. "What do I do with this?"

"With what, sir?" she asked without turning her head.

"This credit card," said Tom, slipping the keycard

back into its protective sheath. Tom knew that these days many people bought almost all their purchases on credit. Mr. Hardly had lectured Billy and him about fiscal responsibility and living within one's means when he had given them each a credit card.

"Do we charge our meals on the card?" he asked the clerk.

She returned her attention to Tom. "Certainly, you may put your meals and any other expenses you incur while you're at the resort on your credit card, Mr. Hardly. Or you can charge them to your room and they will appear on your bill when you check out." She slid three more envelopes across the counter. "Here you are, sir."

"How many credit cards do I need?" asked Tom, picking up the three envelopes and slipping them into his shirt pocket.

She gasped. "I can't possibly answer that question, Mr. Hardly! I have no way of knowing how many credit cards you need!" She was definitely taking tomorrow off. If necessary, she would call in sick.

"I'm sorry, ma'am." Tom could tell he had said something wrong. "I thought since you'd given me these credit cards you might know how many more I was going to need."

"I haven't given you any credit cards," said the clerk.

"You haven't?"

"No sir."

Tom reached into his shirt pocket and pulled out one of the protective envelopes. "Then what is this?" he said, extracting the keycard.

The clerk stared at him blankly then said in a hushed voice, "That's the room key, Mr. Hardly." Maybe she would go home early and also take tomorrow off.

"This is a key!?" Tom held the card at arm's length, turning it one way and then another. "Now that's a big tickle. Must be a strange keyhole. "So these aren't credit cards for hotel purchases?"

"No. No, sir, they are not." She stared fixedly at Tom.

"Oh, boy!" Tom shook his head as he put the envelope back in his shirt pocket. "I tell you what, the way things have changed since the 1950s, I'm not sure Billy and I will ever catch up."

"Indeed," said the clerk. She watched Tom walk away then went in search of her manager. She was absolutely going to take the next day off from work.

Since they had registered as married couples, the boys weren't sure how to proceed. Whit had gone to scope out the restaurants attached to the resort. Tom and Billy stood awkwardly in the hall with the luggage at their feet.

After a moment or two, Jessa and Anne took pity on them and directed the nervous brothers to one room, taking the other for themselves. That night, after everyone had retired for the evening, the women discussed how inept their friends were at this relationship game and wondered how to get the boys to make the next move.

"I think," said Anne, "we may have to take the bit between our teeth if we're going to get anywhere with Tom and Billy. It's so hard to remember there are teenage minds in those full-grown (and not unattractive) male bodies. And 1950s teens, at that!"

Jessa nodded. "I know what you mean. And I do believe you're right. A weekend visit to the beach might be what we need." She smiled at Anne. "Just the four of us. When we get back to Baymoor, I'll see about getting us a cottage."

In their own room the Hardly boys slept soundly all through the night.

The next morning the quintet of friends met early for breakfast on the veranda of the Brownbrier. Fearing they might encounter some of the gang that had kidnapped Billy, the Hardly boys had decided to disguise themselves. Tom had dissuaded his brother from donning the wig and duster coat he had worn to scout the waterfront district. "I keep telling you," said Tom as he helped Billy apply a moustache and sideburns, "keep it simple."

"Right," grumbled Billy. "You and Dad and your 'keep it simple.' I don't see why not wear the blond wig."

"Because in these circumstances, it is likely to attract attention. We want to *deflect* attention. And two elderly gents with mustaches and neatly trimmed sideburns are about as unnoteworthy as you can get."

"There!" said Tom, smoothing down Billy's moustache. "Now, let me put my own mustache on and we'll be ready to go a'sleuthing."

Billy took a last look at himself in the full-length mirror attached to the outside of the bathroom door: dark jeans, light-blue Oxford cloth shirt, navy-and-white suede Adidas. "Not bad," he said. "You may be right about the value of understatement in this situation."

"Much better than a blond wig and scruffy duster coat," agreed Tom, who had donned black slacks, a gray long-sleeved T-shirt, and a pair of black Sperry Top-Siders.

Whit, Jessa, and Anne were waiting on the veranda when the Hardly boys arrived. Whit, pleased at the opportunity to wear some of his dressier clothes, was nattily attired in crisp khakis, white shirt, blue blazer, and Johnston and Murphy loafers.

"I believe," said Jessa, looking around at the assembled group, "that we will fit right in with the Brownbrier's clientele."

"Shall we go in to breakfast?" said Tom, crooking his arm.

"Let's," said Jessa, laying her hand on Tom's arm and walking with him into the restaurant.

"Five?" asked the maître d', checking his seating chart then leading the group to a table near the floor-to-ceiling windows overlooking one of the hotel's formal gardens. "Enjoy your breakfast."

The tuxedo-clad waiter cooked eggs Hussarde tableside for the Baymoor group. Whit moved on from the eggs to a large helping of bananas Foster, followed by a brace of sausages for good measure. As the friends were finishing a final cup of coffee, an aged gardener sidled up to the table from behind a potted maple. "Meet me in the golf cart shed at ten o'clock this morning," he whispered to the Hardly boys.

"Dad!" Billy exclaimed.

"Quiet, Billy," admonished DeVern Hardly. He shuffled slowly away from the group and began working his way across the yard.

Tom and Billy left the girls to their own devices but bade Whit go with them to meet with their father. At 10:00 a.m. precisely, the three chums arrived at the appointed rendezvous. Mr. Hardly was cleaning his gardener's cart and greeted the boys warmly. No one else was around the shed so they were able to chat quietly but freely.

DeVern Hardly told the boys that Buttman and his henchmen had amassed a cache of precious metals and gemstones so large that the federal government had taken an interest. "Not only the FBI," reported the famous detective, "but the CIA and the ATF are involved. The government fears that Buttman is planning to sell most of the loot to help finance the affairs of terrorist groups around the world."

The boys were stunned at the magnitude of this revelation.

"We're flattered, Dad," opined Tom, "that you have enough confidence in us to let us help."

Billy and Whit nodded in agreement.

"The word is," the elder Hardly continued, "that Buttman and his crowd are coming here tonight for confabs and may be plotting how to dispose of the stolen material. We need to find out as much as we can about their plan in the hope that we can put a stop to it."

"Why doesn't the government just arrest these criminals?" Whit asked.

"The federal agents don't have any hard evidence connecting the Buttman group to illegal activities," said DeVern Hardly. "Our job is to find a chink in their very impressive armor."

"How can we help?" chorused the eager lads.

The famous detective studied the faces of the attentive boys. "Here's what I want you to do."

CHAPTER VII

A Daring Plan

There was a nip of frost in the late afternoon air when a motorcade of white Escalades pulled up to the entrance of the Brownbrier Resort.

Simultaneously the six drivers exited and opened the rear doors of the imposing vehicles. The old gardener stopped pruning and looked on. Tom, Billy, and their friends observed the arrival from the balcony of the Hardly boys' room. Bodyguards swarmed around the six-pack of Cadillacs.

Billy recognized the Trafalgar sisters and their friend Clive as they exited and stood by silently. Last out of the third vehicle stepped George W. Buttman himself. He was disgustingly obese and smoking a huge cigar. Several bellhops quickly picked up the mounds of expensive leather luggage and carted them into the hotel. As they entered the lobby, the group were met by well-dressed hotel staffers and shown to their suites.

After the Buttman entourage entered the hotel, the Hardlys put their dad's plan into effect. DeVern Hardly, still disguised as the gardener, was surreptitiously placing tracking devices on the gang's vehicles while Tom, Billy, and the girls were easing around the resort apparently interested in the lovely, well-tended gardens.

"What Dad wants us to do," said Tom, "is listen to as many of the gang's conversations as possible and try to learn whether Buttman is about to sell some of his cache of treasure in order to finance terrorist plots." He looked directly at Jessa and Anne, who were watching him attentively. "Are you willing to try to befriend the Trafalgar sisters?"

Anne and Jessa nodded their heads slowly. "We will do the best we can for Mr. Hardly and you boys," said Anne.

"We'll have to be very careful," opined Jessa. "I've heard you say how ruthless these villains are. We don't want any of our team to get hurt."

"Indeed we don't," Anne agreed.

"If you're circumspect and take it slow," said Billy, "you can ease into a relationship with the Black Widows. But Jessa is right. You will have to be very careful. Don't be fooled by their stylish clothes and well-coiffed hair. These are dangerous women."

The two couples wandered past the bocce court where the Trafalgar sisters were engaged in a heated contest. The boys then headed to the swimming pool. The girls ambled back to the bocce court and prepared to ingratiate themselves with the beautiful but deadly sisters.

Clive Custard and George W. Buttman, wearing swimming togs and sipping rum and tonics with lime slices, were engaged in an animated conversation. Billy sat as close as he dared with his back to the duo while Tom occupied a chair facing them. Clive glanced at the newcomers, saw only two elderly gentlemen, and turned back to continue his discussion with Buttman. With their hearing-enhancement devices on high, the boys were able to tune in to the conversation at the nearby table. Buttman was saying, "Rusty and Blackie got away just before the Guernsey Coast warehouse was raided. I don't know how the feds found out about it, but we need a new hideout."

"We can't trust the security of the cave since those two escaped," Clive pointed out.

"They may have drowned," said Buttman, "but we can't count on it."

Billy smiled to himself.

"I want that golden goblet," declared Buttman.

"I still think it's in Baymoor," answered Clive. "And if it is, we'll find it."

"You take the sisters and go back to Baymoor," said Buttman. "We need a secure site to store the goods until we're ready to complete the transaction, which shouldn't be too much longer. I've got a line on a storage facility in Scranton I'm going to check out tomorrow."

Just as Buttman and Clive left their table, Jessa, Anne, and the Trafalgar sisters came into the pool area together and sat down. "They're quite chummy," Billy allowed as the girls ordered drinks.

"Right," said Tom. "I knew they could do the job. But now we have to find Dad and give him the skinny on what we overheard. We'll talk to the girls later," said Tom. The boys signed for their Cokes and headed for the grounds to find the disguised DeVern Hardly. As they walked through the lobby they ran into their portly pal Whit, who was eating a hotdog, being careful not to drip mustard or relish on his white shirt or blazer. "What's up?" he queried.

On their way out to the gardens, the boys told Whit

of the recent developments. The old gardener was in the flowerbed cutting the last chrysanthemums of the fall. Feigning an interest in the flowers, the boys told the elder Hardly what they had overheard. "I was able to get tracking devices on the six Escalades in the Buttman entourage and the FBI says all the devices are functional. Some of the agents will certainly be going to Scranton, where Buttman is headed. I'll go with them. I want you boys and Whit to take the girls back to Baymoor. Keep an eye on Clive and the Trafalgar sisters. They'll be staying at the Monarch Hotel."

Early Monday morning the boys and girls piled into Whit's roadster and headed for the Guernsey shore. As they wound down the mountainside, one of the white Escalades roared past the yellow roadster, leaving it in a cloud of dust.

"That's a reckless group," Tom said.

"I'll say," replied Whit, as he motored slowly down the mountain.

The friends stopped for lunch at a family-style restaurant Whit had heard about. As they looked over the menu, they boys asked Anne and Jessa to fill them in on their experience with the Trafalgar sisters at the hotel pool. "They looked comfortable with you," Billy said. "Did you learn anything we should know?"

The girls shrugged. "They're pretty superficial, I'm afraid," said Jessa. "They only talked about fashions and make-up...stuff like that."

"Yes," agreed Anne. "They may be proficient criminals, but they are not deep thinkers. Either that, or they were playing coy."

Since they were all on assignment for the FBI, Billy and Tom thought it would be acceptable to charge the meal as a business expense. Billy had not used his credit card since Mr. Hardly had given it to him and he was eager to try it out.

"Do you want me to help?" Anne had stayed behind with Billy when the others left the restaurant.

"No thanks. Dad explained the difference between credit and debit cards. This," he said, holding up the Visa card, "is a credit card. And I need to tell the clerk that. I don't think I'll have any problem."

"OK. I'll be outside with the others." Anne gave Billy a peck on the cheek and turned away, leaving him to deal with the young man at the cash register.

"Was everything OK with your lunch?"

"Yes. Everything was fine," Billy replied.

The clerk sported one earring in his right ear and two in his left. Billy knew that even in Baymoor some men had pierced ears, but he still found it odd to see a man wearing earrings. He gave himself a mental shake and a silent admonition to "get with the program." It was an expression he had learned from Anne, and he found it oddly appealing.

Billy could see a tattoo peeking from beneath the cuff of the young man's shirt. Was it the tail of a dragon? Or was it a snake? Billy wasn't sure. He wondered whether it was impolite to ask about someone's tattoo. Presumably people wanted their tattoos to be noticed, otherwise why would they subject themselves to being pierced over and over again with needles and ink. Billy shuddered.

He had not cared for the greasers in his day, with their slicked-back hair and cigarette packs tucked into rolled-up sleeves. But tattoos? Only thugs and jailbirds had tattoos back then. Anne had told him that having a tattoo in this day and age didn't mean someone was a criminal or even disreputable. But Billy found that hard to accept.

"Is that a dragon's tail?" Billy pointed at the man's wrist.

"Yeah. Pretty cool, eh?" The clerk unbuttoned his cuff and pushed the shirt sleeve up over his bicep. "Isn't she a beauty?"

"I suppose," said Billy. "But I don't really understand the appeal."

"Yeah. Old people usually don't get it," said the man as he rolled down his sleeve.

"I'm younger than you are."

The clerk stared at Billy. He opened his mouth to speak, then very obviously changed his mind. "Whatever," he said with a shrug.

Though Billy had been back in the world a relatively short time, he had already learned to detest the ubiquitous "whatever" and its accompanying shrug. Biting back a sharp retort, he held up his Visa card. "This is a charge card," he said. "It is not a debit card."

"If you say so, guy."

"I do say so," said Billy. "And I want to use it now." He slid the check for the meal across the counter to the tattooed clerk.

Billy waited while dragon boy tallied up the bill.

"That'll be $43.25."

Billy held out the Visa card.

"Swipe the card."

Billy pulled his hand back and stared at the clerk.

"Swipe the card," he said again.

"What did you say?"

"Swipe the card. Please."

Still holding the Visa card in his hand, Billy continued to stare at the clerk.

"You haven't swiped the card."

"Did you ask if I had swiped the card?"

"No. I know you didn't swipe the card."

"I thought you asked if I had swiped the card."

"No. If you had swiped the card, I would be able to tell." The clerk enunciated every word clearly. "I would know whether it's debit or credit. Then I would be able to push a button. A receipt would print out. I would hand you the receipt. And then you would leave."

"It's a credit card," said Billy sharply. He had not understood what the clerk was saying, but he recognized sarcasm when he heard it. "I already told you that."

"But I don't know that until you swipe it."

"I just told you it's a credit card."

The clerk rolled his eyes.

"And I did not swipe it," added Billy.

"I know you didn't. But, you've got to swipe the card or it won't work."

Billy stared at the clerk incredulously. "What in the world do you mean?"

"I mean," said the clerk with an air of exaggerated

patience, "that you must swipe the card if you want to use it."

Billy did not move.

"Just run the card through," said the clerk losing his patience. "Never mind," he reached out to take the card from Billy, "I'll swipe the darn thing."

Billy snatched the card from the clerk's fingers just as Anne walked back into the restaurant. "Is everything OK?" she asked.

The clerk looked relieved. "No, ma'am. He won't swipe the card."

"I don't need to steal the card," said Billy. "It's mine. Dad gave it to me. And you," he glared at the tattooed clerk, "are not going to swipe it from me!"

Anne looked from Billy to the clerk and back again. "'What we have here is failure to communicate—'"

"*Cool Hand Luke*," blurted the clerk. "I love that movie."

"Indeed," said Anne. "OK, Billy, here's the problem." She took the card from him as she was talking and ran it through the card reader. "You have to slide the card through the device. Information is stored on this magnetic strip," she turned the card over, "which the device reads. That information is transmitted to the computer," she pointed at the cash register, "and then the clerk can complete the transaction."

Anne handed the plastic rectangle to Billy who stared at the magnetic strip on the back of the card.

"'Swipe' just means to run the card through the

reader," said Anne.

Mouth open, the clerk gazed wonderingly at Billy. "Where's he from?" he asked in a near whisper.

"It's more like, 'when's he from,'" replied Anne, taking Billy's arm and walking with him out of the restaurant.

The others were waiting beside the roadster when Billy and Anne walked out.

"Is something wrong?" asked Jessa. "Billy, you look sort of, I don't know . . . stunned."

"I'll tell you all about it on the way home," said Anne climbing into Whit's roadster.

The friends arrived in Baymoor in the early afternoon. The boys had to go back to school the next morning, but they agreed to meet after school for malts.

"Boy, things seem downright dull," opined Billy, "after the weekend we had."

"I'll say," agreed Jessa and Anne as they sipped on their chocolate shakes.

"The FBI agents are keeping an eye on Clive and the sisters," said Tom, "but they've been hanging around their hotel mostly."

"Time for us to start thinking outside the blocks," said Billy.

"Outside the what?" asked Anne.

"Outside the blocks."

Anne caught Jessa's eye and then quickly looked away.

"What does that mean?" asked Tom.

"It means," said Billy, "to be creative. To use

building blocks in new and original— What's so funny?"

"It's *box*," said Anne, trying hard to stifle her laughter. "Think outside the *box*."

"You're sure?"

"Positive."

"Oh. Very well then," said Billy, "it's time for us to start thinking outside the *box*."

"And how," inquired Tom, "do you suggest we do that?"

"I don't know."

No one spoke for a few seconds.

"Why don't we get back into our Brownbrier identities and casually run into our quarry. See what we can find out," suggested Tom.

There was general agreement that the plan had merit.

Later that evening, with the boys' mustaches and sideburns attached and the girls dressed in their resort finery, the group went to dinner at the Monarch Hotel. Whit was eating his second dessert when the trio entered the restaurant. The Trafalgar sisters immediately recognized Jessa and Anne and stopped by to greet them. "What are you doing in Baymoor?"

"We're having a few days on the shore," replied Anne, "before the weather turns cold, doing a little antiquing."

"Why don't we have lunch tomorrow?" suggested Lola.

Jessa said they had an engagement for lunch and

proposed tea instead. It was agreed the women would meet at 4:00 p.m. in the hotel atrium. "I hear there's a lovely string quartet during afternoon tea on Wednesdays," said Inez. The sisters then left to join Clive at their table.

On the way home Tom and Billy cautioned the girls to be careful. "Remember these are dangerous people," warned Tom. "Don't take any unnecessary chances."

"You needn't worry about us," chided Anne. "We'll be careful."

"Right," said Jessa. "We'll be shopping, so the only danger is that we'll spend too much money!"

The group agreed to meet at the Hardly home the next day.

After school Tom and Billy headed home along with their hungry pal Whit, who anticipated that Miss Jane and Mrs. Hardly would have spent the day baking pies and cakes. He wasn't disappointed. When the boys arrived at 223 Baker Street they were greeted by the wonderful aroma of apple pies coming from the kitchen. Miss Jane served an extra large piece to Whit.

Mrs. Hardly told the boys that their father had called to say he was staying in Scranton awhile longer to keep an eye on Buttman. It was after 5:00 p.m. and the boys were expecting Jessa and Anne at any moment. By 5:30 the girls still had not showed up or called. "I'm worried," said Tom. "We should have heard from them by now."

"Let's go to the hotel," said Billy.

Miss Jane was in a tizzy. "I knew something like this would happen. I just knew it. You should never have asked those lovely girls to get involved with one of your dangerous schemes. There's no telling what's happened to them. I declare, you boys just never think about the consequences of your actions."

"Now, Jane, that's unfair," Mrs. Hardly interjected. "The girls knew the possible dangers when they got involved. And I think Tom and Billy are quite good at taking responsibility for their actions."

"Well, Hazel, it's just like you to take up for those boys . . ."

Tom and Billy headed out the door, leaving their mother to defend them against unjust accusations. Whit followed quickly behind them.

When the boys arrived at the hotel, they saw neither their friends nor Custard and the Trafalgar sisters. At the front desk the boys were devastated to learn that the slippery trio had checked out an hour ago.

Tom and Billy headed for the FBI's temporary headquarters in the Baymoor Police Department. It was abuzz with activity. Special Agent Lou Steele shook hands with the Hardly boys and Whit. "Good to see you gentlemen again," said Steele. The break room had been turned over to the FBI, and agents were turning dials on their tracking equipment, searching for the telltale hum of the devices planted on the Escalades.

"We've lost the signal for the Cadillac that was in Baymoor," said a dejected Agent Kraus. "About an hour ago the bug stopped sending a signal. We sent agents for a visual but the vehicle was nowhere to be found. They've eluded us," he admitted. "We don't know where they are."

"We've got to find them," said Tom. "We fear they've kidnapped Jessa and Anne."

"We know the vehicle and the license number," said Agent Kraus, "but no reports of the car have surfaced. And the OnStar systems on all their Cadillacs have been disconnected."

"I think," said Tom, "an air search is required."

"We'll start at first light," said Billy. "There's nothing we can do from the air tonight."

Whit dropped the Hardly boys off and went back to his own house to tell his parents the distressing news. Miss Jane and Mrs. Hardly were waiting for the boys in the kitchen. "What have you found out?" asked Hazel Hardly as she brought out a plate of home-made macadamia nut cookies and poured the boys each a glass of milk.

Billy told them about how Custard had apparently disabled the tracking device, and Tom explained the search plan for the next day.

"You'd think," said Miss Jane, noisily emptying the dishwasher, "the FBI would be able to keep track of those villains." She closed the silverware drawer with a bang. "There's no telling what will happen to Anne and Jessa." She glared at the boys. "You and your schemes! I told you how it would be. I told you." She untied her apron and hung it on the back of the pantry door. "I'm going to bed," she announced to the room at large.

Mrs. Hardly tried to console the boys, who were looking quite dejected. "You know Jane's ways," she said, putting away the milk carton. "She doesn't mean half of what she says."

"But the girls *are* in danger," said Billy.

"And it *is* because of us," added Tom.

"Well, I know you'll find a way to rescue them," said their mother. She gave them each a peck on the cheek. "And I know the girls have faith in you. Don't worry. Things won't look so bleak tomorrow."

Indeed, the next morning Tom and Billy felt more confident. "We'll find them today," said Billy as he and his brother finished a hasty breakfast. "I just have a feeling."

They met their pals at the airport a little before six to coordinate the search. Whit, Izzy, and Marco had agreed to search by sea and ground for a couple of hours before school while the Hardly boys were scouring the countryside from the air.

The morning dawned bright and sunny as the biplane roared down the runway.

"Keep a sharp eye out," said Tom. "We need to find them soon."

They flew a series of easy turns up and down the coast. They spotted Marco and Izzy in the *Capri* headed out of the Lockjaw River. Then they saw Whit's yellow roadster on the Coast Highway tooling in and out of driveways along the way.

After about an hour Tom headed inland. They flew along Carol Creek for three or four miles but saw only empty cabins with no sign of life. As they headed back, Tom decided to fly over Richards Mountain before landing at the Baymoor airdrome. And there it was, a white Cadillac Escalade next to a cabin that had smoke coming from the chimney.

So as not to arouse suspicion, Tom did not circle back to the cabin, but flew instead straight to the airdrome. They left the plane with Hoppie's assistant and headed to the office and a telephone.

A call to police headquarters and the FBI led to a plan of action. Tom reached Whit and Izzy on their cell phones and told them to go on to school. "We've got a lead on where the girls have been taken," said Tom. "I've called Mom and she's going to let the principal know that Billy and I probably won't make it to school today."

Izzy said he and Marco would be available in the afternoon if they were needed. Whit insisted on skipping school and helping the boys in their search for Jessa and his sister. Along with local police and FBI agents, they would storm the cabin on Richards Mountain.

By the time all aspects of the plan had been coordinated with various law enforcement agents, the morning was well advanced. The Hardly boys and Whit joined members of the task force in the Wal-Mart parking lot just before noon.

"Sure enough," noted Whit, "we're about to head out for Richards Mountain without stopping for lunch. I was afraid that was how it would be, so I stopped at the deli for a couple of corned beefs on rye." He thrust a paper sack at Billy. "I bought a couple for you and Tom, too."

The three boys wolfed down the sandwiches while they were waiting for Agent Kraus to complete his instructions to the task force members. Billy tossed the sack of empty wrappers in a trashcan. "Thanks, Whit. That really hit the spot."

The white Escalade was parked in front of the bungalow and smoke was still coming from the cabin chimney when the rescue party arrived. The men surrounded the cabin and, on a signal from Agent Kraus, they rushed in.

There was no one in the cabin. Tom pointed to the floor where two lipstick-stained cigarette butts had been ground out.

"The Black Widows' calling cards," said Billy.

CHAPTER VIII

Where Eagles Dare Not

The boys were disconsolate. There was no indication that the girls had ever been in the cabin.

"The license number of this car matches one of the Escalades from Buttman's caravan at the resort hotel," said Chief Langly. "And look at this! There's one set of tire tracks coming in and none going out."

"He's right," said Agent Kraus. "Is there anywhere they could have gotten to on foot?"

"I know of a place not all that far from here—" began the Chief.

"Jacks Peak," ejaculated Tom and Billy simultaneously.

"Right!" said Chief Langly. "It's two miles up the mountain, but it's an easy hike, and there's a small cabin at the top."

"Let's go," said Agent Kraus.

Whit looked dismayed at the idea of a two-mile hike up a mountain. "Shouldn't someone stay here," he asked, "just to be sure the kidnappers don't double back?"

"Actually," said Agent Kraus, "that's not a bad idea. Whit, you stay here with Agent Langford. Everybody else, come with me."

Looking relieved, Whit went to sit on the cabin's stone steps. Agent Langford leaned against the Escalade and began playing Angry Birds on his cell phone.

The rest of the group headed up the trail, hoping to

rescue the girls. The plan was to encircle the cabin and overpower any of the kidnappers on the premises. It took the group about twenty-five minutes to reach Jacks Peak. They quietly surrounded the small cabin, which showed no signs of life.

"I don't like the looks of this," muttered Tom.

"Me either," whispered Billy.

With weapons drawn, the agents and Chief Langly approached the cabin. The two unarmed boys followed close behind them. No sounds could be heard from inside.

Agent Kraus tried the door, which was not locked. Carefully opening the door, he stepped into a single large room. The others crowded in behind him.

Not only was there no one in the cabin, it had obviously been empty for some time. A layer of dust covered the chairs and tables. "They were never here," lamented Tom.

"How," said Agent Kraus, following the group back outside, "did they leave Richards Mountain without leaving any tire tracks?"

"Helicopter," said Chief Langly.

"We'll get a copter of our own," growled Agent Kraus. "I'm tired of being left behind. But we can't begin an air search now. In fact, I don't think we can do anything more today. Let's meet at the police station at sunup and compare notes. I have a feeling things will be better tomorrow."

The boys had left their car at police headquarters, and when they got back there Tom Hardly put in a call to his mom, who answered the phone promptly, as she always did when her menfolk were out on a job. "Mom," said Tom, "the girls are still missing and no one knows what to do next."

"You'd better come home then. That's what your dad would do," said Mrs. Hardly. "Miss Jane has made one of your favorite meals, a nice chicken pot pie. I'm sure it will help you think."

"Right, Mom. We'll see you soon."

The Hardly boys said good-by to Whit and headed to their house. At home, even Miss Jane was solicitous. "I'm sure," she said, as she dished up plentiful helpings of her chicken pot pie for the boys, "that everything will work out. Eat some dinner and get a good night's rest. You'll find the girls tomorrow."

The Hardly boys had a restless night, and after an early breakfast they headed off to the Baymoor police headquarters. Whit was skipping school to stay with his mother, who was understandably concerned about her daughter. "I told Mom that you and Billy will find the girls," he had said to Tom the night before. "And she has great confidence in you, but—"

"But she will feel better if her stalwart son is there with her."

"Something like that," replied an embarrassed Whit.

At the police station, Agent Kraus was on the phone and Chief Langly sat on the visitor's side of the desk listening to Kraus's end of the conversation.

Officer Hunnicut was drinking coffee and eating a jelly donut. He gestured with his coffee cup toward the box of donuts on the table. "Help yourselves," he said. The brothers said that they had already eaten and went to stand near the Chief.

Agent Kraus hung up his phone. "We've caught a break. A satellite photographing the area of the Guernsey Coast for Google Earth—"

"Goo-goo what?" interrupted Tom.

"Google Earth," Kraus repeated.

"What's a goo-goo earth?"

"Not goo-goo. Google."

"Google?"

"Tom," said Billy, pinching his brother's arm. "Do be quiet and let the agent tell us what he knows."

"Thanks," said Kraus, taking up where he'd left off. "The satellite for Google Earth photographed a helicopter leaving the area of the cabin on Richards Mountain just two hours before we arrived. From a series of photos, we have determined that it was on a course for Scranton, Pennsylvania."

"Our dad is there!" exclaimed Billy excitedly.

"We have men there, too," said Kraus. "They're headed for the airport and are checking all possible landing sites in the area. I'm going up there now, myself." He looked at the Hardly brothers. "Can I give you guys a lift?"

"And how!" Tom Hardly avowed. "I hate to miss class again, but the girls are more important than school."

An FBI helicopter was waiting for them at the Baymoor airdrome.

"Wow!" exclaimed Billy. "Our first ride in a

helicopter. Isn't this cool, Tom?"

"I think," said Tom sternly, "you should focus on what's important here: getting the girls back."

"You're right," said a chastened Billy. "I get carried away sometimes."

"I know," replied Tom. Then he flashed his brother a grin. "But you're right. It *is* cool."

There was an expectant air of success as the boys strapped themselves in the Bell JetRanger, along with the federal agent.

When they arrived at the police heliport in Scranton, DeVern Hardly and Special Agent Steele were waiting for them. DeVern had requested that Steele be sent from Baymoor to be his special liaison with the FBI. The two men had worked together before and were pleased to be collaborating on another case.

"We meet again," said Steele, shaking hands with the two boys. "Late yesterday," he continued, "a helicopter landed at one of Buttman's properties, a five-hundred-acre farm in the hills west of town. We think the captives are being held at that farmhouse."

"How do you propose to rescue the girls?" asked Tom anxiously.

"We'll go in under cover of darkness," said Agent Steele.

He explained the plan to the three Hardlys and Agent Kraus. As soon as the sun went down the rescue team would be mobilized. Tom, Billy, and the elder Hardly would approach from the front while Steele, Kraus, and the other FBI agents would enter from both sides and the rear.

When everyone was in place, a signal was given and the three Hardlys headed for the front of the house. Billy knocked on the door. It was opened by Gus from the undersea cavern. He recognized Billy at once.

"I thought you drowned," sneered Gus, as he tried to slam the door in Billy's face.

"You wish," said Billy throwing his full weight forward.

Billy was losing ground against the heavier and burlier Gus when Tom hurled himself against the door and he and Billy surged over the threshold.

Gus staggered but quickly regained his balance and made a dash for the back door.

"I've got him!" yelled Tom, flinging himself onto the ruffian's back. But Gus was too strong for him and Tom was tossed aside, as he later said, "like a sack of feathers."

Billy made a diving tackle and caught the fleeing villain around the ankles, bringing Gus down with a resounding crash. Tom meanwhile had picked himself up and now sat down heavily on Gus's legs. Writhing and bucking, the angry Gus attempted to shed the Hardly boys, but they hung on grimly until FBI agents, flooding in from the back entrance, took over.

"Good work, boys," said Mr. Hardly, who had followed his sons in through the front door. "Well done."

Manny, Gus's cohort, was soon escorted in by two agents. "We caught him trying to make a break for it," said the younger agent. "Get over there with your buddy," he added, shoving Manny toward the kitchen table where a dejected Gus sat glumly staring at the roomful of agents. Gus and Manny were soon handcuffed and Agent Kraus read them their rights.

"Where are Jessa and Anne?" demanded Tom.

"Them crazy sisters and their high-falutin' plans. I tell you they ain't nothin' but trouble. Brought those dames here to prove they're as tough as the rest of the gang. We done told 'em that kidnappin's a federal offense and—"

"Shut up, Manny!"

"I don't have to take no orders from you, Gus!"

"You'll keep your trap shut if you know what's good for you. The big boss don't take kindly to snitches."

"Ain't snitchin'," retorted Manny. "Ain't sayin' nothin' that won't be obvious—"

"I'm telling you to shut up now or you'll be sorry."

One of the agents who had been searching the rest of the house called out from a room toward the back, "The ladies are in here."

Tom and Billy, followed closely by Mr. Hardly, Special Agent Steele, and Agent Kraus, hurried to the study, where they found Anne and Jessa bound and gagged but otherwise unharmed.

"Lordy!" said Anne after Billy had removed her gag. "Are you a sight for sore eyes!"

"You can say that again," said Jessa. She stood up and gave the startled Tom a hug. "We are *so* glad to see the guys in the white hats."

"Where are the wretched Manny and Gus?" asked Anne.

"In the kitchen, surrounded by FBI agents," said Tom.

"Couldn't happen to nicer guys," said the gentle Jessa with unusual venom.

"What happened?" asked Billy. "Those thugs in the kitchen said the sisters kidnapped you to prove something to the rest of the gang. Is that true?"

"Apparently so," said Anne, swinging her arms as she walked briskly about the room. "D-...uh...consarn it!" she stammered, face reddening. "In the movies people who have been gagged and bound for hours are always leaping up when they're released and dashing off to subdue the baddies as if their arms and legs weren't stiff and achy because their circulation had been cut off. *Very* unrealistic. I will never believe one of those scenes again."

"Yes, Anne," said Mr. Hardly with a slight smile. "Could you perhaps bring your attention back to the matter at hand."

"Of course, Mr. Hardly." Anne stopped her pacing. "Sorry. Where was I?"

"You were about to tell us about the Trafalgar sisters' apparent motive for the kidnapping."

"Right. Jessa and I were to meet them for tea at the hotel, which we did. But instead of having tea, they asked us to go for a ride to visit a special antique shop they had found. You remember," she said to Billy and Tom, "that was supposedly one of the reasons we were in Baymoor."

"Right," said Billy. "So what happened?"

"We got in the car with them and they drove to a

cabin up on Richards Mountain. On the way there we began to suspect that something was not right, but we couldn't get out because the back doors were locked."

"I know it would have been risky to jump—"

Anne gave Billy an odd look. "We *couldn't* jump. I told you, the doors were locked."

"Were you tied up?"

"No. We weren't tied up. But the doors were *locked*."

"Well if you weren't tied up, why didn't you unlock the doors?"

"We *couldn't* unlock the doors."

"I'm not saying you should have jumped out. Though maybe when the car slowed down on one of the curves, you might have—"

"It wasn't a matter of *wouldn't,* Billy, it was a matter of *couldn't*," said Anne with a note of asperity. "The back doors were *locked* and—"

"Oh, of course," exclaimed Jessa, interrupting Anne. "They don't know about childproof locks."

"Childproof locks?"

"In lots of cars these days the back doors can't be opened by a backseat passenger until the car stops or the driver flips a switch to unlock the doors."

"Why?"

"To keep children from accidentally opening the doors and falling out."

"Oh," said Billy with a blank stare. "Childproof locks." His face brightened. "I get it. Locks that are secure against the mischievous ways of children— *childproof locks*." Then his brow wrinkled. "But why?

Were lots of children falling out of the backseats of cars?"

"Forget about the locks," said Tom testily. "The point is that Jessa and Anne couldn't get out of the car. Go on with the story, please."

"When we got to the cabin," said Jessa, picking up the tale, "the sisters pulled out pistols and told us to go inside. They said they wouldn't hesitate to shoot us. And we believed them."

"We sure did," interjected Anne.

"We were gagged and our hands were bound. In a little while a helicopter arrived and we were forced to get in," Jessa continued. "When we got here—"

"Where *is* here?" asked Anne. "Sorry, Jessa."

"That's OK. I want to know, too," Jessa agreed. "Where are we?"

"You're at a farmhouse west of Scranton, Pennsylvania," said Special Agent Steele.

"Scranton!" said Anne.

"Scranton?" echoed Jessa.

"Yes, ma'am. The property belongs to George W. Buttman," explained Steele. He turned to address Jessa directly. "You were about to say what happened when you got here, Ms. Sheridan. Please go on."

"The sisters were boasting to those two ruffians," Jessa nodded in the direction of the kitchen, "about how they had single-handedly kidnapped us. They said they were as capable as anyone else in the gang and now they had proved it. They left us with those clowns and said they'd see us later." Then, as an afterthought, "I don't believe they know there's any connection between us and you Hardlys."

"I really do think," interjected Anne, "that they kidnapped us and brought us here just to show the men that they could do it."

"That," said DeVern Hardly, bemused, "is as odd a reason as I've ever heard for kidnapping someone. But all's well that ends well, as the Bard has said. Now," he turned to his sons, "I think you'd better get these young ladies back to Baymoor."

"Yes, sir," replied Tom. "There isn't room in the helicopter for everyone, so I'll arrange for a rental and we'll drive the girls back to Baymoor. Are you coming home, Dad?"

"Yes, Tom. I'll ride back with the FBI, if that's all right with you, Agent Steele."

"We'll be glad to give you a lift, sir."

"Very well," said DeVern Hardly. "I think we'll find that Buttman and his henchmen will be back in Baymoor soon. Buttman covets the golden goblet with the emeralds, diamonds, sapphires, and the occasional garnet. We will use it to set a trap."

As Agent Steele and DeVern Hardly headed for the helicopter and a quick trip to Baymoor, one of the FBI agents gave Tom and his friends a ride to the nearest car rental facility.

"You can just drop us here," said Tom. "We appreciate the lift, sir."

He and Billy shook hands with the agent through the open window, as they stood on the curb.

"My pleasure," replied the young man.

Tom had heard all about Billy's credit card encounter with dragon boy, as Billy had dubbed the young man at the restaurant. As a result, Tom had made a point of going to several different stores in Baymoor to practice using his own card; he was confident he would have no problem renting a car for the drive home.

The rental facility was not much larger than a medium-size storage shed, so Billy and the others waited outside while Tom went in to secure the car.

"Are you sure you don't want me to come with you?" Jessa said. "I can put the car on my credit card and you can reimburse me."

"I'll be fine," said Tom firmly.

Jessa smiled. "Well, give a shout if you need me."

"Evening, sir," said the middle-aged clerk as Tom approached the counter. "What can I do for you?"

"We'd like to rent a car. We need to get back to Baymoor."

"Right. What size car would you like?"

"What size car?" Tom stared at the man. "I don't know," he said. "I've only been driving a year."

The man stared back at Tom with a blank look on his face.

"It's a long story…What do you have?" asked Tom

"Though we are a fairly small facility we have a good selection of cars," the clerk asserted. "Are all your friends going with you?" The clerk nodded toward where Billy and the others were gathered.

"Yes. We're all going back to Baymoor."

"Our economy and compact cars can hold five

passengers." The man leaned forward a little and lowered his voice, "But between you, me, and the lamp post, I think you'll be more comfortable in a midsize or a standard. Maybe even a luxury."

"Luxury is a size?"

"I beg your pardon?"

"Luxury isn't a size. I mean people don't say, 'What size hat do you wear?' 'I wear a luxury.' That doesn't make sense."

"No...sir." The clerk's glasses had slid a little way down on his nose and he peered over them at Tom. "I had never thought of it that way . . . 'I wear a size luxury running shoe.'" He began to chuckle. "'What size jacket are you looking for? An economy or a compact?' Quite funny, sir." He pushed his glasses up on his nose as if to say "now back to business."

"Do you have much luggage?"

"No," said Tom. "No luggage."

"Well, then," the man turned slightly so he could enter information into his computer, "I expect one of our midsize cars will do just fine, though the *luxury size* does tend to impress the ladies, if you know what I mean." He winked at Tom.

Tom looked blank.

"Yes, well," said the clerk, resuming his typing, "I assume you won't be needing an infant or toddler car seat," he smiled at his own joke, "but what about a GPS? Very helpful that can be. Particularly at night. When you don't know the lay of the land as it were."

"Is a Jeepy-S a luxury car?"

"Beg pardon?"

"Is a Jeepy-S a luxury car?"

"It's not a car."

"It's not?" Tom frowned. "Jeeps used to be cars. At least they were vehicles like cars only they were called Jeeps. They were used during World War II. I remember seeing one in Baymoor after the war."

"Yes, sir. I'm sure you did. But a GPS is, nevertheless, not a car." He looked out the window again at the two women and their friends. They were still just standing around chatting with each other. He wondered if he should try to attract their attention. The old man didn't seem dangerous but he was clearly not all with it. On the other hand, maybe his friends were batty, too.

"What is a Jeepy-S then?"

"It's a global positioning system—gee pee ess. It keeps track of where you are and where you want to go."

Tom gaped at the clerk. "It does? Wow! Just like something out of Dick Tracy or Buck Rogers."

"Very high tech, indeed. I was telling my sister just the other day that I sometimes feel like I'm living in the midst of a science fiction novel." The clerk's gaze shifted from Tom to some unknown space just beyond him. "But still no hovercars," he said with a sigh. "You remember they were in all the sci-fi stories: no more roads, no more traffic jams, no more congestion. Ah, well." He shook his head. "Perhaps a GPS isn't the thing for you."

"Probably not," averred Tom. "But I would love to see one operate sometime. Do you think I could get one for my car?"

"Absolutely. The price has come down dramatically, as it always does with electronic gear. Do you want the gasoline option or will you return it with a full tank? If we fill it, it will be $6.00 per gallon," said the clerk.

"Six dollars per gallon!" Tom exclaimed. "Are you crazy? The last time I bought gas it was twenty-five cents a gallon!"

The clerk stared at Tom and shook his head. "Now, sir," he said briskly, turning back to his computer, "I'll need your driver's license and credit card."

"Swell," said Tom reaching into his back pocket for his wallet. "Here you go." He proudly flashed his shiny new license, which the Baymoor police had provided.

The clerk accepted the two cards, entered the information into the computer, and slid the rental contract across the counter to Tom.

"If you'll just sign here and here. And initial here, that you don't want the additional insurance, and here, that there will be no drivers under the age of twenty-five."

"Oh." Tom paused, pen in hand. "I didn't know there was an age limit."

"An age limit?"

" I mean I didn't know you had to be a certain age to rent a car."

"And what is the problem, sir?" he asked. The old man was beginning to get on his nerves. In another fifteen minutes he could close up shop and go home to his apartment. He would fix himself a stiff bourbon, sit in his favorite chair, and download shows from his Netflix instant queue. He had just started the third season of *Have Gun, Will Travel* last night and he was looking forward to more adventures with Richard Boone. No doubt the old man was harmless, but he was clearly a few fries short of a full order. "Do you want to add an additional driver to the contract?"

"No," replied Tom. "I'll drive us home."

"Then I don't see a problem. Just sign here and here, and initial here and here."

"Maybe I should go ask Jessa about this." Tom was turning away from the counter when the door opened and Jessa walked in.

"Hey," she said, looking from Tom to the clerk and back again. "What's up? Can I help?"

"I didn't know there was—"

"He won't sign—"

The clerk stopped speaking and gestured to Tom to continue.

"I didn't know there was an age limit. You have to be twenty-five to rent a car and—"

"Right," said Jessa, stepping up to the counter. She smiled sweetly at the clerk. "It's OK. Sometimes his sense of humor gets away with him."

"But I'm not twenty—"

"Here, Tom," said Jessa handing the ballpoint pen to Tom. "The man has put checkmarks where you should sign."

"Yes, ma'am," said the clerk. "And he needs to initial here and here."

"Right-oh," said Jessa.

"Well," said Tom, as he signed and initialed in all the appropriate spots, "if you think it's OK ..."

He handed the pen back to the clerk. "Sorry for the misunderstanding. Billy and I haven't been back very long and we still tend to think of ourselves as teenagers."

"Uh— I uh—"

"Not to worry," said Jessa, reaching for the keys the man had laid on the counter. "Just point us in the direction of the car and we'll be on our way."

He told them where to pick up the car and watched as they rejoined their friends outside the building. "That," he said aloud to the empty room, "was an oddly disorienting experience. I shall lock up now and go home."

And so he did.

The Hardlys and their pals found the rental car without any problem. Tom familiarized himself with the car's controls and they started on their journey home.

Anne had called her parents and Mrs. Hardly while Tom was renting the car and told them that everyone was fine. The foursome stopped along the way for a bowl of chili and rolled into Baymoor after midnight.

The girls were worn out from their ordeal. Whit and his parents were thrilled to welcome Anne back and invited Jessa to spend the night. She was happy to accept their kind offer.

Tom and Billy got to 223 Baker Street at 3:00 a.m. Their mother had waited up for them. "Your dad got home several hours ago and told Jane and me about your adventures in Scranton. I'm so glad Anne and Jessa are safe at home now. Those Black Widows are ruthless women."

"They sure are," mumbled Billy, trying to talk and yawn at the same time.

"You boys go on to bed," said Mrs. Hardly. "And sleep as long as you'd like. I'll tell your aunt not to wake you."

"Thanks a million, Mom," said Tom. "You're the best."

The boys slept late, and when they came downstairs they learned that their father had gone to Washington, D.C., to confer with Homeland Security on another assignment. He had left word that they would continue the case of the golden goblet when he got home at the end of the week.

Not surprisingly, the boys were a little behind in their schoolwork, so they spent part of the weekend doing homework and reviewing notes from Izzy and their other chums. By the time Monday rolled around, they had caught up on their assignments and their sleep.

This was the week that Baymoor High played football against their cross-county rival Marshall High for bragging rights to "best in the county." Coach Thomas put the players through their paces and was satisfied that Whit and the Hardly boys could perform as usual.

On Friday night the stands were filled with excited fans, including the Hardly family. DeVern, back from Washington, was on the 50-yard line with his wife and sister to cheer the boys on.

The Marshall team took the opening kickoff and marched down the field for a quick score. With Tom Hardly at the helm, the Baymoor eleven returned the favor and scored 7 of their own. The see-saw battle continued through the first two quarters. The score was tied at 21 at the half.

Coach Thomas took Tom and Billy aside. "The defense isn't doing as well as I had hoped," he said. "We're going to need all the points you can muster." Tom and Billy nodded in agreement. As the team returned to the field for the second half, the cheerleaders from Baymoor were doing their job. The crowd was vocal in its support of the home team.

Baymoor kicked off to the boys from Marshall, who returned the ball to their own 39 with a 1st and 10. On the first play from scrimmage the Marshall Mavericks executed a long stop-and-go pass play to perfection and scored 6 more. The point after made the score 28 to 21.

Tom Hardly took his brother and Whit Moore aside before the Marshall kickoff. "If we don't step up and get some quick scores we're in for a long and depressing evening," he said. Whit and Billy agreed. "Let's tell Coach Thomas what we've been working on," said Tom.

When Baymoor took the field at their 27-yard line the boys were ready to run their own special play, the Statue of Liberty. Whit snapped the ball to Tom who feigned a pass. Billy circled around and took the ball around the left end and streaked down the field for a quick 6 points. The successful point after had the game tied again.

The quick score invigorated the Baymoor defense, who held on throughout the next series of plays. The boys got the ball back on their own 16 with 1st and 10.

With two first downs in succession, Baymoor was quickly on the Mavericks' side of the field. Tom called a time-out and ran to the sideline to talk with Coach Thomas. He returned to the huddle and the play was called.

Whit snapped the ball to Tom as Billy ran down the sideline headed for the end zone. The Marshall lads had put double coverage on Billy but failed to cover Marco on the other side of the field. Tom lofted the pigskin to Marco who snatched the spiraling object from the air and scored for the lead.

Baymoor played inspired football the rest of the game and won by two touchdowns.

Tom and Billy had another reason to celebrate after the game: they had gotten their cell phones. "Verizon on the horizon no longer," Billy had crowed that afternoon. "Verizon is here!"

After the game, the gang met the girls at the malt shop and savored their victory as they sipped chocolate shakes. Seated in a booth at the drugstore, Billy took out his iPhone and showed it to Anne Moore. "Isn't it swell! Watch what happens when I touch this button!"

"It's not a button," said Whit, looking over Billy's way.

"Huh? Sure it is."

"No, it's an icon."

"A what?"

"An icon—an image, a graphic symbol, a pictorial representation."

"If you say so," responded Billy. "It works like a button. Look at this . . ."

Saturday morning dawned bright and clear, and the boys were eager to resume their investigation of Buttman and his crew. DeVern Hardly had arranged for a meeting with the local police and the FBI agents from Washington. Tom and Billy were invited to attend.

"We need to set a trap to catch a rat," said DeVern Hardly. "The golden goblet is just the kind of object that Buttman would love to have for his private collection of priceless treasures. Let's make it available."

"What," asked Special Agent Steele, "do you have in mind?"

"We'll put it on display at the art museum," suggested the world-famous detective, "and hope he will send someone to steal it."

"What!?" exclaimed Chief Langly. "Why would we want to do that?"

"I get it," said Tom. "The thief will take the golden goblet to George W. Buttman, who will want to show it off as he does his other loot. And if you can catch him with the goblet in his possession, you'll have proof positive of his connection to the theft."

Chief Langly looked pensive as he mulled over this scheme.

"Billy and I can help stake out the museum," exulted Tom. "We have a bone to pick with these hooligans."

The goblet was installed in the museum in a locked case. Guards were posted inside and outside the museum, and the security cameras were focused on the Plexiglas cube that housed the artifact. Tom and Billy devoted as much time as they could spare from class and after-school activities to helping with the stakeouts.

On Tuesday evening, after three days of stakeout duty, Tom and Billy were looking forward to a special meal prepared by Miss Jane and Mrs. Hardly. They had been allowed to invite Jessa, Anne, and Whit to dinner that evening.

The rotund boy and his sister were ushered into the sitting room, where the boys were entertaining Jessa Sheridan with a recording of the Tommy Dorsey orchestra. DeVern Hardly was tapping his foot in time to the familiar music. Tom solicited Jessa's hand for a dance and they twirled around the room until Miss Jane announced that dinner was ready.

She and Mrs. Hardly had outdone themselves that evening. They served up a sumptuous feast: a standing rib roast of beef, baked potatoes, a grand green salad, and home-made Parker House rolls.

After finishing seconds, Whit Moore was ready for the apple pie a la mode served by Hazel Hardly. "That's the best dinner I've had since last night," Whit exulted.

The ladies smiled at Whit's enthusiastic praise of their culinary efforts.

As Whit was polishing off the last of his pie and ice cream and everyone else was finishing their decaf coffee, the doorbell rang. DeVern Hardly opened the door to be greeted by a crestfallen police chief and Special Agent Steele.

"They've taken the goblet," said Langly.

"That's just what we wanted them to do," said DeVern Hardly. "Why do you fellows look so despondent?"

"The security guards saw nothing; they heard nothing; and nothing recognizable is on the security cameras."

The HARDLY Boys

CHAPTER IX

On the Trail of George W. Buttman

"I see," said Mr. Hardly. "That does alter the situation a bit." He invited Chief Langly and Special Agent Steele to join him in his home office. "If you ladies will excuse us," he said with a bow. Then, turning to his sons, "We have business to discuss. Boys, come with us, please."

"They tunneled under the museum," reported Chief Langly as he took a seat in one of the green leather chairs facing DeVern Hardly's desk.

"They cut a hole," said Special Agent Steele, "in the bottom of the case. They snatched the goblet and were gone within seconds after the alarm sounded."

"All we see on the security recording are arms and hands covered in black cloth," reported Chief Langly. He leaned forward, put his elbows on DeVern's desk, and rested his chin on his clasped hands. "We failed," he said quietly. "It was a good plan but . . ." His voice trailed off.

"Where did the tunnel start?" queried DeVern Hardly.

"In the basement of the storage building next door," said Steele.

"We've been watching all roads out of Baymoor," reported the federal officer. "And the Coast Guard has been alerted. There has been no sign of Buttman or his known associates."

"Maybe they are still in Baymoor," exclaimed Tom

124

Hardly.

"Let's have a look at the tunnel," suggested
DeVern.

Whit and Anne agreed to drop Jessa off at her house on
their way to the Moore family farm. Tom, Billy,
DeVern, and the law officers piled into the Chief's
patrol car and headed to the scene of the crime.

The world-famous Hardly detective examined the
tunnel entrance for clues. "I don't see anything that
points to the identity of the culprits. There's little doubt
that the Buttman gang is behind this, but some proof
would not be unwelcome."

Tom and Billy agreed to crawl from one end of the
tunnel to the other. When they returned to the entrance,
Billy held in his hands the only clue the group would
find: two Mexican cigarette butts with lipstick stains of
different colors.

"I knew it!" roared DeVern Hardly. "The Black
Widows were here. Good work, boys!"

The boys were thrilled to have their father's
approval. "We'll find these villains, Dad," exclaimed
the brothers. "And get the goblet back."

"We'll keep watching the exits out of town," said
the FBI agent, "although I agree with Tom that there's a
strong possibility Buttman and his crew are hiding out
somewhere in Baymoor."

"Let's meet at headquarters in the morning," said
Chief Langly.

"Right," Tom replied. "It's time to implement
plan B."

"And what might plan B consist of?" queried Billy.

"I don't know," admitted Tom. "But surely we can think of something in the morning. And then we can implement it."

When they arrived at 223 Baker Street, DeVern Hardly revealed to his boys that he had to return to Washington early the next morning. "I want you boys," said the elder Hardly, "to take charge of this investigation and bring the blackguards to justice."

"We'll make you proud, Dad," chorused the boys.

"I know you will," said DeVern Hardly. "I'll see you in a few days."

Miss Jane had made hot chocolate for the boys, which they drank before heading off to bed.

When they got up the next morning, their dad had already gone. Hazel Hardly insisted the boys have breakfast before they joined the lawmen in town.

"Youngsters," complained Miss Jane. "They're so busy rushing from one place to the next, they don't take time for a proper repast. 'Sink meals,' my grandmother used to call that kind of rushed eating, a meal where you're leaning over the sink to keep from dropping crumbs on the floor." She was frying eggs and buttering hot toast while she fussed. "Now in my day—"

"Yes, Jane. We know things aren't what they used to be in the good old days," said Mrs. Hardly, taking the plate of buttered toast from her sister-in-law. "The problem," she added, with a wink at her boys, "is that they weren't like that back then either."

The boys ate their breakfast as quickly as good

manners would allow, then headed off to the police station. Officer Hunnicut was eating a jelly donut when they arrived. "You boys already had breakfast, I suppose."

"We did," said Tom.

Hunnicut snared himself another donut and headed out on patrol.

Agents Kraus and Steele were in Chief Langly's office. Steele, sitting on the corner of the desk, looked up and motioned for Billy and Tom to join them. Kraus had swung one of the side chairs around and was straddling it; he turned his head when the boys walked in and nodded a greeting.

"Morning, boys," said Zack Langly from behind his desk. "Come on in and take a seat. We were just talking over our next step."

"What can we do to help?" asked Tom.

"Put us to work," begged Billy.

"All right, boys," said the Chief. "We've decided an air search might reveal something. Can you take your plane up and have a look around? See if something turns up?"

"I think we can get an excused absence for this," said Tom. "Come on, Billy. Let's go.

"We'll report to you after our flight, Chief." He was punching in a number on his cell phone as he walked out of the office. "May I speak to Principal McCafferty?"

Hoppie had their biplane warmed up and ready when they arrived at the airdrome at a quarter to seven. They flew along the coast looking for anything to suggest where the Trafalgar sisters were hiding out. DeVern Hardly and the law officers hoped the Black Widows would lead them to Buttman—and the golden goblet encrusted with diamonds, rubies, sapphires, emeralds, and the occasional garnet.

As the boys flew low over the upper Lockjaw River they saw smoke coming from the chimney of the old Burchfield Mansion, which had been abandoned for fifteen years. "We'd better tell the Chief about this," urged Billy. Tom radioed the tower at the Baymoor airdrome with the information and instructed that it be passed on immediately to Chief Langly. Then he turned the biplane toward home.

The boys burst into police headquarters and began pelting the Chief and the FBI agent with questions. "Did you find anyone?" "Were the Black Widows in the mansion?" "Did you find Custard and Buttman?" "Have you called Dad?"

"Whoa!" said Chief Langly. "One question at a time, boys."

"Did you find anyone in the mansion?" repeated Tom.

"We haven't been out there yet. We were just discussing how to proceed. Can you boys miss school for the rest of the day?"

"Yes," replied Tom. "I cleared it with Principal McCafferty. She said not to worry about school. So we're at the ready."

Special Agent Steele asked the boys to take their

boat up the Lockjaw River to the Burchfield Mansion and scout around outside. "Don't go into the house," cautioned Steele. "I'll be going out there myself later this morning and I don't want anything disturbed."

"You got it," said Billy as he and Tom headed out the door.

Taking the *Flatfoot*, they arrived at the Burchfield dock around ten in the morning. Officer Hunnicut had been posted at the old mansion after the boys had radioed in their report of smoke from the chimney. "Haven't seen hide nor hair of anyone since I've been here. Of course I didn't get out here until about 9:30. Plenty of time for those scoundrels to beat a hasty retreat. What are you boys doing out here?"

They explained that Special Agent Steele wanted them to look around outside the mansion. "He said he'd be out himself later today to search the house," added Tom. "We're going down to look for clues on the riverbank. We'll check in with you again before we leave."

Tom followed Billy down to the edge of the river. Billy turned downstream; Tom headed upstream.

"Billy," cried Tom, "look at this." Billy hurried over to where Tom stood pointing at the ground.

"Ah hah!" exulted Billy. "The litterbugs have been here."

Tom bent over to pick up the evidence and drop it into a plastic evidence bag. "Maybe," he said.

"What do you mean, 'maybe'?! Do you think someone else is smoking Records con Filtros with two different shades of lipstick and throwing the butts on the ground?"

"No," said Tom slowly. "I think these cigarette butts were left by the Trafalgar sisters."

"Well, then," said Billy irritably, "why did you say 'maybe'?"

"Because I don't think they were littering. I don't think they dropped the butts accidentally."

"What do you— Oh." Billy looked thoughtful. "You think they're dropping them on purpose."

Tom nodded. "Yep. I think they're taunting us." He slipped the evidence bag into a pocket. "OK. Let's get on with our sleuthing."

The brothers decided to finish their search together, heading downstream.

"All the footprints in the mud lead to the river," noted Tom. "There are no footprints leaving the riverbank."

"The submarine," ejaculated Billy.

"No doubt," said Tom.

The boys hurried back to Hunnicut and instructed him to report their findings to the Coast Guard and Chief Langly. They hopped into the *Flatfoot* and headed downriver toward the open sea and Blackbeard's Island. As they motored into Welsley Bay they could see a Coast Guard cutter headed on the same course. They pulled alongside the cutter and hailed Lieutenant Shaeffer.

"We'll check out the island," said Shaeffer, when Tom had explained to him what they had found near the Burchfield mansion. "You boys head on back. We'll keep you posted. I'll dispatch a helicopter to check out the situation on the island and in the underwater cavern."

The boys motored back to Baymoor, put the *Flatfoot* away, and headed to Chief Langly's office. Langly, who was there with Special Agent Steele, expressed his gratitude for the boys' discovery at the Burchfield Mansion. "The Coast Guard called and said the helicopter had arrived but found no evidence that anyone had been on the island," said the Chief.

"When the cutter arrives," added Steele, "Lieutenant Shaeffer plans to send a team of frogmen into the cave. In the meantime," he said, addressing the Hardly boys, "what do you say we take a run out to the Burchfield Mansion? See what we can find inside the house."

"Let's go," chorused the boys. "See you later, Chief."

"Let's grab a bite of lunch on the way," Steele suggested, as they got into his car.

"If Whit were here you wouldn't have to remind us about lunch," laughed Tom.

"That's the truth," chimed in Billy. "That boy does not like to miss a meal."

Steele made a U-turn and headed out of town toward the Burchfield Mansion. "We can stop at that new fast food joint. Does that suit you two?"

The meals were quickly dispatched and they continued on their way.

Officer Hunnicut was still at the mansion; he

showed the boys and Steele into the parlor. "There's dust on everything," said Steele.

"It's been closed up a long time," agreed Billy.

The three investigators worked their way around the ground floor looking for clues.

"Look here," cried Tom. "Several footprints lead to the basement door."

"Over here," yelled Billy at the same time. "Footprints headed upstairs."

Agent Steele examined the prints carefully. "It looks like two women and three men were here at the basement door and at the stairs leading to the upper stories. Let's check out the basement first," said Steele.

The boys followed the FBI man slowly down the dark stairway, which was illuminated only by their flashlights and the small amount of daylight coming in through the head-high basement windows. A stack of firewood, a few pieces of tattered wicker porch furniture, and some old yard tools were all they found.

"Let's have a look upstairs, boys," said Agent Steele. "Maybe we'll have better luck there."

The trio climbed the rickety stairs of the old mansion. They looked carefully around the second floor of the three-story mansion but found nothing of interest.

The dust revealed more footprints headed to the third floor. As the boys arrived at the top of the stairs, a curious sight greeted them. The footprints stopped and the dust was not disturbed beyond the landing. As the boys pondered this peculiar discovery, Agent Steele joined them.

"Gentlemen," said Steele, "look up." They turned

their attention to the ceiling. The mystery was solved. A short rope hung from a set of pull-down stairs that gave access to the attic. Steele led the boys up the stairs and into a wonderland of modern technology. Unlike the rest of the house, the attic was spotlessly clean. No dust or cobwebs were visible. What was visible was communications equipment capable of sending audio and video signals around the world.

"Wow!" exclaimed Tom, "Look at those machines! What could they want with all this stuff?"

"I don't know," said Steele. "But there's enough computer equipment here to open a Best Buy."

"Look at this," exclaimed Billy. He had discovered an electric panel.

"Don't touch anything," said Steele just as Billy flipped a switch on the panel. Overhead lights came on. "Don't throw any more switches, please."

"Sorry," said Billy, stepping away from the panel and making his way toward a small stack of boxes.

"Well, boys," said Steele, "we may be able to get some information from this equipment. I'll have a tech crew retrieve the computers and see what they'll tell us."

Billy chimed in from across the room, "Look at this, a street address on the Fruitville Pike in Lancaster, Pennsylvania, on this small shipping carton. The label's torn, but you can read the street number."

"We'll check it out," said Agent Steele.

"Why don't we go?" said Tom. "We know what these crooks look like. We can fly down there in our plane in no time. Maybe they'll be holed up at the address."

"Good idea," said Steele "but remember they know what you look like, too."

The FBI agent placed a phone call to one of his team members telling her to send some people to retrieve the electronics at the mansion.

When he and the Hardly boys arrived back in Baymoor, Tom and Billy excitedly told Chief Langly about the equipment in the attic and the torn address label they had found.

"We're flying down to Lancaster to scope things out there," said Tom. He glanced at the large clock on the wall. "Almost five," he said aloud. "I guess we'll have to leave in the morning."

"That's OK," said Billy. "We don't want to leave until we hear what the Coast Guard finds in the underground cavern at Blackbeard's Island."

"Right," agreed Tom.

While Billy and Tom were discussing their plans for the next day, the Coast Guard cutter was anchored just outside the entrance to the cavern. Lieutenant Shaeffer's frogmen were receiving last-minute instructions before swimming into the tunnel. The four frogmen were outfitted with audio and video communication equipment so they could be in constant contact with the cutter. They were also armed.

The briefing finished, they entered the water and made their way to the cavern's opening, as Lieutenant Shaeffer headed to the communications center. Only the lead frogman's camera was activated, and at first all the lieutenant could see was a murky image of seawater. When the first frogman emerged inside the cavern, he swung his powerful waterproof halogen lamp in an arc until it illuminated the side of the *Sneaky Fish.*

"OK, men," said Lieutenant Shaeffer, "let's see what's inside the sub."

Everyone in the communications center watched tensely as the frogmen climbed onto the hull, opened the hatch, and clambered inside. They moved carefully through the boat from stem to stern, but found no sign of life.

CHAPTER X

A Flight Back in Time

"I wonder how they got out of the cavern?" puzzled Billy Hardly.

"They may have had a mini-sub on board," said Agent Steele. "Shaeffer's men are securing the *Sneaky Fish* now. We'll know more about what's on board—and maybe know how our quarry escaped—after the lieutenant's men report in."

"You boys did well," said Chief Langly, "noticing the smoke from the chimney. Too bad those rascals got away. But you may find out something about their whereabouts when you get to Lancaster."

"We'll head out there first thing in the morning," said Tom.

"Keep us posted. And be careful. Don't do anything but observe," cautioned Agent Steele.

The brothers took their leave and headed to Baker Street. When they walked into the kitchen, Miss Jane was just taking a casserole out of the oven. "There you are," she said over her shoulder. "Your mother said you skipped school today. I don't know what the world's coming to. Skipping school and gallivanting about with FBI agents." She put the bubbling casserole on a trivet to the left of the stove. "There's no telling what you've been up to or where you've been. Go wash your hands. It's time for supper."

The boys hurried away and were back in short order. "Mmmm," said Billy leaning over and taking a sniff of the dish that was now on the dining room table. "Chicken and macaroni casserole. My favorite."

"Get your nose out of that dish," admonished Miss Jane. "Now sit down so we can eat."

During supper the boys told their mother and Miss Jane about seeing smoke from the chimney and finding the lipstick-stained cigarette butts. Miss Jane, as was her wont, predicted that the trip to Lancaster would not end well. "Why you can't stay home and let the police handle these matters I do not know. It is almost more than body and soul—"

"Now, Jane," said Mrs. Hardly soothingly, "you know DeVern and the FBI have asked for Tom and Billy's assistance on this case. I'm sure the boys will be careful, won't you?"

"We sure will, Mom," said Tom.

"You can take it to the bank," declared Billy.

"Slang," sniffed Miss Jane as she got up from the table. "If your grandfather had caught me using slang . . ." Her voice trailed off as she headed into the kitchen. Mrs. Hardly followed her, letting the door swing shut behind her. Just before it did, however, she turned and gave the boys a wink.

"What do you suppose the Colonel would have done to her?" mused Billy.

"Not a thing would be my guess," replied Tom with a smile. "C'mon. Let's call Whit and find out if we missed anything in school."

No homework assignments had been given out that day, so Tom and Billy took turns telling Whit about their day. Whit was chagrined to learn that he had missed so much excitement. "Next time," he vowed, "I'm skipping school too."

Tom asked Whit to keep his eyes open around the waterfront for the return of the *Lizzie Borden* or any of the Buttman gang. Whit said he would take care of it.

The boys were up early the next morning eager to follow up on the clue they had found in the attic. They packed a small overnight bag since they weren't sure how long they might be away. They hated to miss more school, but clearly the case took precedence.

Miss Jane had made them a picnic lunch. "You never know when you'll be able to get a decent meal," she said.

"Whit would certainly agree with that," said Billy under his breath.

"What was that, young man?"

"I was just saying thank you for the lunch, Miss Jane. We really do appreciate it."

"Now you boys be careful," she admonished. "You don't know what those ruffians might do if they recognize you. Tom, you're the oldest, so you take care of Billy."

"We'll be fine, Miss Jane," said Billy. "There's no need to worry."

Tom called Hoppie at the airport to have their plane ready. When the boys arrived at Linberg Field, Hoppie had already rolled the biplane out onto the tarmac.

"I've called the manager at the Lancaster airport," said Hoppie. "He's arranged a motel room for you in

Lititz near the airport."

"Thanks," chorused the boys.

The early morning fog was just lifting as the boys rolled down the runway and headed southwest toward Lancaster. After an uneventful flight they landed and checked in with Henry Sauter, Hoppie's friend. Henry gave them directions to their motel and the keys to his pickup truck to use while they were in town.

"What a swell fellow," said Billy as they headed south to check into the motel.

The boys stowed the overnight bag in the room and set out to search for the address they had found in the Burchfield Mansion. As they headed down the highway they fell in behind an Amish horse-drawn buggy.

"What a way to travel," said Billy. "It looks like fun."

As they passed the buggy they saw a lot of activity on the roadside ahead.

"Look at that," said Tom. A group of tourists were at a cider stand. Tom pulled into the parking lot. He and Billy hopped out of the truck to buy a pint of cider and a few apples.

"That was grand," said Billy as they got back in the truck and headed for the Fruitville Pike.

"When we find the address," said Tom, "I'll drive by slowly and you take a good look at the premises."

As the boys drove along they were impressed with the amount of land being used for agricultural purposes. The fields were neatly laid out and well tended. As the buildings got closer together, Billy began to read aloud address numbers. When they drew closer to the address they had found at the Burchfield Mansion, Tom slowed down.

"There it is!" yelled Billy. "On the right."

Tom drove slowly past the building. The brothers were astonished at what they saw. "It's the Maggio Chocolate Factory," Tom said. "We better stop and check it out."

Tom was able to turn around about a block past the chocolate factory, and drove back to the building and parked. The boys were shown to the shipping department where a young man about twenty years old greeted them. "What can I do for you gents?"

Tom explained that they were working on a hush-hush government case with the FBI and showed him the credentials Special Agent Steele had given them.

The clerk examined the credentials. "Wow! The FBI! I've never worked with the FBI before. This is just like *Mission Impossible*."

"I don't think it will be that bad," said Tom, taking back his credentials.

"Huh? That's not bad, dude. That's like totally awesome. Tom Cruise. Ving Rhames. I loved him in *Striptease*. And *Dave*. When I like an actor, I try to watch all his movies. Most people don't know how many movies, well, and TV shows, Ving Rhames has been in. Did you know that he was in *Lilo and Stitch*. Well, he wasn't *in* it because it was a cartoon. He was the voice—"

Billy held up his hand to stop the young man's rambling.

"Sorry," he said. "I get carried away sometimes.

Anyway, I'm like totally into those old movies like *Mission Impossible*. And I am so down with this."

Tom frowned at the young man. "I'm sorry you're depressed, but—"

"I'm not depressed. I'm pumped. I'm like, you know, ready to rock and roll."

Tom was beginning to wonder if he should ask for the manager. "OK. Right. Do you think you could check your records to determine if you have recently shipped an order of chocolate to an address in Baymoor on the Guernsey Shore? We're not sure of the recipient's name."

"Dude, I am all over it," said the bespectacled clerk. He was singing to himself as his fingers moved quickly across the keyboard. "'*Saturday night I was downtown, working for the FBI, sitting in a nest of bad men, whiskey bottles piling high.*'" He looked up briefly from the computer screen. "Lots of people think that's CCR but it's not. It's the Hollies. The same Hollies who did *Bus Stop*. Hard to believe, isn't it? Remember that one? '*Someday my name and hers are going to be the same.*' Like, I mean is she, like, going to change her name to Fred or Larry or Richard?" He returned his attention to the computer. "A Mr. Clive Custard and a Miss Jane Hardly both received small shipments in Baymoor last week."

Miss Jane's sweet tooth was well known around Baymoor, nonetheless the boys were taken aback to hear their aunt's name mentioned in the course of a criminal investigation. Recovering, Tom asked the clerk if he had a man named Buttman in the computer.

"Lemme check," said the clerk. "Nope. No Buttman on the list. Man, this is so exciting. What else you wanna know? I'm the one who set up all the cross-indexing for the customer list. I can make it tell me about anything you can think of. I'm taking computer courses at the community college and—"

Billy interrupted the young man again. "Thanks. That's about it." He turned to Tom. "Maybe we should take some chocolates home to Mom and Miss Jane."

"Good idea," said Tom.

The young chocolatier helped them pick out several selections and packaged them in a fancy box. "You're gonna be heroes back home. These chocolates are the best."

Billy paid cash for their purchases and thanked the young man for his assistance. "Good luck with your computer courses. "

"Thanks, dude."

The boys were headed for the door when the clerk called out to them. "Wait a minute, fellows. I just thought of something."

The boys returned to the counter.

"I've got a pretty good memory," said the young man. "All my teachers tell me that I need to go on from community college and get a degree from the university. But I don't know. I like this job. And old man Johnson says if I'll stay, he'll promote me once I've got my associate's degree. Well, anyway, I thought that name Custard rang a bell. Remember how I told you I could get the computer to cross-check different things? I just ran his name through and sure 'nuff, I received a new order from Mr. Custard just this morning. It's not in Baymoor though. It's a different address. I suppose it could be another Clive Custard. But really that doesn't seem likely does it? It's not a very common name. At least I wouldn't think so."

The clerk tore a piece of paper from a word-a-day calendar. "The order was sent to a hotel in Scranton," said the clerk. "I'll write the address down for you."

It was beginning to get dark as the excited boys headed back to their motel.

"What a find!" exclaimed Billy. "Now we know where Custard is. And I'll bet we find the Black Widows there, too!"

"Indeed," agreed Tom. "We'll call Agent Steele as soon as we get to the motel. He may know how to get in touch with Dad in Washington, D.C."

"Good work, boys," commended Steele when he received the call. "I'll get a message to DeVern telling him where Custard is. What's your plan?"

"We're leaving at sunup and flying to Scranton," said Tom.

"I'll meet you there," said Steele. "It's just possible we'll be able to catch Buttman with the goblet."

With time on their hands that evening, the boys decided to go to one of those great all-you-can-eat Pennsylvania Dutch restaurants. After a very satisfying meal of corn chowder, chicken and dumplings, cabbage slaw, and shoofly pie the boys retired to their motel room and went to sleep almost immediately.

Early the next morning they drove to the airport, where they delivered a large assortment of Maggio chocolates as a thank-you for Henry Sauter, the airport manager.

Tom and Billy rolled down the runway that chilly morning and headed north toward Scranton and a rendezvous with the FBI.

The boys flew low and slow over the Pennsylvania countryside and arrived in Scranton just after nine in the morning. They were met at the airport by Jon Keener, the FBI agent in charge in Scranton. As they drove to FBI headquarters Keener told them that their father had arrived the night before and was waiting for them. The job he was working on in D.C. was on hold and he had decided to check back in on the Buttman case.

When they arrived at headquarters, the boys were greeted warmly by their father. "I'm proud of you boys," said the world-famous detective. "You've done really good work on this case."

"Thanks, Dad," said the boys, beaming.

"Clive Custard checked in to the Bellmont Hotel with one of the Trafalgar sisters yesterday. We don't know where Buttman is holed up, but the FBI has agents on the lookout for him here, at the farmhouse the girls were taken to, and at the Brownbrier Resort. And of course they're watching in case he turns up in Baymoor."

"Do you know where the golden goblet is?" asked Tom.

"We suspect Custard brought it with him, but we're

not sure," said Agent Keener.

DeVern Hardly said to his boys, "We want you two to check into the Bellmont and see what you can find out."

"We've got our disguises from Brownbrier," said Tom. "We'll check in right away." The boys put on their moustaches and sideburns and headed for the Bellmont. After checking in, they went down to the atrium restaurant for lunch and a look around.

Clive Custard showed up with Inez Trafalgar and ordered lunch. Both had a Caesar salad with grilled chicken.

But where was the other sister, Lola? they wondered.

Billy went out to the lobby and phoned Agent Keener

"We'll check their rooms," said Keener, "while they're at lunch."

Billy returned to the dining room. Tom was eating a Philly cheese steak and Billy dug into his meatball sandwich as he reported to his brother. Clive and Inez were deep in conversation as the boys finished their lunch.

The waiter handed Tom Hardly a sealed note. Tom tore open the envelope and read a note from Agent Keener. "The other sister is nowhere to be found; the goblet is not in the room. Keep your eyes open."

When Clive and Inez finished eating, they got up and headed for the Bellmont Resort Hotel's nine-hole golf course. As the boys followed the suspects, they recognized two FBI agents who were also following the couple. Clive and Inez picked up golf clubs and headed for the first tee in their cart. Tom and Billy followed suit.

Clive and Inez were halfway down the first fairway when the Hardlys were ready to tee off. Tom sliced his drive into the right rough. Billy followed with a drive down the middle of the fairway. Tom had found his ball and was just about to hit when the pair in front headed to the second tee. Even though he was in the rough, Tom connected with a great shot and was only ten yards short of the green. Billy, from the middle of the fairway, was able to reach the green thirty feet from the cup.

The boys both finished with pars and headed to the par three second hole. When they reached the tee, the pair in front were already walking off the green headed for the par five third. Both boys bogeyed the second and headed for the next tee. When they reached the tee, Inez and Clive were hitting their third shots.

After their drives, the boys hopped into their cart and headed down the fairway. Two shots later they were on the green and made pars. The next hole was a long par four into the wind. When they arrived at the tee, Clive and Inez were nowhere to be seen.

"They couldn't have finished the hole already," said Tom.

The boys pushed their cart to the limit but never caught up to the twosome.

Tom and Billy returned to FBI headquarters crestfallen that Custard and Inez Trafalgar had eluded them.

They found Special Agent Steele in the office talking with Agent Keener. "We've received word that Buttman is back at the Brownbrier," said Agent Steele. "Inez and Custard almost certainly got a phone call from Buttman while they were on the golf course and have gone to meet him. Your dad has resumed his cover as the resort's gardener. We want you boys to head up to the Poconos and lend him a hand."

"Proud to do it," said Tom.

"We have a car waiting for you," said Steele. "And I'm going to ride along if you don't mind. Your plane will be put in a secure hangar while you're gone. You can either pick it up later or we'll have one of our agents fly it to Baymoor."

"OK," said Tom. "We're ready when you are."

Still wearing their disguises, the boys arrived before dark at the Brownbrier. Steele's driver dropped them off at the front of the hotel. They were welcomed by the manager, who recognized his former guests.

The boys headed out to the lovely gardens of the resort hotel. DeVern Hardly was pruning the roses as the boys walked by.

"Meet me at the gardener's shed," he whispered.

The boys took a slow walk around the garden and ended up at the shed. The elder Hardly shuffled up to his sons. "Buttman is here," he said. "A companion, a thin man in a dark suit and sporting a butch haircut, showed up yesterday. He had a lot of luggage. I didn't recognize him, and I haven't seen him since."

"How can we help?" queried Tom.

"I want you boys to keep an eye on Buttman and

see if you can find out who his mysterious cohort is," said DeVern Hardly. As always, the boys were pleased to help their famous dad.

Nothing untoward happened the rest of the day, and in the evening the boys headed down to dinner. They were almost finished with their meal when Clive Custard and Inez arrived. They were soon joined by Buttman and his mystery guest.

Billy stared at the stranger. "I know that guy," he said to Tom. "It's Lola, dressed like a man. Both of the Black Widows are here."

Billy headed out of the restaurant to report the news to DeVern Hardly.

"Good work," said the famous detective. "Now we know where all four of those scoundrels are. We should be able to discover whether they have the golden goblet with them. I'll alert the FBI. You and Tom can call it a night."

When Billy got back to the restaurant, Buttman and the others had just been served cocktails and were looking over the menu. Billy reported to Tom on his conversation with their dad. "So," he concluded, "I guess we can go on up to our room."

"Right," agreed Tom. The brothers walked toward the exit. "There's a James Dean movie on TV." He signed his name and room number on the bill and handed it to the young man at the cash register whose badge proclaimed that his name was Parker.

"Oh yeah!" exclaimed Billy. "The one with Natalie Wood."

"*Rebel without a Cause,*" said the young man with

a grin. "I'm a huge fan. I've seen everything she ever made."

"I know it's not likely to happen, but I would love to meet her someday," said Billy.

"Huh? Dude, she's dead."

"Dead?!" exclaimed Billy. "What happened? When did she die? How old—"

Tom took Billy by the arm and began pulling him toward the door. "We can find out about Natalie Wood later," he said. He turned back to Parker, who was staring in stunned amazement at the Hardly boys. "Sorry," he said. "It's a long, complicated story. Good night."

When the boys arrived for breakfast the next morning, Buttman was alone at a table for two. Where were Clive and the Trafalgar sisters?

Billy and Tom ate a hasty meal, then went in search of their father. They saw Special Agent Lou Steele in the hotel lobby talking to a couple of his agents. As they approached, he was wrapping up his instructions. "So that's it, men. We'll turn surveillance of that trio over to our counterparts in Los Angeles. Meanwhile, let's keep an eye on Mr. Buttman. He's too canny to carry the goblet with him while he's traveling. But he has homes all across the country. And it's possible he'll have someone bring the goblet to him at one of his residences. I want to know where he is at all times, and we—"

"Custard and the Black Widows weren't at breakfast," blurted Billy.

"I know," replied Steele. "They checked out last night. They're headed for Los Angeles. Agents are waiting at the airport to tail them to their hotel."

DeVern Hardly had walked up in time to hear Billy's exclamation. He was smartly turned out in a three-piece suit, crisp white shirt, and club tie. He looked not at all like the stooped and slightly scruffy resort gardener. He shook hands with Steele and laid a hand on Billy's shoulder. "It's all right, son. You and Tom have done a fine job of surveillance."

"But, Dad," said Billy, "Special Agent Steele says Custard and the Black Widows have gone to California."

"So I heard. Interesting. I wonder what Buttman's up to. He always has a reason for his actions, though the reason isn't always obvious."

"Should Billy and I go out to California to help keep an eye on those villains?" offered Tom.

Steele and Mr. Hardly exchanged glances then looked at Tom. "I think," said DeVern slowly, "that might be an excellent idea. I have to get back to D.C. for a meeting with the head of Homeland Security. The FBI might appreciate the extra pairs of eyes. What about it, Steele?"

"I don't know of any law enforcement officer who would turn down help from your sons, sir. I certainly wouldn't."

"Do you think Whit would be willing to go with you?" asked Mr. Hardly. "There are some excellent restaurants in Los Angeles," he added with a chuckle.

"He'll be glad to help," said Tom, "even without

the promise of great restaurants."

"But that won't hurt," added Billy.

"I'll leave Agent Steele to make arrangements for your flight to California. I've got to get on the road."

CHAPTER XI

Where Are They Now?

Whit readily agreed to join the Hardly boys for the trip to Los Angeles. Steele arranged for an early morning military flight that would get the boys to LA just before ten.

Though Tom was a licensed pilot and the Hardlys owned an airplane, none of the three boys had ever flown in a jet plane. They were thrilled. The flight across country was pleasant and uneventful. The weather was clear and the boys had a good view of the Grand Canyon on their way to California.

When the boys arrived in LA, they were met by an FBI agent, who told them the suspects had checked into the Chateau Marmont in Hollywood. Rooms overlooking the swimming pool had been booked there for the boys. Whit had put his time on the plane to good use, and when he joined Tom and Billy in their room he was quite familiar with what the AAA book had to say about restaurants in LA.

"Can we go to Pink's for chili dogs?" asked Whit.

"We're not here for food," said Tom.

"But Pink's," begged Whit, "is world famous."

"World famous or not, we have work to do," said Billy.

Whit walked past the brothers, who were discussing what Buttman's next move might be, and looked out the window to the swimming pool below. "Oh boy!" he gasped.

Tom and Billy stepped over to see what had caught Whit's attention. Several young women were sunbathing by the pool in very revealing bikinis. The three chums were transfixed for a moment.

"OK, boys," said Tom, regaining his composure, "we have work to do, let's go."

"Come on, guys," said Whit, who had already lost interest in the sunbathers, "let's get a Fatburger."

"My rotund friend," said Billy, "forget the food. We'll eat when we're done."

FBI agent Fred DiMarco picked up the boys at their hotel. "Our intelligence says a man named Shorty Bernard, one of Buttman's henchmen, works at the Santa Monica Pier," said the agent. "He runs the bumper car concession. Custard made arrangements to meet him a little before two o'clock. Steele doesn't think Buttman would trust Bernard with the goblet, but he thought we should keep an eye on Custard."

The boys were astonished at the volume of traffic on the 405 freeway and were agog at the freeway interchanges. "I've never seen anything like this," said Tom, "even in New York City."

Agent DiMarco pulled on to the Santa Monica Pier and led the boys to the bumper car concession. "Let's buy tickets and take a ride, pretend to be tourists," he said.

"The last time I drove one of these," said Billy, "I was in junior high school and Dad took us to Coney Island."

"I remember," said Tom. "Whit was with us but he

was eating hot dogs instead of driving the cars."

"Those dogs were great," said Whit. "Which reminds me that I'm really hungry now."

The Hardly boys promised Whit that, after the bumper cars, the next item on the agenda would be lunch. He took what comfort he could from that assurance. Then all three boys drove around the rink, crashing into each other and having a splendid time.

Agent DiMarco kept a sharp eye on the bumper car operator and alerted Tom and Billy when Clive Custard approached the ticket counter where Shorty Bernard sat on a high-back stool.

Tom pulled over near the two men long enough to overhear Clive Custard say he and the Trafalgar sisters were meeting Buttman at the Universal Studios tour at five o'clock that afternoon. "I don't know what the boss's game is," said Custard, "but I'm willing to play along."

"Yeah," growled the other man. "As long as he's payin', I'm playin'."

Tom sped away and crashed hard into DiMarco. Before their cars separated he reported the overheard conversation to the FBI agent.

"Excellent," said DiMarco. "I think you boys deserve a trip to Universal Studios. I'll make a few phone calls and get back with you."

Leaving the bumper car concession, the three boys walked to a pier-side restaurant that was well known for its overstuffed burritos. Agent DiMarco was to meet them there. As they were eating, Tom explained to Whit and Billy that their next assignment would require them to take a ride on the tram at Universal Studios.

FBI agent DiMarco dropped the boys off at their hotel, where they donned their disguises then went down to the lobby to wait. Agent DiMarco was dressed in khakis and a knit shirt when he picked up the boys for the short ride to Universal Studios.

"This is exciting," said Whit. "Is this where they film *Our Miss Brooks?*"

The boys laughed at their portly pal, who failed to catch the anachronism, as they headed for the agent's car.

"We should split up into pairs," said Agent DiMarco. "Billy, you stay with me. Tom and Whit, you go on ahead of us."

"Good idea," said Tom.

At Universal Studios, Tom and Whit walked up to one of the ticket booths. "Two, please," said Tom, giving the ticket taker his credit card.

"Yes, sir," said the young woman behind the Plexiglas shield. She swiped the card then slid it and two tickets through the narrow opening. "Two senior citizen tickets. The ticket operates like a credit card. You swipe the—"

"No," said Tom, sliding the tickets and his credit card back toward the young woman.

"No, what, sir?"

"We are not senior citizens. We need regular tickets."

"But, sir, the senior discount is available to anyone

sixty-two or older." She slid all three cards toward Tom again.

"We aren't sixty-two," replied Tom, pushing the cards back. "We can't accept the senior discount."

"Very well, sir," she said, shaking her head as she ran the credit card through again. "Here are two regular tickets."

"Thank you," said Tom. As he turned away he heard her mutter something about people in denial.

Tom and Whit were waiting at the head of the line when none other than George W. Buttman appeared, followed by Clive Custard and the Trafalgar sisters. Billy and Agent DiMarco were not far behind them. When it was time to board the tram, Tom and Whit were in the seat just in front of Buttman and Custard. DiMarco and Billy occupied the seat behind the beautiful but deadly sisters.

Despite having on their enhanced listening devices, which they had become quite adept at using, Tom and Whit were able to overhear only snippets of Buttman's conversation with Clive Custard. They caught the words "golden goblet," "San Francisco," "Captain Folsom's ship," "Washington, D.C.," and "substantial payment," but nothing else. It was like a game of connect the dots without all the dots. They did not learn where the goblet was nor what Buttman intended to do with it.

And then they heard quite clearly "that busybody detective from Baymoor" and knew Custard was referring to Tom and Billy's internationally renowned father. "If he becomes a nuisance," replied Buttman, "we will take steps." He did not elaborate on what those steps might be, but Tom and Whit had no doubt that they boded ill for DeVern Hardly.

When the tram returned to the terminus, Buttman headed toward the amusement park entrance while Custard and the Black Widows strolled over to a picnic area and sat down. "Billy," said Agent DiMarco, "you and I will follow Buttman. Tom, you and Whit stay with Custard and the sisters."

"What if they split up?"

"You'll have to act in the light of your 'intelligence, guided by experience.'"

"Our dad loves Nero Wolfe," replied Tom.

"Come on, Billy, let's move," said the agent

DiMarco and Billy reached the entrance just in time to see Buttman turn right. They followed him as he strolled down the sidewalk. They had not gone far when Buttman stopped in front of an art gallery. Pushing open the glass door, he walked inside. His followers watched him climb a set of circular stairs to the mezzanine overlooking the gallery. He walked into an office and shut the door.

"Quickly," whispered DiMarco scooting into the gallery. "Let's get behind that statue." Suiting the action to the words, he crouched down behind a sculpture of three scantily clad nymphs cavorting in a "fountain" of thin stainless steel streamers. The whole piece, set on what must have been a battery-operated turntable, rotated slowly, causing the metal ribbons to sway gently. Billy joined DiMarco and they moved a little farther back into the alcove that housed the sculpture.

They had not been waiting long when they heard footsteps descending the circular staircase. Two pairs of legs appeared, then Buttman and a young man with neatly trimmed mustache, goatee and gallery badge could be seen walking toward the front door. Without warning, the sculpture of the three nymphs began to emit a series of wailing notes clearly composed on a Moog synthesizer. The eerie tones echoed off the marble floor and cascaded down from the high ceiling. Billy, who had just taken his cell phone from his pocket, gave a start. The phone dropped from his hand and slid a few feet across the highly polished floor. "Drat," he said under his breath.

The music emanating from the sculpture muffled the sound of the falling phone, but Billy could not retrieve it while Buttman and the gallery employee were in sight. He and DiMarco remained motionless in the alcove. The music faded away and they could hear Buttman speaking to the thin, dark-haired man. "Very well, Antoine, I am pleased with your efforts thus far. I will let you know when my latest acquisition will be available for display. In the meantime, keep your eyes out for other items I might want to acquire."

"*Oui*, Monsieur Buttman. Always am I on the search for *objets d'art* that will have appeal for your most discerning appetite. Allow of me, please, to secure the gallery and then great pleasure will I receive by walking with you to the street."

The man called Antoine turned a key in a panel

beside the door and metal screens began to descend from the ceiling in various parts of the gallery. Billy and Agent DiMarco watched in horror as metal mesh slid down in front of the sculpture, sealing the alcove off from the rest of the gallery—and blocking their escape route. They dared not cry out, for Buttman and Antoine were still inside the gallery.

Antoine dimmed a few lights then held the door for Buttman. Billy and DiMarco heard the click of the lock as Antoine turned the key in the door. In the silence that followed their departure, the FBI agent's voice echoed through the gallery, "What a total goat cluster this is." He had pulled his own cell phone out and was staring at the display. "I have no signal. And you," he looked at Billy, "have no phone."

"I know. I feel like a dolt, but that music startled the spit out of me." Billy sat down on the edge of the nymphs' fountain and rested his chin on his clasped hands. "So what," he asked, looking up at the FBI agent, "does our 'intelligence, guided by experience' suggest we do now?"

Back at Universal Studios, Whit and Tom had followed Custard and the Black Widows as they made their way from one concession stand to another, buying a T-shirt at this one, ice cream at another, and a huge, stuffed Curious George figure at a third.

"I wonder why we haven't heard from Billy and Agent DiMarco," said Tom. He and Whit were trailing along behind their quarry as they headed out of the amusement park. "And what are we going to do if

Custard and the sisters get in a car and drive off? I
didn't think to ask Agent DiMarco about that."

"Maybe we can get a cab," said Whit.

"Maybe," replied Tom. "But they seem to be
headed to that hotel." As he spoke the trio were
crossing the street to the Hilton. "And look!" said Tom,
pulling a protesting Whit behind a clump of palm trees.
"There's Buttman!"

Indeed the notorious Mr. Buttman was strolling
along the sidewalk toward the hotel. Spotting his
minions, he waved a languid hand in their direction.
Custard and the two sisters picked up their pace and
joined Buttman at the hotel entrance.

"Where," asked Tom, peering out from his hiding
place, "are Billy and Agent DiMarco?"

"Maybe they're hiding behind a palm tree, too,"
said Whit, moving slightly to avoid being poked by a
spiky bit of vegetation. "Or maybe Buttman came here
in a car and they weren't able to follow him. Or
maybe—"

"Those are all fine explanations for why we can't
spot them tailing Buttman, my portly friend. But they
do not answer the more pressing question: Why haven't
we heard from them?"

There was a long silence before Whit responded.
"That," he said, "I don't know. And I fear the answer
may not be to our liking."

"If I owned this monstrosity," said Billy, casting a
baleful look behind him at the nymphs twirling slowly
through their cascade of metal water, "the very first

thing I would do would be pull the plug on that obnoxious caterwauling." The Moog synthesizer music had cycled on about every ten minutes, filling the gallery with a plaintive and mournful sound that grated on Billy's already-jangled nerves.

"I'm with you there," said DiMarco.

The two prisoners were standing at the metal gate staring morosely at Billy's phone, visible but unreachable. "Too bad my phone has a signal and yours doesn't," said Billy, watching as the phone once again vibrated on the slick marble floor. "That's probably Tom. He and Whit will be worried."

"They aren't the only ones," replied Agent DiMarco.

He and Billy had pulled, pushed, tugged, and kicked at the gate separating them from the rest of the gallery—and the exit—to no avail. Billy had taken off his belt in hopes of snaring his phone with it, but had been unable to slide the belt through the finely latticed mesh. DiMarco still had no signal on his Blackberry.

"Maybe we can dismantle this thing and use one of the nymphs as a battering ram." The FBI agent walked the few steps to the sculpture and began to investigate its construction.

"Look!" said Billy.

DiMarco turned quickly and rejoined Billy at the gate.

"Someone's at the gallery door."

Sure enough, a silhouette, backlit by a nearby street lamp, was visible through the glass door. After a click and a rattle, the door opened slowly inward.

"Move back," whispered DiMarco, tugging on Billy's sleeve.

"Holy mackerel! It's Tom!" exclaimed Billy, pulling away from DiMarco. "Tom, we're over here. How in the world did you find us?"

"Mr. Techno-Nerd to the rescue," said Whit, following Tom into the gallery. "When we couldn't reach you and you didn't phone or text us, I used the Find My iPhone app to locate a GPS signal for your phone and hey, *presto!*" Whit executed a sweeping bow, "here comes the cavalry."

"Boy are we glad to see you!" cried Billy.

"Yes indeed," said Agent DiMarco.

"How did you get into the gallery?"

Tom held up a set of lock picks.

"Ah hah!" crowed Billy. "Those lessons with the locksmith paid off."

"May I suggest, gentlemen, that we postpone further conversation until we are safely off the premises,," said DiMarco. "You will find the lock for this gate over there by the door. If you would be so kind as to release us, we can make tracks."

"Good idea," agreed Billy. "Maybe we can get out of here before we have to hear another rendition of 'Cats Squalling in the Night.'"

"Cats squalling . . . ?" said Tom.

"Never mind," said Billy. "Just get us out of here."

In less than a minute Tom had the gates throughout the gallery raised. Billy picked up his cell phone on his way to the door.

Meanwhile, Tom had brought the mesh screens

back down. "Better if no one knows we were ever here."

"Good thinking," said DiMarco. "Can you lock the gallery back up?"

"You know it," said Tom, closing the door behind him. "Now," he said, slipping the lock picks into his jacket pocket, "let's make like a tree and leave."

Back at the hotel the detectives compared notes. As soon as Billy heard about the threat to DeVern Hardly, he wanted to call and warn him, but Tom and Agent DiMarco persuaded him to wait. "Dad knows how dangerous Buttman is," said Tom. "He's in important meetings in D.C. You know full well he wouldn't thank us for interrupting him for anything less than a dire emergency."

"I think a threat from a villain like Buttman is fairly dire," grumbled Billy under his breath. But he agreed to let the FBI agent pass along the information through regular channels.

DiMarco jotted down the other snippets of information Whit and Tom had overheard. "I'll have someone check out this Captain Folsom."

"Were you able to overhear anything the sisters were saying?" asked Whit.

"Yes," said DiMarco. "Custard is heading to San Francisco to meet up with this Captain Folsom, though for what purpose the sisters didn't say. I've alerted the FBI in the Bay Area; they will keep a close watch on Custard and this Folsom character."

"Are the Black Widows staying in LA?" asked

Whit.

"Apparently they are going with Buttman to Santa Fe. Though again they did not say for what purpose."

"What can we do to help?" asked Tom.

"I'm going to check with headquarters—and Mr. Hardly," said DiMarco thoughtfully, "but I'm inclined to think that you three should follow Buttman and the Trafalgar sisters."

"We're ready whenever you need us," said the elder Hardly brother.

"Whenever you need us *after* we've eaten supper," interjected the ever-hungry Whit. "I haven't had anything to eat since those burritos on the Santa Monica pier. I'm famished."

"I don't think we need to keep Whit from his next meal any longer," said DiMarco with a smile. "If you're going to New Mexico, I'll arrange a military flight out of Burbank. In the meantime, have a good dinner. Maybe go to a movie tonight. You deserve a rest."

Whit picked up right away on the good dinner suggestion. "You heard the man," said Whit with a sigh of relief. "A good dinner is what we need. Let's go to Musso and Frank. It's the oldest restaurant in Hollywood. We might see a film star."

"Unless it's John Wayne or Gloria Swanson," said Billy with a grin, "I wouldn't recognize a film star."

"We'll go to the restaurant and then the Chinese Theater," said Tom, "but we must get to bed early for we have a lot to do tomorrow."

The next morning Agent DiMarco met the boys in the hotel restaurant. Whit had just made his third trip through the breakfast buffet line and was settling in with French toast, sausage patties, and a serving of fresh fruit.

"A Gulfstream departed a few minutes ago with a flight plan for Santa Fe, New Mexico. Buttman and the Trafalgar sisters were on the plane."

"What should we do?" asked Tom.

"You've got a flight in two hours out of Burbank," said DiMarco. "I have a car waiting, so finish up your breakfast and go pack your bags. I'll meet you in the lobby in forty-five minutes."

CHAPTER XII

High and Dry

The boys were met at the Santa Fe airport by FBI agent Mike Martinez, who had driven up from Albuquerque as soon as he was notified of Buttman's flight plan.

"We've booked rooms for you at La Fonda, a great hotel on the plaza. Buttman and his crowd are nearby at the Inn of the Anasazi."

As the boys were being driven to their hotel, Whit was reading about restaurants in the area.

"It says here," Whit reported, "that the Pink Adobe is a top-notch place for dinner, and on Water Street, Pasqual's is highly recommended for breakfast. La Fonda has a good restaurant, also," he added. "Up Canyon Road is an excellent—"

"Whoa, big fella," said Tom, cutting him off. "Our purpose here is not to eat our way through town. We'll eat when we can; first, we have work to do."

"Do you know, Agent Martinez, what they're doing here?" asked Billy.

"We were at the airport when they arrived," said the federal agent. "They had only overnight bags with them."

"If," mused Tom, "they had the goblet when they headed out West, where is it now? I'm beginning to wonder if we're on a wild goose chase."

"Me, too," chimed in Billy.

"You're not the only ones," said Agent Martinez. "Mr. Hardly and some of the FBI honchos suspect as much. But they want us to follow Buttman and the sisters for the next few hours, just in case. After that, I'll check in with the powers that be and see if they have new instructions for us."

The boys checked into La Fonda and were delighted with the architecture and the furnishings. "This place is beautiful," said Tom. "I wish we had time to really enjoy it."

"Why don't you have a walk around the plaza," suggested Martinez. "I'll keep you posted by phone."

The boys strolled around looking at the turquoise and silver jewelry displayed by the Native American crafters and in the surrounding shops.

"The air is sure thin here," said Whit.

"Yes it is," said Billy, "but you're not."

Whit convinced the boys that a meal was in order. They wandered down to Pasqual's and had huevos rancheros at a community table, where they struck up a conversation with a man and a woman from Wisconsin.

"I'm Louise Ware," the woman volunteered, "and this is my husband, *Jim*."

"Pleased to meet you," said Tom, introducing himself and the others.

"We're visiting our son," Louise continued. "He's on the *golf team* at the University of New Mexico. We're spending a few days sightseeing in Santa Fe before heading back to Albuquerque.

"Are you gentlemen here on *business* or *pleasure?*" She smiled at the Hardly boys and Whit.

"Sort of a combination," said Tom.

"Those are the *best* kinds of trips," said Louise.

"Jim tries to combine business and pleasure all the time, *don't you,* sweetie?" Jim glanced up briefly from his French toast, nodded, then returned his attention to his plate.

Louise Ware was a talker who needed no encouragement to carry on a nearly nonstop monologue. She chattered away while the others ate their food and listened to her with varying degrees of attention. Having lauded her son's accomplishments as a high school golfer and now a college standout ("he didn't start as *young* as Tiger Woods, but he is absolutely *devoted* to the game and *quite* good"), she moved on to her daughter's cheerleading accomplishments ("no matter *what* the university says about cheerleading not being a *sport,* I assure you that it requires *great* athletic ability"), and then to her husband's outstanding career in the recording industry.

"Jim has really made a *name* for himself, *haven't* you, honey?" She did not pause for Jim to acknowledge this accolade. "He was actually instrumental in the *success* of the British invasion."

Billy, who had finished his meal and was looking idly around the restaurant, turned back to Mrs. Ware. "The British invasion?"

"Yes. Are you surprised?"

"But, ma'am," began Billy—

"I *know* what you're going to say. He doesn't look *old enough* to have been involved with the British invasion, but I assure you he played a pivotal role, a *pivotal* role."

"But, ma'am, I've read a good bit about the British

invasion. The Napoleonic Wars were—"

"I know, *I know,*" said Mrs. Ware, steamrolling over Billy and the Napoleonic Wars, "people are *always* surprised when they learn about his involvement."

"Ma'am, the British invasion of Rio de la Plata took place—"

"Rio de what?"

"Rio de la Plata."

"I don't remember them."

"It's not a them, ma'am; it's a place," said Billy.

"Oh. Like Liverpool. Such an *unlikely* place for famous people to be from, don't you think?"

"Not like Liverpool, ma'am. Rio del Plata was—"

Mrs. Ware shook her head. "I never heard of a place called Rio Della Plata, though *Jim* might have. He has a *wonderful* memory for names."

"But ma'am," said Billy returning to the crux of his concern, "the British invasion was—"

"He can meet someone *once,* meet them again six months *later,* and remember their name *and* where he met them. It's been a *great* asset to him in his rise up the corporate ladder. But I don't ever remember him mentioning a Rio Della Plata. You don't mean *The Platters,* do you?"

Billy gave up the unequal struggle and let Louise Ware's words flow over him unchecked.

Whit, like the laconic Mr. Ware, was finishing up the last of breakfast. Tom had walked away from the table to talk on the phone. When he returned, he explained, "That was Agent Martinez. Buttman and crew are on the move." He nodded to Mr. and Mrs. Ware. "A pleasure meeting you both. If you'll excuse us, we have to join someone."

Whit and Billy stood up and said their good-byes. Tom paid the check and the trio left the restaurant and headed up the street. They joined Martinez outside a curio shop. "They seem to be shopping," Martinez reported. "Nothing out of the ordinary."

"They never," said Tom, "do anything out of the ordinary. They must be up to something."

"Agent Martinez," said Billy, while they were waiting for Buttman and the Trafalgar sisters to emerge from the shop, "do you know when the British invasion occurred?"

"Sure, 1964, when the Beatles came to the U.S. That's generally considered the start of the invasion."

"Insects?!" queried Tom. "There was an invasion of insects from England?"

Martinez frowned. "Insects? What are you talking about? I didn't say anything about insects."

"Yes, you did," asserted Billy.

"He's right," said Whit, joining the conversation. "You said there was an invasion of British beetles."

Still frowning, Martinez looked from Billy to Tom to Whit. Then his brow cleared. "Oh. That's right. You were asleep, weren't you? Not insects . . . the Beatles, *B-E-A-T-L-E-S,* a rock band, also known as the Fab Four: Ringo, Paul, George, and John. They are generally considered to be the start of what's called 'the British invasion.'"

"A band invaded the United States?"

"Not just one band, Billy. There were dozens of British bands that were incredibly popular in the States. The Beatles were a British band from Liverpool—"

"Ah ha," said Billy, "that explains Mrs. Ware's reference to Liverpool."

"Mrs. Who?"

"A woman we met at the restaurant. She was very proud of her husband. Said he played a '*pivotal role*' in the British invasion," said Billy. "I thought she was a total kook."

"Why?" asked Martinez. "What did you think the British invasion was?"

"Attempts by the British army to take over Spanish colonies in South America between 1806 and 1807 during the Napoleonic Wars."

Martinez smiled, then chuckled, then laughed out loud. "Oh, my!" He patted Billy on the shoulder. "That must have been *quite* an interesting conversation. I can see why you were surprised that her husband was involved in the invasion." He laughed aloud again. "The Napoleonic Wars. Oh, my! The British invasion of South America . . ." He was still laughing when Buttman and the girls left the curio shop.

Lola had a small Navajo rug tucked under her arm. The three crossed the plaza and headed toward the front entrance of the Anasazi.

Martinez and the boys watched them go into the hotel.

"What now?" asked Billy.

"I'll be right back." Martinez strolled into the hotel lobby.

He returned to the group waiting on the sidewalk and motioned for them to follow him. "Our agent inside is undercover as a hotel clerk," said Martinez. "Buttman has booked a car for a trip to Taos this afternoon. Our agent said the car was to arrive at about 2:30."

"Oh, good!" exclaimed Whit. "We have time for lunch."

The others laughed and let Whit lead them to the restaurant he had picked out for the noontime meal.

Buttman and the girls got into their hired car at 2:25 p.m. and headed north.

The Hardlys, Whit, and Agent Martinez followed at a discreet distance. Behind them was a car with two more FBI agents. The caravan passed through Espanola just after 3:00 p.m. and headed up the Rio Grande Valley toward Taos.

"Wow!" exclaimed Billy. "This is beautiful country."

The cars rolled through town just after 4:00 p.m. and headed to the Taos airport northwest of town. Just a few minutes after arriving at the airport, Buttman and the girls were headed aloft in a hot air balloon.

Martinez and the Hardlys were mystified.

"What are they doing!?" asked Tom.

"I don't know," said Martinez. "Let's see what we can find out."

He and the others got out and walked toward a small shack with a miniature hot air balloon on its roof. Agents Azzari and Scott left the second car and joined the small group at the door to the building. Martinez introduced the agents to the Hardly boys and Whit.

"Now let's see what's what with the balloon riders," said Martinez, opening the door.

He presented his credentials to the concessionaire, who told Martinez the balloon had been booked for a short sightseeing trip. "The concierge at the Inn of the Anasazi arranged the excursion for Mr. Buttman and the two ladies this morning. Bookings through Santa Fe hotels are not uncommon," explained the concessionaire.

"When will the balloon land?" asked Martinez. "And what happens then?"

"The flight will take about an hour. The chase car will be leaving soon. It will pick up the passengers where they set down and take them to their own vehicle. Then it will return to get the balloon and the pilot."

"Thank you for the information," said Martinez. He and the others left the small office and walked back to their cars.

"I'm beginning to think we may be on a wild goose chase, boys," Martinez echoed earlier sentiments. "But we might as well see where they land. Then we can decide what our next step will be."

The boys and Martinez followed the slow-moving craft in their car as it floated eastward on the prevailing winds. The chase car, a small white van with hot air balloons painted on the side panels, led them toward the landing site in an open field near the small town of Arroyo Seco at the base of the Sangre de Cristo mountains, which were covered with golden aspens.

In the basket of the balloon, Buttman, on his cell phone, was giving instructions to Captain Folsom on the *Lotus Maru* in San Francisco. "Set sail for Anchorage, Alaska, as soon as Custard is back on board. He will explain to you what happens next." As he finished the call, Buttman smiled at the Trafalgar sisters. "If the FBI and our friends the Hardlys are aware that Clive is in San Francisco, as I expect they are, his rendezvous with Folsom aboard the *Lotus Maru* should keep them guessing. We will stop for dinner soon."

Shortly after that, the balloon landed and the passengers alit.

Agent Martinez received a call from the San Francisco office saying that the *Lotus Maru* had set sail moments before and that Clive Custard was on board. The San Francisco Port Authority reported that the *Lotus Maru* was headed for Anchorage, Alaska.

Buttman and the girls climbed into the small van and were driven to Sabroso in Arroyo Seco. Their hired car was waiting for them at a restaurant. Buttman spoke to the driver briefly then followed the sisters into the historic 150-year-old adobe.

After watching the trio enter the restaurant, Martinez and the boys decided to head back to Santa Fe. Agents Azzari and Scott were instructed to keep a watch on the quarry. "Call me if they do anything suspicious," said Martinez. "But I have a feeling they're just going to eat supper then head back to their hotel." He turned to Whit, "Before you ask, we'll grab a pizza at Paisanos on the way out of town."

Back at La Fonda, Martinez talked with his superiors at the FBI. It was agreed that the Hardly boys would head home the next day.

"We do need to get back for football practice," said Billy. "And we don't want to get too far behind in our schoolwork. Finals will be coming up before long."

"Ugh," groaned Whit. "Don't remind me about that."

Martinez had men waiting in Anchorage for the *Lotus Maru* and in Santa Fe to keep tabs on Buttman and the Trafalgar sisters. He promised to keep the Hardly boys up to date with relevant information.

"It's been a pleasure working—and eating—with you," said Martinez, shaking hands with Whit and the Hardlys. "We'll keep in touch."

Before heading up to their rooms, the Hardly boys decided to take a walk around the plaza. "Help clear out the cobwebs," said Tom.

"I'm going up to watch a little TV before bedtime," Whit responded. "I'll see you fellows in the morning."

Billy and Tom headed off toward the plaza. They were talking about the brave new world to which they had returned, not paying much attention to their surroundings.

"Language is the biggest hurdle for me," said Billy. "I'm always tripping over words that don't mean what I think they should. Like 'swipe' meaning 'to process a credit card.' Then, the other day I had a totally embarrassing conversation with our English teacher."

"Mr. Johnson?"

"Yeah. We don't have another English teacher, do we?"

"No. But you might have meant some other English teacher at school."

"Then I wouldn't have said 'our' English teacher."

"All right," said Tom. "I was just yanking your chain."

"What?"

"Teasing. Joking with you. Pulling your leg."

"Well that's just what I'm talking about," said Billy with a frown. "Everybody knows what pulling somebody's leg means. So why do we need to have 'yanking your chain'? And—"

Knowing that, once mounted on his high horse, Billy could gallop for an exceedingly long time, Tom interrupted. "Tell me about the embarrassing conversation."

Billy walked a few more paces before he continued his tale. "I was talking with Mr. Johnson when George Miller walked into the room. I said, 'George is so gay you just can't help but like him, can you?' I knew right away I'd said something wrong 'cause Mr. Johnson's eyes opened wide and he sort of held his breath for a second. I asked him what was the matter.

"'Gay,' he said, dropping his voice to a whisper, 'means homosexual.' I just stared at him so he went on to explain that 'gay' and 'lesbian' refer to male and female homosexuals. Though 'gay' is sometimes used for men and women both." Billy stopped walking and turned to face Tom, who listened in amazement. "You see what I mean? Why take a perfectly good word and turn it on its head so that it means something completely different? Not even in the same general category as 'happy, excited, merry.' Why couldn't they go on using homosexual? Or make up an entirely new word?"

"I don't know," said Tom, non-plussed. "But thanks for the tip. I will try to remember not to call people 'gay.'"

Suddenly, they both chuckled, shaking their heads. "It *was* rather funny," Billy admitted. "Poor Mr. Johnson was terrifically embarrassed. And so was I."

The boys crossed the street and continued walking north, heading away from the plaza.

"I wish we could take a crash course in 'words and expressions that have changed over the past fifty years.' I hate making mistakes like that."

"I know you do," replied Tom. "But you understand lots more than I do about all the new gizmos and gadgets."

"Maybe. Though I can't hold a candle to Whit— Hey! Look at that!"

Thirty yards in front of them, a couple were being set upon by muggers. The woman was shouting and swinging her purse at a young punk in jeans and a purple sweatshirt, who was trying to snatch her bag. The man was fending off blows from another hoodlum, who was dressed in black from head to toe.

"Looks like they could use some help," said Billy, heading toward the couple.

"I'm with you, Crusader Rabbit," said Tom, following close behind.

The thugs were startled to see two elderly men approaching them, clearly intent on interfering. Turning their attention from their original victims, they began to taunt the Hardly boys.

"Wha'cha doin', ol' man," said purple shirt. "You wanna piece-a the action? Come-on, come-on. I give ya some action."

"Yow," said the thug in black. "You geezers wan' excitement, you come t' da right place."

"The Jujitsu Kid and Super Slugger to the rescue," said Billy. "You hit 'em low and I'll hit 'em high."

Their hearts pounding with excitement, the Hardly boys entered the fray and brought the miscreants quickly under control. Billy coldcocked purple shirt, who now lay unconscious on the grass. His brother dispatched the man in black with a few swift and well-placed jujitsu moves. Tom then used his belt to lash the groggy adversary to the wrought iron fence that ran along the sidewalk. Billy was sucking his knuckles and complaining under his breath about ill-mannered, hard-headed punks.

"Oh, my goodness!" gasped the woman, now clutching her purse to her chest. "Oh, my goodness! How amazing! Both of you! We can't thank you enough. Oh, my goodness!"

"Indeed," said her companion, slipping his cell phone back into his pocket. "The police should be here any minute."

"OK," said Tom. "We'll wait with you. Ma'am, why don't you have a seat on the curb here. Sorry there isn't a bench."

The woman lowered herself to the curb, still hugging her purse and muttering "Oh, my goodness!" over and over.

True to their word, the police were soon on the scene.

"I'm Detective Beck and this is Detective Waters. What happened here?"

"I'm Steve Perry," said the man who had been attacked. "There really isn't much to tell. My wife and I were strolling along the sidewalk when those hoodlums attacked us. We were trying to fend them off when these two gentlemen appeared on the scene—for which they have our sincere thanks. You hear so much these days about people not wanting to get involved. It is gratifying to know that there are still people who will come to someone's aid—even that of complete strangers."

Billy and Tom acknowledged Mr. Perry's thanks with a nod.

"It's our mom," said Billy. "She raised us to respect our elders."

Mr. Perry and the policemen all turned to look at Billy.

"Respect your elders?" said Detective Beck.

"Yes, sir," said Tom. "Billy's right. Our mom drilled that into us from a very early age."

The three men stared at the Hardly brothers.

"Respect your elders?" repeated Detective Beck.

"Yes, sir. When we saw the attack, we knew we couldn't just walk away. Our mom would *not* have been happy with . . ." Billy's voice trailed away as the men continued to stare.

"Oh." Billy and Tom exchanged a look. "We forget. It's . . . uh . . . it's . . . well, uh, sort of like a . . . like a . . ."

"Like a family joke," said Tom, coming to Billy's aid.

"Right," said Billy. "Sort of a family joke. It started when we were young and then it just 'grow'd.'" His comment was met by three blank looks. "Like Topsy?" Still no reaction.

"*Uncle Tom's Cabin?*" offered Tom. "No? OK. Well, sorry to have confused the issue, Detective Beck. We couldn't simply walk away when we saw Mr. and Mrs. Perry being set upon by ruffians."

"I see," said Beck, in a tone of voice that clearly meant he did not see at all. He walked back to the patrol car, reached through the open window, and brought out an iPad. "Very well, gentlemen. Let me just get names and addresses, then we'll get these punks out of here and you can be on your way."

"We're planning to go back east tomorrow. Will that cause a problem?" asked Tom.

"There shouldn't be any difficulty," replied Detective Waters, while Beck was taking down information from Mr. and Mrs. Perry.

The policemen got the information they needed and bundled the muggers into the backseat of the squad car. After handshakes all around, the Hardly boys took themselves back to their hotel.

"That was an exciting ending to an otherwise tedious day," said Tom as he and Billy were getting ready for bed.

"It was indeed," agreed Billy. "Do you think Whit will be sorry he missed the excitement?"

"I do *not*," said Tom with a laugh. "I think he will say that Moore's luck came to his aid and kept him from joining us on our walk."

"I believe you're right," replied the younger Hardly. He reached for the bedside lamp and turned it off.

The boys flew home to Baymoor the next morning, and the rest of the week passed slowly. Martinez reported that Buttman and the sisters were doing touristy kinds of things, and the *Lotus Maru* was taking a slow trip up the coast to Alaska. The boys tried to concentrate on their schoolwork while waiting for instructions from their dad and the FBI.

Jessa and Anne were glad to have the boys back in Baymoor, and decided to prepare a welcome home dinner for them and their chums on Thursday night. Whit, Marshall, Izzy, Marco, and Sophia joined the Hardlys for a repast at Jessa's home. The Hardly boys regaled their pals with stories of their adventures out West, and Whit recounted details of various meals they had enjoyed during their travels.

As the group was finishing a dessert of strawberry shortcake, there was a knock at the door. Chief Langly greeted the gathering, then took the boys aside. "I just heard from FBI agent DiMarco in Los Angeles," said the Chief. "The *Lotus Maru* has arrived in Alaska. The local authorities working with the FBI boarded the ship. They found nothing of interest."

"What about Clive Custard?" asked Tom. "What did he have to say?"

"Custard was not on board," reported the Chief.

"But he was on board when they left San Francisco," exclaimed Billy. "Where did he go?"

"We don't know," said the Chief. "He either left in a helicopter or transferred to another vessel. We know the *Lotus Maru* made no stop until Anchorage."

"He must have taken the goblet with him," opined Whit.

"The FBI is checking all West Coast ports of call," said the Chief, "but so far they've found no trace of Custard or the goblet."

Early the next morning DeVern Hardly called the boys with some startling information. A commercial fisherman in Florence, Oregon, was boasting in a local bar about a big fee he had gotten for rendezvousing with a ship off the coast and taking a passenger back to shore. A Coast Guardsman in the bar overheard the tale and called the state police. Under questioning, the fisherman described the man.

"It was almost certainly Clive Custard," said Mr. Hardly. "And he was carrying a large parcel. The ship was the *Lotus Maru*."

"When did this happen?" asked Tom.

"Three days ago. The fisherman, Evan Rothfii, took Custard to the airport at North Bend. We're checking now with the airport authorities to find out where he went from there."

"Well, I'll be dogged!" lamented Billy, who was listening on a cordless handset.

"Buttman and the girls are also on the move," DeVern continued. "They left Santa Fe this morning headed for Albuquerque. Agents Azzari and Scott are following Buttman and will keep us informed."

"What can we do to help?" asked Tom.

"I want you boys and Whit Moore on standby. Be prepared to go wherever you're needed on a moment's notice."

"All right, Dad," said Tom excitedly, "we'll be ready."

"We've traced Clive Custard's movements," said DeVern Hardly. "From Oregon he flew to Seattle in a small charter. At the SeaTac airport he flew in Buttman's Gulfstream to an airport near Manchester, Vermont, where he checked into a resort hotel. Buttman and the Trafalgar sisters left Albuquerque on a commercial flight. Their destination is Albany, New York, just a short drive from Manchester, Vermont. The FBI will follow them. My guess is they're planning to meet up with Custard."

"What should we do?"

DeVern Hardly was silent for a few seconds. "I have a hunch that Vermont is a red herring. I have learned over the years neither to totally disregard nor totally rely on hunches. So . . . I think we will let the FBI keep Buttman and company in their sights in case this is not a red herring. Meanwhile, you, Billy, and

Whit remain on standby in case it is a ruse."

"Right. Do you know when you'll be home?" Billy asked.

"No, son."

"OK. Well, be careful, Dad," Tom interjected.

"I always am," replied DeVern Hardly.

CHAPTER XIII

Where Do We Go from Here?

The Hardly boys were beginning to worry about keeping up with their schoolwork. And they did not want to miss any more football practice.

"It's time for us to get back into our regular routine," opined Tom.

"Yep. It's been exciting," said Billy. "But finals are not going to wait because the Buttman gang is rampaging about stealing golden goblets."

The big surprise that evening was DeVern Hardly's presence, after two weeks away on his last mission. The lads had missed their famous dad and were grateful for his advice and words of encouragement. "I'm proud of you fellows," said Mr. Hardly. "You've done a good job so far. Buttman is a devious man and he delights in concocting schemes to fool—" The internationally renowned detective stopped in midsentence. He looked pensive. "Delights in concocting schemes to fool law enforcement officials . . . I wonder if . . ."

He brought his attention back to Whit and his sons, who were looking at him anxiously. "We'll talk after supper. Let's not keep the others waiting," he said, walking into the dining room. He gave his wife a peck on the cheek and smiled at his sister before taking his seat at the head of the table. "Looks like you and Hazel have outdone yourselves this time, Jane."

While the ladies cleaned up after supper, DeVern Hardly took the three lads into his study to bring them up to date on the Buttman case. He unrolled a large map of the United States. It was marked with circles showing the places Buttman, Custard, and the Trafalgar sisters had been in the last two weeks.

"This map shows Buttman's recent travels," said Mr. Hardly. "Unfortunately, it doesn't tell us where he's going next."

"Nor where the goblet is."

"You're right, Billy. And I'm beginning to believe," said DeVern Hardly, "that if the goblet is not still in Baymoor it has been moved to a totally unexpected location. Somewhere far removed from New York, Vermont, California, New Mexico—"

"But what about all the travel?" interrupted Tom. "What about the package that Custard took when he left the *Lotus Maru?* What was that all about?"

"I think," said the elder Hardly slowly, "yes, I think Mr. Buttman has been wasting our time. He has a reputation for deceit and trickery. And he would delight in leading my sons, not to mention the FBI, on a pointless trip across the country and back."

"Good grief," moaned Billy. "You mean we traipsed from East Coast to West and back again for nothing?"

"I don't know, Billy. I'm not positive that I'm right. But my theory does make sense of the seemingly aimless travel from one city to another, and the rather blatant transporting of packages from ship to shore and back again. I think I will convey my suspicions to

Special Agent Steele and see what he thinks.

"In the meantime, if I'm right," continued Mr. Hardly, "Buttman, Custard, and the Trafalgar sisters will return to Baymoor to retrieve the stolen goods. Or, if the goblet has already been removed from Baymoor, they will eventually go to wherever it has been taken. Buttman has our forces spread out and looking in all the wrong places. We'll let the federal men keep tabs on the *Lotus Maru* and search the other possible hiding places, for we cannot afford to act on my theory to the exclusion of all others. But I believe, yes, I do believe that we should concentrate our efforts on this area and on keeping the Black Widows in our sights."

The day dawned cold but sunny. The boys went to class and to football practice. DeVern Hardly spent the day reviewing the case with Chief Langly. The citizens of Baymoor were unaccustomed to the sort of machinations perpetrated by the Buttman gang, and the chief of police wanted to bring this chapter of criminal activity to a close.

The next day Chief Langly posted a man at the Monarch Hotel where Custard and the Black Widows had stayed the last time they were in Baymoor. The hotel had no reservation for them but the Chief was taking no chances on missing the trio should they reappear. When the boys got home after school their father was not there. Miss Jane said he had received a phone call and left in a hurry.

"He told me it didn't have anything to do with the case you're working on," said Hazel Hardly, walking into the room with an armload of folded sheets. "He took the grab-and-go bag he keeps packed for emergencies and said he'd be back when he could."

"Here, Hazel," said Miss Jane, taking the laundry from her sister-in-law. "I'll put these away." She walked off down the hall toward the linen closet.

"Thank you, dear." Mrs. Hardly turned back to address her sons. "Your dad said Chief Langly could tell you about where he's gone, and why."

"OK, Mom," said Billy. "Come on, Tom, let's check in with Chief Langly."

Tom and Billy Hardly drove to police headquarters to see what Chief Langly knew about the summons that had taken DeVern Hardly away in such a hurry.

Sergeant Blith was at his desk and looked up when the Hardly boys walked in. "Afternoon. I got some new crossword puzzles," he said, holding up a softbound book in proof of this assertion, "and I don't mind telling you that some of these clues don't make a bit of sense to me. For instance, what do you suppose this means: 'A thrifty wife's helpmeet?' There's a question mark at the end of the clue."

Tom thought for a few seconds. "Does the answer have seven letters?"

The sergeant looked down at the crossword and counted off the squares with the eraser end of his pencil. He looked up in amazement. "I'll be blessed. It does have seven letters. How did you know that?"

"The answer is 'husband,'" said Tom with a grin.

"H-u-s-b-a-n-d," said Sergeant Blith carefully

filling in the letters. "Husband?"

"Look it up in a dictionary," said Billy, who was also grinning. "But first, would you please tell the Chief we're here."

The sergeant announced the Hardly boys then went back to his desk. Tom and Billy heard him muttering "husband? a thrifty wife's helpmeet?" to himself as they went into the Chief's office.

The Chief was at his desk sorting through a stack of file folders. "Paperless office," he muttered as the boys entered.

"Paperless office?" echoed Billy. "What does that mean?"

"Nothing. It means absolutely nothing," replied Chief Langly. "It was just a pipe dream. What can I do for you two?"

"Dad's gone out of town and Mom said you'd know about the case he's working on."

"That I do, Tom. Your dad is hoping to tie up the loose ends of a case that's more than a decade old." The Chief leaned back in his chair and gazed at the ceiling. The silence was broken by the whine of the old furnace cycling on. "Don 'Dogface' Roscoe," said the Chief.

"Who's Don 'Dogface' Roscoe?" asked Billy. "I've never heard of him. Have you, Tom?" Billy had been leaning against the doorjamb. Now he hooked one of the two side chairs with his foot, pulled it toward himself, and sat facing the chief.

"Nope." Tom turned the other chair around and straddled it. "Do tell."

"It was while you were asleep," said the Chief,

leaning back in his chair and propping his feet on the desk. "Dogface and his gang went on a real crime spree, everything from bank robbery to extortion to kidnapping. Your dad played a big role in bringing the gang down. But Dogface, himself, was never caught."

"And Dad's gone after him?"

"Yep," said the Chief, putting his feet on the floor and sitting up straight in his chair. "He got a tip that Dogface had been spotted somewhere in Alabama, some little town with an odd name. Farina? Restina? Verbena! That's it. Verbena."

"So Dad's gone to Alabama? To try to catch this Dogface person?"

"Your father has a highly developed sense of civic duty."

"Don't we know it!" said Tom.

"Dad's a believer in that saying, 'If you're not part of the solution, you're the problem.' He never wants to be the problem."

The Chief started laughing.

"What?" said Billy. "What did I say?"

"You're not *the problem,* Billy."

"I know I'm not. Who said I was?"

"No. It's not that 'you're the problem.'"

"That's what I said. Why would you *think* I'm the problem?" He turned toward Tom who looked equally puzzled.

"I mean," said the Chief, reaching for a tissue to wipe his eyes, "you've got the *saying* wrong. 'If you're not part of the solution, you're *part of* the problem.' Not 'you're the problem.'"

"Got it," said Tom, starting to laugh.

"Oh," said Billy looking chagrined.

"It's OK, little brother," said Tom, standing up. "Let's let the Chief get back to work. Let us know if you hear anything from Dad. And, of course, if you get any news about Buttman and his crew."

"I will," said the Chief.

The boys decided to take a walk around the waterfront. "Let's check out the Thirsty Eye and see what Sonny Stufflebean is up to," suggested Tom Hardly. "Maybe we can get a line on when—or if—Custard and the sisters are coming back to Baymoor."

When they entered the smoky, dim-lit dive, Stufflebean was on the phone behind the bar. He recognized the boys and turned his back on them while he finished his call. Tom thought he had a caught a flash of fear in Stufflebean's eyes before he turned away. He and Billy took seats at the bar, hoping to overhear Stufflebean's end of the conversation.

"What sissy drink this time?" quipped Stufflebean, hanging up the phone as the boys sat down.

"Diet Cokes," said Tom.

As Stufflebean went for the drinks, Tom leaned over and whispered to Billy. "I think he knows something of interest to us."

"I think you're right," said Billy. "I wonder if he's in touch with Buttman?"

Stufflebean brought the drinks and set them in front of the Hardly boys. "That'll be three dollars. Unless," he sneered, "you want to run a tab."

Tom took a sip of his Diet Coke, then looked directly at Sonny Stufflebean. "What do you hear from George W. Buttman?"

Sonny's face went white, his eyes shifting from Tom to Billy and back again. "I...I don't know what you're talking about," he whined. "I don't know nobody named B...Buttman." He picked up the money Billy had put on the counter and walked to the other end of the bar, avoiding looking in their direction again.

"He's lying," said Tom.

"Of course he is," replied Billy. "But we have no way to prove it."

The boys finished their sodas and decided to stop by police headquarters to tell Chief Langly about their encounter with Sonny Stufflebean.

"He'll bear watching," said Chief Langly when they had reported their conversation. "I'm sure you're right that he knows more than he's telling.

"I tell you what," said the Chief standing up and reaching for his gun belt. "Let's head down to the Thirsty Eye and have an *official* chat with Sonny Stufflebean."

"We're right behind you," said Billy.

The Chief and the boys drove down to the waterfront and parked in front of the Thirsty Eye. The Hardly boys did not recognize the bartender, who looked up when they walked into the bar. "Whatcha want?"

"Where is Stufflebean?" asked the Chief, flashing his badge at the surly man behind the counter.

"He ain't here," said the barkeep.

"I can see that," said the Chief. "Where is he?"

"Took the night off. Said he had somethin' he had to do. I don't know where he's at." The bartender picked up a glass and began polishing it with a dirty rag.

"Did he say when he'd be back?" asked Billy.

"Nope." The man put the glass under the bar and picked up another one. "That be all for you gents?"

The Chief and the Hardly brothers left the tavern without answering. They stopped by Stufflebean's apartment on the way back to the station, but no one was home.

"We must have spooked him by asking about Buttman. I shouldn't have said anything," said Tom morosely.

"We'll keep an eye out for him," said Langly, as he pulled into his designated parking place at the police station. "I'll let you know when he's spotted."

"Thanks," said Billy. "Come on, Tom, let's go home. Tomorrow's a school day."

"I'm coming," said Tom glumly, as they left the police car. "G'night, Chief."

"Good night." The Chief called back as he headed for the station. "Don't worry, Tom. Stufflebean's like a bad penny. He'll turn up again."

At breakfast the next morning the Hardly boys were discussing Stufflebean's disappearance.

"Stop blaming yourself," said Billy around a mouthful of cinnamon toast.

"Don't talk with your mouth full!"

"Sorry, Miss Jane. Will you please tell Tom that it's not his fault that that weasel Stufflebean is missing."

"Maybe not," said Tom glumly. "But I don't like coincidences. And it sure does seem like an odd coincidence that he should go missing right after I challenged him about knowing Buttman."

"OK," said Billy snaring another piece of bacon from the serving platter. "You're right. Not only is it your fault that he's disappeared, but he's the key to the mystery of the missing goblet and unless we find him we will never solve the case. In addition you have set back the cause of world peace by—"

Tom balled up his napkin and threw it at his brother.

"You know what Dad says," Billy continued.

"I know, I know," replied Tom. "You shouldn't let a setback discourage you. You have to keep pursuing your goal with unflagging enthusiasm. Disappointment must not beget despair because despair begets failure."

"I have heard DeVern say those very words," chimed in Miss Jane. "A very wise man, your father."

"Yes he is," said Billy, pushing back his chair from the table. "You ready to head to school, bro?"

"Bro?"

"Yeah. Don't you think that's a really cool word?"

"I do not," said the elder Hardly boy.

"OK, bro," said Billy as he dodged a playful punch from Tom. "I'll try to remember not to call you that, bro."

"You boys stop your roughhousing," chided Miss Jane. "You'll break something for sure."

"Come on, bro, let's boogie," said Billy as he headed out the door.

"Don't forget to brush your teeth," called Miss Jane.

"We won't," said Tom.

When the Hardly boys arrived at school they found Whit in something of a dither. He was pacing back and forth in front of his locker.

"Hey, bro," said Billy. He twirled the dial on the combination lock, opened his own locker, and put up his math book.

"I've been waiting for you," said Whit. "Do you know about the special assembly this morning?"

"Sure," said Tom. "They told us about it in homeroom yesterday."

"But they didn't tell us what it was about."

"And?" queried Tom.

Whit looked up and down the hall, stepped closer to the brothers, and lowered his voice. "It's about *sex*."

"About what?!" chorused the brothers.

"You heard me," said Whit.

"Who told you this?" asked Billy.

"Izzy."

"He was pulling your leg."

"No," insisted Whit. "He was serious."

"Come on, Whit," said Tom. "You know what a kidder Izzy is. He would joke with the grim reaper."

"I tell you he was serious! Here's Marco. Ask

him."

"Hey, guys," said Marco, joining the group. "Ask me what?"

"Whit's fallen prey to one of Izzy's jokes—" began Tom.

"I keep telling you," Whit interrupted, "he wasn't kidding. If you'd been here you'd believe it."

"What did he say," asked a puzzled Marco.

"He said," Whit whispered, "that today's assembly is about sex."

"Yeah. That's right."

"We're really going to have an assembly about *sex?*" exclaimed Billy.

"Keep your voice down," hissed Whit.

Billy and Tom began pelting Marco with questions.

"Who's giving the talk?"

"Will girls be there?"

"Do we have to get a note from our parents?"

"How long will the assembly last?"

Marco stepped back and held up both hands, palms out. "Whoa, guys! One at a time."

Billy nodded at Tom. "You first."

"Will there be girls at the assembly?"

"I doubt it," said Marco. "The girls get their own lecture. At least they always have before."

"Before?"

"Sure. We've been getting this lecture since junior high school."

"What lecture?" asked Whit in hushed tones.

"The one about safe sex."

"*Safe sex?*" chorused Marco's listeners.

Marco stared at Whit and the Hardly brothers.

"Didn't you learn about safe sex before you were frozen?"

The three guys shook their heads.

"We didn't learn about sex at all," said Tom. "At least," he looked from Whit to Billy then back at Marco, "not in school."

"Hey, fellas. What's up?" a female voice called.

"Hi, Sylvia. Whit and the Hardlys were asking about—"

"Calculus homework," said Whit. "There were some problems that . . ." Whit's voice trailed off at Marco's look.

"Good grief, Whit. It's not like Sylvia doesn't know what the assembly's about. I told you, we've been getting the same lecture about practicing safe sex since we were eleven. Or maybe it was twelve. Anyway, seems like forever."

"Supremely boring at this point," said Sylvia. "Like there's anybody in the whole school that doesn't know to use a condom. Hey, Billy, did you see that Amy Lee is going to be part of the Star-Palooza-Charity-a-Ganza next month? Are you going?"

"I don't know," said Billy, still reeling from the idea of a school assembly to talk about sex. *Safe* sex, at that! Whatever *safe* sex was. "I just read about it on the Net this morning."

"You better move fast if you want to see the show, 'cause tickets are going to sell like beer at a frat party. There's the bell. Gotta run. See you guys, later."

"Me, too," said Marco.

"Wait," said Tom. "You've got to tell us what safe sex is before you leave."

"No time," replied Marco, already headed down the hall. "You'll find out at the assembly." He looked back at the trio of bewildered guys and grinned. "You'll be the only people there not bored out of their skulls."

CHAPTER XIV

Lost and Found

Marco had been right. The Hardly boys and Whit were the only ones at the assembly who had shown any interest in the presentation. They were too embarrassed to ask questions, but they had listened closely and Tom even took a note or two.

"You fellas are something else," said Izzy after school. "I can't believe no one ever talked to you about safe sex before."

"Well, you might as well believe it," said Billy, "because we are here to tell you that no one ever did."

"So I guess maybe you haven't had the MADD and 'just say no' lectures either."

"We have no idea what you're talking about," said Tom.

"Say no to what? Who's mad? About what?" asked Whit.

"Never mind," replied Marco. "You'll hear all about it at another assembly some day. I don't want to spoil the surprise for you."

"But—"

"Nope," said Marco as he slipped his arms through the straps of his knapsack, "you'll just have to wait."

Then, shaking his head, he laughed, "Gosh, you fellas remind me of an old song my grampa sings." Turning down the hall, he jived and snapped his fingers to a tune that he crooned over his shoulder:

Shooby-doo, shoo-bop-a-doo-oo
White buck shoes and button-down collars
Shooby-doo, hear us holler...
Slicked back hair and rolled up sleeves
We're 50's guys, if you please...
Just 50's guys, we don't apologize...

"Let's stop by the police station and see if the Chief's heard anything about Stufflebean or any of the other Buttman crew."

"OK," said Billy. "You coming, Whit?"

"Count me in," replied their stout friend.

At headquarters the three guys chatted with Sergeant Blith while they waited for Chief Langly to finish up a phone call.

"Need any crossword help?" asked Tom.

"Not today. I'm taking a break from crossword puzzles. How are you at Sudoku?"

Tom had heard of the newfangled game, but had had no success with it.

"No good at all, I'm afraid. Whit's your best bet when it comes to anything to do with numbers."

"Let's see what you've got." Whit leaned over Blith's shoulder just as Chief Langly emerged from his office.

"What a coincidence! You're just the fellows I want to see. Come on in.."

"Let me grab an extra chair," said Tom. "Anyone using this one?" He rolled a desk chair from the reception area into the office and sat down. Whit and Billy occupied the straight-back chairs.

"What's up, Chief?" asked Tom.

"That was your dad I was talking to on the phone. He had some startling news."

"Is he still looking for that Dogface person?"

"Don 'Dogface' Roscoe? Yes. He's gone undercover and has a good lead on the whereabouts of Dogface. But that wasn't his news."

"What was it then?"

"While he was waiting for his snitch at a hotel, he saw Buttman with Custard and the Black Widows."

"In Alabama?!" exclaimed Billy.

"Yes. Buttman and his cronies were still there when Foxy Fairfield, the informant, showed up. Foxy told DeVern that he, Foxy, had heard that Buttman had gone down south to meet up with an arms dealer. DeVern wants the three of you to try to catch him making a deal. That should be enough to get Buttman off the streets for a while."

"Mr. Hardly wants us to go to Alabama?" exclaimed Whit. "People say that for good home-cooking you cannot beat the Deep South, Alabama in particular. When does he want us to go?"

Tom laughed. "Honestly, Whit, do you ever think of anything but food?"

"Of course I do," replied his indignant pal. "Just not often," he added with a sheepish grin.

"All right, Chief, looks like Billy, Whit, and I will be making tracks for Alabama."

"I think the first thing to do is contact the FBI and police down there to get you some local backup. You boys get packed so you can leave in the morning for

Birmingham. I'll make all the arrangements while you head home to get ready."

Whit and the Hardlys thanked the Chief and agreed to meet the next morning at the airport. When the brothers got home, their mother was interested to hear that they would be going to Alabama the next day.

As usual, Miss Jane was concerned and began to fret. "You need to be careful down there," said Miss Jane stirring ingredients in a large bowl.

"Why?" asked Billy. "I expect Alabama is pretty much like any other state, only warmer."

"Hmph! Little enough you know about it." She added vanilla to the bowl and continued stirring.

"What do I not know, Miss Jane?"

"You just keep your eyes and ears open." She began spreading dough into a pan.

"But, Miss Jane, if you don't tell me what to look and listen for how will I know if danger lurks?"

"Billy, stop your teasing,'" admonished Mrs. Hardly.

"All right, Mom." Billy walked over and gave his aunt a hug. "Thanks for the warning, Miss Jane. We'll be careful. I promise."

He reached out a finger toward the bowl of dough and his aunt promptly slapped his hand away. "Stop that!"

"What are you making?" asked Tom.

"Butterscotch brownies."

"My favorite," said Billy, trying once more to get a taste of the raw dough. This time Miss Jane rapped his knuckles with a wooden spoon.

"Ow!" Billy withdrew his hand.

"Billy and I are going to go pack now. We'll need a disguise when we're shadowing Buttman and the others, and I don't want to be down in Alabama wishing for that one piece of gear that I don't have."

"Supper in twenty minutes."

"OK, Mom. Thanks."

Upstairs in Tom's room the boys surveyed the trunk in which they kept wigs, false beards and mustaches, makeup, and small clothing items such as scarves, gloves, and ball caps.

"What do you think we should take?" Billy held up a heavy woolen scarf in a muted green-and-blue plaid.

"Not that," said Tom, taking the scarf from Billy and putting it back in the trunk. "We're going to Alabama not Minnesota."

"Let's see what weather.com has to say about conditions in the Deep South." Billy sat down at Tom's computer.

"Good idea." Tom continued to sort through the trunk, pulling a few items out and putting them on the bed, while Billy checked the five-day forecast for Birmingham, Alabama.

"Sounds wonderful. Highs in the 70s, lows in the 50s, no rain for the next week."

"I wonder if weather forecasts in Alabama are any more reliable than they are up here?"

"Probably not," said Billy, logging out. "But I don't think we have to worry about snow. Shall we just wear our Brownbrier gear?"

"I don't know, Billy. I have a feeling . . ."

"A hunch? You know Dad says never ignore a hunch. Don't place all your chips on it, but don't ignore it." Billy picked up a black baseball cap with the Hard Rock Cafe emblem. "Here's something I don't understand," said Billy grasping the cap by the brim and holding it at arm's length.

"What's that?" Tom placed a salt-and-pepper Vandyke beard and mustache back in the trunk and picked up a blond goatee.

"Advertisements."

"You don't understand advertisements?"

"On headgear," said Billy, still holding the Hard Rock ball cap, "on T-shirts and jackets, on plates, glasses, and silverware, on underwear and key rings, on ladies' purses, men's wallets, and children's backpacks—in short, on merchandise. Consumers now pay for the manufacturer's advertising. And I," he tossed the Hard Rock cap on Tom's bed and picked up a cap with the unmistakable Nike swoosh, "don't understand why."

"Good question,'" said Tom, "although not, perhaps, of pressing importance at this point in time."

Billy put on the Nike cap then picked up the Vandyke that Tom had replaced and held it up to his face. "What do you think? Dashing yet casual? Debonair yet charmingly informal?"

"I think you're a total goofball," said Tom, "and that supper will be ready soon."

"Right, as usual, big brother." Billy grinned. "At least about supper. So what's this hunch of yours?"

"I don't think we should wear the Brownbrier

disguises again. Maybe it would be fine, but . . ."

". . . why risk it? OK. Let's pick out some other gear for our first visit to Dixieland."

They began to paw through the hairpieces, caps, and makeup in earnest.

The next morning the brothers put on their disguises before leaving home. Billy wore acid-washed jeans, a plain black T-shirt, a red zippered hoodie, and a pair of Nike walking shoes. He had elected to wear the blond goatee with a matching chevron moustache that covered his upper lip. Tom had suggested that he also brush his hair forward, creating short bangs. "I don't think even Mom would recognize you on the street," averred Tom.

Tom, who had wavered back and forth between the Vandyke and a petit handlebar, had finally gone downstairs the day before to elicit an opinion from his mother and aunt. They thought the Vandyke made him look quite debonair. He had on black jeans, a yellow Lacoste polo shirt, an olive drab windbreaker, and black Skechers. They each had an overnight bag with toiletries and a change of clothes.

Jessa and Anne had volunteered to drive the Hardlys and Whit to the airport. Jessa picked up the Hardlys right on time and they were at the airport promptly at ten. The Moore siblings drove up moments later. Whit was wearing his usual khakis with a white button-down shirt, gray Harris tweed jacket, and a pair of short Frye boots. He also sported a reversible Harris tweed hat that his sister deemed "quite dashing."

Chief Langly was waiting for them in Hoppie's office. "There's a government plane waiting out there to take you to Birmingham. I've arranged for you to be met at the airport by Joe Morgan, an Alabama State Trooper, and FBI agent Carlos Hyche. They have been briefed on the Buttman situation and are ready to assist in whatever way they can."

"Thanks, Chief," said Tom Hardly. "We'll be in touch."

The Hardlys and Whit said quick good-byes to Anne and Jessa and walked to the waiting plane. Two hours later they were in Birmingham.

DeVern Hardly's informant had said Buttman was meeting his contact in Tuscaloosa, a university town about an hour's drive southwest of Birmingham. Buttman had reserved three rooms at a local hotel. According to the FBI agent, Buttman and the others had checked in the day before.

"We've gotten you fellas rooms at the same hotel," said Joe Morgan.

"Thanks," said Tom. "Buttman has evaded the law for long enough. It's time someone put a stop to his nefarious schemes."

"Can we do that after we eat?" asked Whit plaintively. "I read about a local barbeque restaurant that isn't too far from the airport."

"You can't be hungry," complained Tom. "It's barely twelve o'clock."

"It's past one in Baymoor," replied his corpulent comrade. "I'm starving."

Trooper Morgan laughed. "There's a meat and three in Tuscaloosa that is justifiably famous. We'll get a bite there and check in with the local cops."

"What's a meat-and-three?" asked Whit, always on the lookout for new dining experiences.

Carlos Hyche turned his head to look at the boys in the backseat of the patrol car. "It's a type of restaurant. It offers a meat and three vegetables as its standard fare. We have a goodly number of meat-and-threes in the South."

"Oh, boy!" exulted Whit. "I can hardly wait."

In less than an hour the Hardly boys and Whit were seated at a round table in the Kountry Kitchen along with Trooper Morgan. Agent Hyche had left to make some phone calls and would join them later.

Whit was mulling over his lunch options when Henry Turnipseed, a local police officer, approached the table. Trooper Morgan made the introductions and Turnipseed pulled up a chair.

"Been a while, Henry."

"Indeed it has, Joe. Good to see you."

"Would you recommend the country fried steak or the fried catfish?" asked Whit. "Or should I get two meats and a three?"

"Portions are right big here," said Henry Turnipseed. "I 'spect you can make do with just the usual meat and three." He looked Whit over. "But you may want to get dessert, too. The Kountry Kitchen makes a mighty fine cobbler."

Whit set down his menu as the waitress walked up to the table. "OK. Thanks for the suggestion."

"What can I get you gents?"

"Afternoon, Maybelle," said Office Turnipseed. "I'll have my usual."

"Chicken pot pie, collard greens, black-eyed peas, peach cobbler, and sweet tea. You got it, Henry."

The Hardly brothers both ordered country fried steak with mashed potatoes, black-eyed peas, and green beans.

"You want sweet tea?" asked Maybelle.

The brothers exchanged glances.

"When in Rome . . ." said Billy, handing his menu to the waitress.

"Is that a yes?"

"Yes, ma'am," replied Tom, casting a disapproving look at Billy.

After Trooper Morgan ordered, Maybelle turned to Whit. "And for you?"

"I'll have the fried catfish, mashed potatoes, mac and cheese, and fried okra. Do the potatoes come with gravy?"

"Sure do," said Maybelle.

"Good. And I'll have peach cobbler with vanilla ice cream for dessert."

"And to drink?"

"Diet Coke."

Restraining a grin, the waitress left to put in their order and was back quickly with their drinks and a basket of hot rolls and cornbread.

Whit buttered a piece of cornbread and took a bite. "Golly, but that's good!" he said as he finished off the square of cornbread and reached for the bread basket.

Their food arrived in short order and everyone dug in. Other than an occasional "pass the salt, please" there was little conversation while they were eating.

As they were finishing lunch, a local farmer came by their table and spoke to Turnipseed. "War Eagle, now, ya hear?"

"Roll Tide, you ignoramus," replied Turnipseed.

Morgan noted the questioning looks the chums from the north gave each other. "The University of Alabama plays Auburn soon," he said. "It's a big game locally."

"Oh, yeah," said Billy. "Bart Starr's the quarterback at Alabama."

Officer Turnipseed looked puzzled. "Your information is a trifle out of date." He looked from Tom to Billy to Whit. "Where you fellas from?"

"I haven't had a chance to fill Henry in on your situation," Morgan said to Billy. "Why don't you give him the short explanation while I pay the check."

With an occasional assist from Tom and Whit, Billy told Officer Turnipseed about their capture and cryogeriatric incarceration.

"So you see," he finished up, "our current events are other people's history."

"Amazing. I've never heard the like."

Trooper Morgan walked back to the table and took a seat. "Agent Hyche said he'd meet us here. Anyone want a refill on tea while we wait?"

Everyone passed.

Just then, Hyche walked over to the table. "Let's get y'all checked in to the hotel. Then we'll decide on on our next step."

"Sounds good," said Tom.

"Henry," said Morgan, "are you goin' to be our liaison with the Tuscaloosa police?"

"Yep," said Officer Turnipseed, "that I am."

"OK. We'll meet you at the Crimson Hotel."

"See you there."

The boys had checked into the hotel and met up again with Officer Turnipseed in the lobby, which opened onto a large conference center. Built in a circle around a large indoor garden that was often used for weddings and other celebratory occasions, the hotel–conference center boasted an entire mall, with shops, restaurants, an indoor pool, and the usual fitness area, meeting rooms, and business center.

"This is the biggest hotel/conference center in West Alabama," said Officer Turnipseed. "'Course, to be totally honest with you, it's the *only* one, but we're still mighty proud of it." Whit and the Hardly boys followed Turnipseed through the lobby to the east entrance, where they were to rendezvous with Joe Morgan and Carlos Hyche.

"I need to catch this call," said Turnipseed, checking the caller ID on his phone, "then I'll be right with you." He was talking on his phone as he walked back toward the lobby.

The Hardly boys and Whit took a few steps into the atrium, where skylights flooded the area with natural light.

"This is stunning," said Tom. The garden in the

center of the atrium had benches placed asymmetrically around a tiered fountain. Some of the benches faced the fountain; others looked out on the shopping area.

"Look at that!" said Billy, pointing to the fountain. "Ducks."

"It's like that hotel somewhere that has ducks in the lobby. Is it in Mississippi?" asked Tom.

"The Peabody Hotel," said Whit. "It's in Memphis, Tennessee."

"You have the oddest assortment of factoids floating around in that head of yours," said Billy.

"Factoids?" queried Tom. "What the heck is a factoid?"

"A small fact," replied Billy, walking toward the fountain for a closer look at the ducks, which paddled round and round.

"Facts," said Tom scornfully, "do not come in sizes. They either are or they are not."

Intrigued with the ducks, Billy was paying no attention to his brother until he felt a grip on his arm. "Ten o'clock," whispered Tom. "It's Buttman, Custard, and the sisters."

"Golly!" exclaimed Billy looking in the direction Tom had indicated. "You're right."

"What should we do?" asked Whit who had followed Billy over to the fountain and was now staring at Buttman and his cronies.

"I think we'd better shadow them. Whit, you head counterclockwise. Billy and I will go clockwise."

"Shouldn't we let Officer Turnipseed know what we're doing?" asked Whit.

"I didn't get his cell phone number," replied Tom. "There they go! Don't lose them!"

He gave Whit a shove, then he and Billy began walking in the direction that Buttman had gone.

"I have a bad feeling about this," muttered Whit as he headed in the opposite direction from the brothers. "A very bad feeling."

Whit was circling around the fountain when he was nearly run down by a young woman. Her arms were full of packages, and boxes went flying as she collided with Whit.

"Oh my paws and whiskers!" she cried as she stooped down to pick up some of the boxes at her feet.

Whit was gathering up the smaller packages, which had skittered across the marble floor. "Very sorry, ma'am," he said as he made his way toward her.

"It's not your fault," said the young woman. "My grandmother always said 'haste makes waste.' I didn't really understand what that meant until I was grown. Now I do, and I *still* don't always live by Gramma's maxim." She sighed. "I don't know why I have to do everything at warp speed.

"Thank you very much," she added, accepting some of the boxes from Whit. "I appreciate your helping me gather up my belongings, particularly after I nearly bowled you over."

Whit smiled as he handed her the last of the packages. "It's all right, ma'am. No harm done."

"Well, thanks again," said the young lady.

Whit watched her for a few seconds then turned

around and began walking in the direction he had been going when the young woman had barreled into him. "Got to keep your mind on the job," he admonished himself. He saw no sign of Buttman and crew or the Hardly boys.

He moved over closer to the shops that lined the mall in hopes of spotting his quarry. Suddenly, headed straight toward him were Buttman, Clive Custard, and the beautiful but deadly Trafalgar sisters. Forgetting that they did not know who he was, Whit panicked. Turning around he found himself facing a door that was slightly ajar. He pulled the door open and slipped inside, leaving the door slightly open. Peeking through the crack he watched as the quartet of villains settled themselves on one of the benches. Their backs were to the fountain, which meant they were looking straight at the door.

"I could use a dose of Moore's luck about now," said Whit. Unfortunately, his luck was about to get worse instead of better.

As he moved a little farther from the door, he brushed up against a shelf. Turning around he saw that it was filled with flowers, some in vases, others in buckets, still others made up into corsages. All the walls were lined with similar shelves, also filled with flowers. "I'm in a flower shop," he said.

He heard a click and turned around just in time to see the door completely shut. The overhead lights went out and the room was plunged into total darkness. Only then did Whit realize that the room was quite chilly. "Oh no," he muttered, "I'm not in the flower shop. I'm in the walk-in refrigerator used to store the flowers. I wonder if I'm going to be a human Popsicle again!"

Outside in the mall area, Tom and Billy were making their way cautiously around the fountain. "Do you see them?" asked Billy.

"No," said Tom, peering around one of the columns that dotted the mall. "Let's hope Whit has them in his sights."

"Should we go back to the hotel lobby and wait for Officer Turnipseed? He's bound to be through with his phone call by now. He'll be wondering where we are."

"I know," replied Tom. "But we can't afford to lose Buttman. After all, that's why we're in Alabama— to catch him red-handed in some felonious transaction."

"All right," said Billy, "let's go."

Slowly moving out from behind the column, the brothers found themselves standing under a flowered arch. The group of people seated in front of the arch stared and whispered among themselves, shaking their heads and shrugging.

"Sorry," said Tom, looking around. "Um, we're... uh . . ."

"Lost..." said Billy, his voice trailing off.

A man in a black shirt and white clerical collar, holding a Bible, stepped toward the bewildered lads. Suddenly, he offered a handshake, and Billy, befuddled, gripped it lamely

"Hello, gentlemen," said the cleric. "I'm Reverend Thorndike. We meet at last! I must say, I've never performed a gay wedding, but I guess it's high time … eh?

He nodded to them warmly, stepped to the podium beneath the arch, and directed them to face him."

Now," he said, with a wink, "we begin with the traditional 'Dearly beloved, we are gathered together here, before God and in the sight of this company…'"

Aghast, Tom and Billy bolted, turning and running down the aisle of the gathering like scared rabbits, until they came to another twosome, young men holding hands, and sporting earrings, making ready to enter the aisle, from the back.

The gathering laughed uproariously at the fiasco, and the minister cleared his throat.

"Shall we begin, again?" he said, as the two partners came forward.

Tom and Billy headed into the mall area, where they fell against a pillar to catch their breath. There was no time to discuss what they'd just endured, however, before they saw Buttman and crew getting into an elevator.

"Oh no!" wailed Billy. "We've lost them."

"And where's Whit?" asked Tom looking around for a sign of their corpulent chum.

"This is a real mess."

"I'm afraid you're right, Billy."

Meanwhile, inside the flower locker, Whit had positioned himself next to the door, both to keep from knocking over the flowers—"I do not want to douse myself in cold water," he said aloud—and in hopes that perhaps someone would hear him. As he rubbed his arms, trying to stay warm, he would occasionally give a shout, but his calls for help had gone unanswered.

His cell phone cast enough light to dispel the inky blackness that had descended with the closing of the door. "It's a swell flashlight," Whit said to the empty room, "but what I need in the present circumstances is a phone that works as a phone."

Once again Whit put his mouth near the door and yelled. "HELP!" No one answered. "I've read," said Whit into the silence, "that some flowers are edible. But some are poisonous. And as I do not know which are which, I think I'd best not sample any of the merchandise. In any case, I would have to eat great quantities of flowers to assuage my current hunger pangs."

Whit turned off his phone to conserve the battery and the refrigerated space was plunged once again into pitch-black darkness.

Suddenly, a young man in a green apron opened the door. "OK. I'll just be a— Criminy!! What are you doing in here?!" he gasped. He jumped back as Whit lunged out of the walk-in refrigerator.

"Oh, boy!" Whit exclaimed. "Am I glad to see you! *Brrr!* You keep that place cold." Whit rubbed his hands together and stamped his feet. "I really thought I was going to be a human Popsicle again."

"What were you doing in the flower fridge?"

"Being cold," replied Whit. "And wanting very much to get out."

"I mean how did you get in there? That door is

always locked."

"Well, it wasn't locked when I walked into the room."

"And why did you walk into it?"

"It's rather a long story."

"Whit! Whit! Where have you been? We've been looking high and low for you."

Tom rushed up with Billy close behind.

"I was trapped in a refrigerator."

"A refrigerator?" exclaimed Billy.

"It's our flower fridge and he had no business being in there," said the irritated clerk.

"What were you doing?" asked Tom.

"That's what I want to know," said the clerk.

"Harvey?" A woman called, stepping in from the front of the shop. "Stop gabbing and get me my orchids. I have to get this order made up before five o'clock."

"I'm not gabbing, Miss Abernathy. This man was in—" But Miss Abernathy had gone back to the counter and was out of earshot.

"This seems like an excellent time to take our leave," said Billy quietly.

"I believe you're right," agreed Tom. "Come on, Whit. Let's go find Officer Turnipseed."

"Thanks for the rescue," said Whit to the man called Harvey.

"OK, fellas," said Tom, "let's go." He began walking toward the entrance to the hotel lobby.

"What happened to you?" asked Billy, as he and Whit followed Tom across the atrium.

"It was Buttman," said Whit.

"He locked you in the refrigerated room?!" exclaimed Billy.

"Not exactly."

"Then what *exactly*?"

"I'll tell you all about it over supper," said Whit. "I'm famished."

"Good to know that some things never change," said Tom with a chuckle. "You'd never believe what almost happened to us!"

Trooper Joe Morgan and FBI agent Carlos Hyche were waiting with Officer Turnipseed when Whit and the Hardly boys approached the rendezvous point.

"We were beginning to get worried," said Hyche. "I'm glad I didn't have to call your dad and explain how we lost his sons and their pal."

"Dad wouldn't have blamed you," said Billy, as they walked through the hotel lobby. "We're supposed to be able to take care of ourselves."

"Still," said Hyche with a wry grin, "I wouldn't want to be the one to tell him you were missing."

Tom gave a brief account of what had happened in the hotel mall, deftly avoiding any mention of the "wedding."

"I am really sorry that we couldn't keep tabs on Buttman. When the elevator door closed we knew we'd lost him. At least for the time being."

Hyche had made a couple of calls and learned that Buttman and his entourage had checked out of the hotel. "He must have already completed his transaction by the time you saw him in the conference center. So even if you'd been able to follow him, all you would have seen was the bellboy coming to get the luggage from his room."

Officer Turnipseed suggested that they go to the police station to discuss the recent turn of events. "We have a conference room we can use."

"What about supper?" asked Whit plaintively. "We aren't going to miss supper, are we?"

"Whit!'" said Tom sharply. "Stop whining about food."

"I wasn't whining. I was merely inquiring," said Whit dejectedly.

"I expect we can order in a pizza," said Joe Morgan. "No reason we have to skip a meal."

Whit was profuse in his thanks as they left the hotel. In the parking lot, he pointedly ignored Tom as he got into the highway patrol car with Morgan and Hyche. The others rode to the station in Turnipseed's unmarked police car.

CHAPTER XV

Gone but Not Forgotten

At police headquarters, Carlos Hyche checked in with his office and learned some startling news. "It seems that Clive Custard was down in this neck of the woods for about a week before Buttman and the Trafalgar sisters arrived. He was staying in a cabin that belongs to a man named Scott Bullard. It's one of several rental properties that Bullard owns. Do you know him Henry?"

"More like I know *of* him. He's one of our more prominent citizens."

"Hmmm. I think we need to have a talk with Mr. Bullard," said Agent Hyche. "He may not know anything about Mr. Custard, but we'll feel mighty foolish if we don't check him out and then find that he was knee deep in Buttman's affairs."

"I've never heard anything to his detriment," said Turnipseed, "but I agree someone needs to check him out. He keeps a boat down in Pensacola, which is where he is now. Do you have an agent down there who can talk with him?"

"I don't, but I can dispatch someone by tomorrow."

Tom and Billy exchanged a glance, then Tom spoke up.

"Since we're down in 'this neck of the woods,' would you like for us to talk with Mr. Bullard?"

"If you can spare the time, I'd be pleased to have your help. I'll run Bullard's name through the FBI database, see if we come up with anything."

Agent Hyche arranged for a government plane to the naval air station in Pensacola for the Hardly boys, Whit, and himself. They arrived just after noon and the navy provided lodging for the detectives. The boys were greeted by base commander Kevin Aitken, who had worked on a highly classified government case with DeVern Hardly and was happy to entertain his sons and their chum, Whit.

While waiting for information about Bullard from the FBI, the Hardlys and their friend were treated to a tour of an aircraft carrier and a look at the navy's Blue Angels. Whit Moore had heard of a restaurant on Palafox Street and convinced the boys to have supper there. Agent Hyche declined the invitation to join them. "The soft shell crabs are supposed to be great," said Whit. "You ought to come with us."

"Another time," said the agent. "I've got some paperwork to take care of. I'll just grab a bite in the base cafeteria."

Whit shook his head at such misplaced priorities, then he and the Hardly boys left to catch a cab downtown. Returning to the naval base after supper, they learned that information from the FBI would not be available until the next day.

Hyche met the boys for breakfast next morning at the base. "As we suspected, Bullard has no criminal record," he reported. "A real estate agency handles his rental properties in Verbena. The cabin was rented for a week to Clive Custard, who paid cash in advance.

"Bullard is in Pensacola," Hyche continued, "and has agreed to meet with us on his boat at a nearby marina. I doubt that he can tell us anything about Custard and the rest."

"I agree," said Tom, "but now that we're here we might as well talk to him."

When they arrived at Bullard's boat, he was getting ready to head out on a fishing trip into the Gulf of Mexico. "Why don't you gentlemen come with me. We can talk while we fish," suggested Bullard. Agent Hyche declined but encouraged the boys to go out and have a good time. "I'll meet you back at the base late this afternoon," said Hyche.

Scott Bullard proved to be a good host. The boys caught several mackerel, and Whit landed a dolphin. "What a beautiful blue green color," said Whit before releasing the fish. It turned out that Bullard almost never had any contact with his renters and had not even heard of Custard, Stufflebean, or the Trafalgar sisters.

They returned to the marina after a pleasant day of fishing in the Gulf. Bullard dropped the three lads back at the naval base. "Now you gents stay in touch," said Scott Bullard after shaking hands with the Hardlys and Whit. "Y'all come back when you've got more time so we can spend a weekend out on the boat. We'll have a grand time."

"Maybe we could come back during spring break," said Billy.

"You're teachers?" asked Bullard, opening the driver's side door of his car.

"Oh no," said Whit. "We're high school seniors."

Bullard looked startled. "High school seniors?" He paused with one foot in the car and one out.

"You see," began Whit, "there was this mad scientist—"

"Not now, Whit," said Tom, interrupting his pal. "But we would like to come back, sir. And I promise we'll give you the full story then."

"All right," said Bullard, getting into his car. "I'm gonna hold you to that."

Agent Hyche joined the boys at the officers' club for supper with Captain Aitken. The boys had decided to return to Baymoor on Monday. "We really need to hit the books," said Tom as they took their seats at the table.

Whit Moore complimented the base commander on the excellence of the food. He was particularly pleased with the dessert of baked Alaska. "I thought military food was supposed to be barely edible," said Whit, running his spoon around the edges of the plate to get every remaining morsel.

"We are extremely fortunate," said Captain Aitken, "to have a young woman who was studying to be a chef before she joined the military. By an amazing stroke of luck, her chef's credentials were taken into consideration when she received her duty station assignment." He added under his breath, "It almost never happens that way."

The boys flew out of Pensacola early the next morning and were back home just after lunchtime on Monday.

The three lads spent all that afternoon and part of the evening catching up with schoolwork. "I don't think I was cut out to be a detective *and* a student," complained Whit as he flopped down on a sofa in the Hardly family's den. "One or the other, but not both. Thank goodness we're off Thursday and Friday for Thanksgiving. I don't think I could go to school for four whole days this week."

"I know what you mean," said Billy and Tom in chorus.

"Jinx, jinx, you owe me a Coke," crowed Billy.

Whit left shortly after this exchange and the Hardly boys went into the kitchen to tell their mother and Miss Jane goodnight.

"Your father called," said Hazel Hardly. "He said to let you know that Dogface Roscoe has been apprehended and is in jail in Alabama. He also said to tell you not to be too despondent about George Buttman getting away."

"'Even the best detective sometimes suffers a setback,'" said Billy. "I think I've heard Dad say that before."

"One or two times," added Tom with a smile. "Did Dad say when he would be home?"

"Tomorrow," said Hazel Hardly, giving each of them a quick hug. "Your father and I are very proud of you."

With a bottle of spray cleaner in one hand and a damp rag in the other, Miss Jane was busily wiping down the kitchen counters. "Flying off to Birmingham," she sniffed. "Gallivanting around in the wilds of Alabama. Nobody knows where you'll be off to next. I declare—"

"Now, Jane," chided Hazel Hardly in her soft-spoken manner. "Don't fuss."

"I'm not fussing," said her sister-in-law. She gave the front of the refrigerator a swipe with her cloth. She then rinsed the cloth in the sink, wrung the water out, and laid it over the dish drainer to dry. "I'm going to bed."

The boys looked at each other then back at their mother. "We know," said Tom with a grin, "her bark is worse than her bite."

Tuesday and Wednesday were uneventful and the boys devoted themselves to their schoolwork. Billy was in his room late Wednesday afternoon, working on an English assignment, when Tom knocked on his bedroom door.

"Enter."

"Criminy!" Tom exclaimed as he nearly tripped over a leaning tower of books. "Obviously Miss Jane hasn't been in your room in a while." He pushed a pile of clothes to one end of the bed and sat down.

"True," replied Billy, swiveling around in his clear acrylic desk chair to face Tom. "The last time Miss Jane ventured past the doorway she was quite distraught, *quite distraught,* I say. I know this," continued Billy with a wink, "because she told me so. More than once. But...being a trained detective, I deduce that you did not come in here just to discuss my untidy ways."

"You have that right. No, I was wondering if Anne," Tom looked down at his hands, which were folded in his lap, then back up at his brother, "had talked to you. About the cottage. At the beach."

"Oh. That." Billy raised both arms above his head, twirled twice around on his chair, crossed his legs up under him, and sat with his back to the desk, once again facing Tom. "Did you know schoolkids don't sit 'Indian style' any more? When teachers want them to sit Indian style, they say 'criss-cross, apple sauce' and kids know to sit down cross-legged." Billy stared into the distance for a few seconds before bringing his gaze back to meet Tom's. "I wonder if they still walk Indian file. Probably not." He sat frowning into the distance again. "I don't know whether that's a good thing or a bad thing."

"I don't either," said Tom irritably. "Nor do I know what it has to do with us and a beach cottage."

"Nothing. Absolutely nothing. Sorry. I get distracted."

"Don't I know it," muttered Tom. He waited but Billy did not speak. "Well, has she? Talked to you?"

"Actually, she has. I gather that Jessa has talked to you?"

"She has," agreed Tom.

"And what did you say to the fair Jessa?"

Tom smiled shyly. "Probably the same thing you said to Anne: you and I would talk about it and I'd get back to her."

"Yes," said Billy, setting his feet on the floor and leaning forward in his chair, "that is exactly what I said."

"Well, then, let's talk."

"Yes, let's."

The brothers sat without saying anything for several seconds.

"There is—"

"Obviously we—"

They both stopped talking and Billy nodded at Tom. "I yield the floor to my older brother."

"There is," Tom began again, "no question that the idea of going away with the girls for a weekend has great appeal."

"No question at all," agreed Billy.

"There is, however, the question of what would we tell Mom and Dad."

"And Miss Jane."

"Ouch. Yes, and Miss Jane."

The brothers sat again without speaking.

"I really don't think," said Tom slowly, "that Mother and Dad would mind. At least I'm pretty sure Mom wouldn't."

Billy raised one eyebrow. "Why do you think that?"

"You remember when we told her that the FBI wanted us to take the girls to Brownbrier and pose as two married couples?"

"Sure."

"Well, think about it. She told us that of course if Dad needed us we had to help him out. Did she seem upset?"

"No," said Billy after a few seconds. "You're right. She didn't." Then, reflecting, "However, her acceptance was in the context of us 'helping our country,' remember? Besides, I doubt she expected any…"

"Indiscretions?" Tom filled in.

"Good word," Billy replied.

Tom blushed. "Yes, well, anyway…if it *were* OK with Mom, you know it'd be OK with Dad."

"True." Billy crossed his legs again and played a quick drum solo on his knees. "Miss Jane, on the other hand . . ."

"Ah, yes," replied Tom. "An entirely different kettle of fish."

"Well," said Billy, "maybe we shouldn't actually tell everybody that we're going off with Anne and Jessa. I mean—"

"I know what you mean. And I agree with you. I don't think an announcement at the dinner table is the way to handle this."

"Decidedly not," said Billy. "I don't want Miss Jane to collapse face first into her mashed potatoes."

Tom laughed. Then, holding his chin at a bold angle, he declared, "No. I think if we just say we're going off to the beach for a weekend, we don't have to go into details about who's going with us."

Billy looked at his hands and ran them down his pants legs. "Whatever you think, big brother."

Tom gazed out the window, both boys avoiding each other's eyes.

"Well," Tom gulped, "you know what dad says…"

"'It's always best to sleep on it, before making a major decision,'" they chorused.

The boys laughed together and Billy quipped, "'Jinx, jinx, you owe me a Coke!"

On Wednesday evening, DeVern Hardly asked the boys to join him in his study after supper.

"I've been reviewing my files on the Buttman case," said DeVern Hardly. "And I believe that the golden goblet is back in Baymoor. Buttman is a devious scoundrel and it would be in keeping with his wily ways to move the treasure and then return it to its original hiding place."

"What can we do?" asked Tom.

"I want you boys and some of your chums to be on the water, in the air, and on land looking for any sign of movement from our suspects. I have a hunch that Buttman may make a move on Thanksgiving Day. Do you think your buddies will be willing to give up part of their holiday searching for these villains?"

"You bet," said Tom. "They'll be right on top of it."

"We may have to offer to feed Whit," Billy said with a laugh. "His parents have gone out of town for Thanksgiving and I was thinking of asking Mom if we can invite him and Anne for turkey and trimmings anyway."

"By all means, invite the Moores to share Thanksgiving dinner with us. And perhaps Jessa will join us too."

"I'll check with Mom and Miss Jane," said Tom. "I

know they'll say it's fine, but—"

"They'll like it if we check with them ahead of time," said Billy with a knowing smile.

"Very well," said their father. He picked up the book he was reading and settled back in his desk chair, signaling the end of the conversation. "Tomorrow you and your pals will take to air, land, and sea in search of any sign of the Buttman gang. Good hunting, sons."

The boys called Whit, Izzy Lipman, Marco Remo, and Marshall Johnson and enlisted their aid in the next day's search.

They also invited Whit, Anne, and Jessa for Thanksgiving dinner. "Mom and Miss Jane said there was plenty of food," Tom assured Jessa when she said extra guests might not be welcome. "And I would like for you to be here."

Jessa was pleased with that declaration and happily accepted the invitation.

The plan was for Marco and Izzy to take the *Capri* and scour the rivers and the bay for unusual activity. Marshall and Whit on their motorbikes would drive the back roads of Baymoor. Tom and Billy would fly their two-seater biplane over the entire area.

Thanksgiving morning found the Hardly boys and their pals on their assigned routes, looking for any clue to the whereabouts of Clive Custard, Sonny Stufflebean, or the Trafalgar sisters. The sleuths had agreed to meet at the Baymoor airport at noon to talk over their morning search.

The Hardly boys landed just before noon and refueled the Stearman so they were ready to head out again after meeting with their friends.

Marshall and Whit rolled up on their motorcycles and reported no luck.

Marco and Izzy had not arrived by 12:30, and repeated phone calls went unanswered. "We'll start a search," Tom said. "Billy and Marshall, you take the *Flatfoot* and retrace the search route of the *Capri*. Whit, you come with me for an air search."

Tom called Chief Langly and reported the situation as he and Whit taxied for takeoff. Once airborne, the anxious lads flew down the Lockjaw River to Welsley Bay and on out to Blackbeard's Island, but saw no trace of the *Capri*. As they headed back up the Lockjaw, Whit spotted the *Flatfoot*.

Billy and Marshall, motoring slowly down the river, were making a thorough search of the coves and inlets along their route. Billy steered the *Flatfoot* into the mouth of Wehner's Creek and let out a whoop as he spotted the stern of the *Capri* visible through the branches and twigs that covered the boat. There was no trace of Marco or Izzy in the abandoned boat. Billy phoned Tom to report the situation.

"You fellows tow the *Capri* to the boathouse," said Tom. "Whit and I will meet you there along with the police. Be sure not to disturb anything."

When Tom and Whit arrived at the boathouse, the police had already arrived and were dusting the *Capri* for prints. Clearly, two sets of prints belonged to Marco and Izzy, but no other fresh prints were found.

While the police were searching the boat, Marshall was looking at Izzy's cell phone, which had been found in the boat.

"Look at this," Marshall exclaimed. "There's a partial text message on this phone. It was keyed in but not sent."

"Old Warehouse Clinton's Cree"

"Izzy must have been stopped before he could finish," Marshall said.

Tom said excitedly, "It must have something to do with the abandoned warehouse on Clinton's Creek. It's about an hour from here by boat, but closer by car."

"We'll take the squad car," said Chief Langly.

The boys piled into the vehicle, and with sirens wailing the Chief led another police car toward the warehouse on Clinton's Creek. Twenty minutes later the police cars approached the warehouse, sirens blaring. There was no activity outside the building and no sign of a vehicle.

Everyone got out of the cars and walked quickly in the direction of the warehouse. The large double doors were standing open and the Chief told the three boys to stay back while he and his men entered the building. Inside, they found Marco and Izzy tied up to pipes along the wall. Two burlap sacks lay beside them. One of the policemen quickly cut through the ropes binding the boys.

"Oh, man! Are we glad to see you!" cried Izzy. "I don't think I've ever been so scared in my life."

"Ditto!" exclaimed Marco.

The Chief led the boys outside to the delighted

---

whoops and cries of their chums.

"Tell us what happened, son," said Chief Langly to Marco.

"When we moved up Wehner's Creek, we saw the *Lizzy Borden*, and before we were spotted we overheard a man on the phone telling someone named Sonny—I presume it was Sonny Stufflebean—telling him to bring the girls and the goblet to the old warehouse on Clinton's Creek. Izzy started a text message but we were interrupted by two men who threw burlap bags over our heads, grabbed us, and tossed us in the *Lizzy Borden*. The next thing we knew we were being tied up in this warehouse. Although we didn't know where we were at the time. We just knew we weren't on the boat any more. We got the sacks off our heads—"

"That was after the men left—"

"Right. While the men were in the warehouse we didn't speak. We didn't even move. I guess maybe we were hoping they would forget about us." Marco stopped talking and gazed off into the distance.

Izzy waited a few seconds and then took up the tale for the eager listeners.

"And in a certain way, that's just what they did. The men seemed to be loading things onto a truck. We could hear them grunting, and every now and then one of them would curse. I don't think they were happy about being the ones doing all the heavy lifting.

"When they heard your sirens," continued Izzy, "they had a quick confab and decided to bolt. 'What about them?' one of them said. And we knew he was talking about us. 'Forget about 'em,' said the other one.

`Let's get out of here while we still can. Custard can worry about them.' We heard them running to the door and then we heard tires screeching—"

"And that's when we got the sacks off," concluded Marco.

"Whew," said Whit. "I wonder what they were planning to do with you two."

"I don't know," said Izzy with a shudder.

"And I don't want to know," added Marco.

"All right, boys," said Chief Langly. "I'm going to have one of my men drive you home. You should be just in time for Thanksgiving dinner."

"Tell Bernie we said hi," Whit called out as Izzy and Marco got into the patrol car. "We'll stop by to see him once this case is wrapped up." Bernie Lipman, Izzy's grandfather, had been in school with Whit and the Hardly boys back in the day, and he enjoyed hearing about his grandson's adventures with his old pals.

The Hardly boys and Whit piled into the Chief's car and headed to Baker Street.

Chief Langly dropped Whit and the Hardly boys at number 223. He had declined an invitation to eat Thanksgiving dinner with the Hardlys and their friends. "Cora's as patient a woman as I've ever known," said the Chief. He got into his car and rolled the window down. "She's been a policeman's wife long enough to know that the job has odd hours and I can't always be home when I say I will. So I try extra hard to be there for special events."

He stopped the window halfway up and added, as the boys were walking away, "And she's a terrific cook."

"Happy Thanksgiving," said Billy over his shoulder as the boys reached the front porch.

They headed straight to the kitchen, lured by the aromas of the sumptuous Thanksgiving feast their mother and aunt had prepared. Anne and Jessa were also in the kitchen. They had helped when they were allowed to, but mostly they had sat at the kitchen table and chatted with the Hardly women.

"Yumm," said Billy, "as he gave Miss Jane a hug. "It smells good enough to eat."

"Get away with you," grumbled his aunt, pushing him aside as she went to the stove. "Good enough to eat, indeed. Humph."

Mr. Hardly walked into the kitchen to invite his sons and Whit to his office for a talk.

"DeVern Hardly, don't keep those boys in there while you go maundering on about golden goblets and the like. Dinner will be on the table in ten minutes." Miss Jane brandished the large wooden spoon she had been using to stir the green beans. "Don't be late."

"I wouldn't dare," said her brother with a smile. "You three come along. Let's have a quick confab then get to the dining room for Thanksgiving dinner." Tom, Billy, and Whit followed him from the room.

"Boys," said Mr. Hardly, taking a seat behind his desk. "We've had a tip that the Buttman gang will effect some sort of disturbance in New York City this weekend. We have no specifics. We aren't even sure this tip is legitimate."

"You mean this could be another of Buttman's red herrings?"

"Yes, Tom. He could be using the magician's ploy of directing attention to the right hand while the left prepares the magic trick. But we cannot afford to ignore the possibility that Buttman does indeed have some scheme in mind."

"Do you think this has something to do with the men who snatched Izzy and Marco?" asked Billy. "Izzy said the men seemed to be loading things onto a truck. I meant to ask before what you thought that could have been. They wouldn't need to grunt and curse if it was just the golden goblet."

"It's a lot more than the goblet," revealed the famous detective. "Do you remember I told you that Buttman has a stash of illegal weapons and explosives that the government has been searching for?"

The three boys nodded solemnly.

"I think that was what was stored in the warehouse at Steele's Creek and loaded onto the truck. But—"

"Golly!" blurted Whit. "Sorry, Mr. Hardly."

"All right, Whit," said the elder Hardly. He took back up his tale. "But those weapons are not the worst of what Buttman has acquired."

Mr. Hardly leaned back in his chair and stared at the ceiling for a moment. Silence filled the room.

"What he has," said DeVern Hardly, sitting upright and looking directly at the boys, "is enough germ warfare agent to wipe out New York City."

CHAPTER XVI

The Big Apple Had Worms in It

The boys were stunned at this revelation.

"How can we help?" asked Tom.

"I want you three to go to New York City tomorrow. The Trafalgar sisters have been spotted there. I believe they might indeed have proven themselves when they kidnapped Anne and Jessa. Buttman admires what it pleases him to call 'derring-do.'" DeVern's eyes narrowed and he glared at the far wall, seeing something visible only to himself. "'Villainy' is what I call it.

"In any case, it's possible the Black Widows will be the ones responsible for putting Buttman's scheme into effect."

"But, Dad," said Tom, "that assumes there *is* a scheme."

"We cannot afford to assume otherwise," replied Mr. Hardly. "I've arranged for FBI agent Susan Leslie to meet with you in the city and bring you up to date.

"Are you ready to take on this assignment?"

"You bet," said all three boys.

"Then let's get on into the dining room before Miss Jane comes hunting for us with a butcher knife in her hand."

On Friday morning the boys climbed into Whit's roadster to make the short drive in to the city. Whit insisted they stop for an early lunch on the way. "After all," he pointed out, "we don't know when we'll have another chance to eat."

After hearty bowls of clam chowder in Hoboken, the lads rolled on in to the Big Apple. As they were checking in to their hotel, FBI agent Susan Leslie entered the lobby. She had been given descriptions of the trio and walked over to introduce herself. "Your dad's told me a bit about you two," she said shaking hands with Tom and Billy. "And about you." She shook hands with Whit. "You guys get settled, then we'll meet with Adams of the NYPD. I'll wait here for you."

The boys went up to their rooms. A few minutes later they were back in the lobby and ready to go.

"I've arranged for us to meet with Chief of Detectives Carol Adams," said Leslie. "The precinct is just around the corner."

The temperature was in the mid-fifties and the boys and Agent Leslie enjoyed the short walk to the police station in the bright autumn sunshine. "Here we are." Leslie led the way up the broad, shallow steps of a red brick building and into a large reception area. "We have an appointment with Chief Adams."

The duty clerk swiveled to face his computer screen and pulled up the chief's calendar with a few keystrokes. "May I see some identification, please?" He checked the ID cards the boys had been given by the FBI, looking at the faces of the quartet in front of him. "Have a seat. I'll let the chief know you're here."

They waited only a few minutes before they were escorted to the chief's office. After introductions were made, the chief took her seat. The others sat in the chairs drawn up in a semicircle facing her desk.

"Your father," said Chief Adams, addressing the Hardly boys, "tells me that you and your friend," she nodded in Whit's direction, "are familiar with some of the Buttman gang."

"Yes, ma'am," replied Tom. "We've been after these crooks for quite a while and have a debt of our own to settle. Tell us what we can do to help."

"You're aware that Buttman has a formidable stash of weapons and explosives in addition to the germ warfare agent he recently acquired. We have been told that the gang is planning some sort of demonstration this weekend. We don't know the identity of the tipster, so we don't know if her information is good or not. But we cannot afford to disregard the tip."

The three boys nodded in agreement.

"We're glad to have your help," Adams continued, "but you must not take any unnecessary risks or interfere with the government agents."

"Ma'am," said Tom, "we have no intention of getting in the way of your investigation or that of any government agents. We just want to help bring this evil crowd to justice. What do you recommend we do?"

"We don't know," said Captain Adams, "where Buttman is holding the vials of germ warfare agent or the conventional weapons. We do know the Trafalgar sisters are in New York City. They arrived less than twenty-four hours ago and have done nothing out of the ordinary. They appear to be sightseeing, just like ordinary tourists. As far as we know, they have not made contact with Custard or the others.

"The sisters are staying at a hotel in the Village. It would be helpful if you fellows could keep tabs on them while we try to locate the cache of weapons."

"We'll start right away," said Tom. "Where are the sisters now?"

"The last report had them shopping on Fifth Avenue. I'll check with our tail and find out where they are now," said Adams.

As Chief of Detectives Adams phoned Lieutenant Jenkins, who was following the sisters, Billy, Whit, and Tom prepared to begin their assignment in the Big Apple.

"It's a good thing we had lunch," groaned Whit. "I'm already hungry again."

"You're always hungry," Billy laughed. "We won't let you starve."

"They've just gone into Tiffany's," said Chief Adams. "We'll take you there now."

The boys were in place when the sisters emerged from Tiffany's, each carrying one of the store's distinctive blue bags. The trio followed the women for a few blocks until the sisters joined a crowd queued up to board a sightseeing bus with "Kenny Kramer's Seinfeld" in large letters on the side.

"What's a Seinfeld?" asked Whit Moore.

"I don't know," answered Billy.

"I think," said Tom, "it's an old TV show and Seinfeld is the district where the family lives."

"Like Soho?" said Billy.

"Exactly," said Tom.

The boys joined the line but were turned away

because the bus was full.

"We'll get a cab and follow the bus," said Tom. "Probably they're just doing touristy things, but as Dad and Captain Adams have pointed out, we can't afford to assume that's all they're doing."

Billy flagged down a taxi and instructed the driver to follow the bus. The tour lasted more than an hour and the boys ran up quite a large cab fare. Finally, the sisters disembarked. The boys set off in pursuit, as the Trafalgar sisters continued their shopping spree.

"We're getting nowhere," lamented Tom. "These women are just shopping."

"I'm hungry," Whit complained. "When do we eat?

The boys followed the sisters back to their hotel in Greenwich Village and turned surveillance over to the police stakeout posted there.

"We'll see you tomorrow," said Tom as the boys walked away.

"Come on, guys," whined Whit. "The Carnegie Deli is near our hotel. I hear it's a must-eat destination."

The brothers agreed to go to the deli to assuage Whit's hunger pangs. "Look at the size of this thing," Tom said in awe as the waiter set a roast beef sandwich in front of him. "I'll bet I can't even eat half of it."

"Don't worry," said Whit. "I'll help." After eating his pastrami sandwich and half of Tom's roast beef, even Whit was full.

The boys walked around Times Square. "Remember the last time we were here?" asked Tom. "It seems like last week, only those huge TV screens weren't here. I know a lot has happened in the last fifty years, but this takes the cake."

"Yeah," said Billy. "Mom and Dad took us to the automat. That was fun."

A scantily dressed woman wearing very high heels and heavy makeup approached the boys. "You fellows looking for a party?"

"No thank you, ma'am," replied Tom. "We need to get back to our hotel. It's past our bedtime."

The woman stared blankly at the boys and wandered off mumbling to herself.

After breakfast the next day, the boys met with the stakeout crew outside the sisters' hotel. "They stayed in all night," reported Officer Kelly of the NYPD. "We'll meet back here at the end of the day."

It was after ten o'clock before the Trafalgar sisters emerged from their hotel. The boys tailed them as they headed uptown on Fifth Avenue. At Central Park South the Trafalgar sisters hired a horse-drawn carriage and headed into the park. The Hardlys and Whit Moore followed in a carriage of their own.

"This is great!" exulted Whit. "All we need is a Sabrett's hot dog."

The air was a little nippy, but not bad for late November. After the carriages emerged from the park on upper Fifth Avenue, the sisters alit and headed into the Guggenheim. The boys followed them into the famous art museum. While a visit to the Guggenheim was a treat, the Hardly boys began to suspect they were once again being led astray.

Where was Custard?

Where was the cache of weapons and the germ warfare agent?

Was Buttman really planning a demonstration this weekend?

These were the questions that ran through their minds as they left the museum and taxied to the Empire State Building for a trip to the observation deck. At the end of the day, back outside the sisters' hotel, the boys turned over the tailing duties to the NYPD officer then went back to their hotel. They would head back to Baymoor the next morning, to prepare for final exams.

Tom called his father to report their disappointing results. DeVern Hardly was in Scranton and reported a similar lack of success. "Tend to your schoolwork and I'll see you in Baymoor in a few days," said the elder Hardly.

After breakfast, Sunday morning, the boys piled into Whit's roadster to make the trip back to Baymoor.

Miss Jane and Hazel were thrilled the boys were returning and spent the day baking cookies and pies. Jessa Sheridan and Anne Moore had been invited to dinner to celebrate the boys' return. When the travelers pulled into the driveway on Baker Street, they were greeted by the four women.

Whit was overcome by the wonderful aromas and immediately headed for the kitchen. He ate a couple of cookies that were cooling on a wire rack before heading to the dining room.

"We saw a lot of New York City," said Tom as everyone sat down to dinner, "but we didn't make any progress in the case."

"What were the Trafalgar sisters doing?" asked Jessa.

"That's just it," explained Billy. "They seemed to be seeing the sights just like any tourist. They had no contact with the others."

"They may be acting as a diversion so that Buttman and Custard can carry out their evil plans," said Tom.

"The pizza in New York," opined Whit, between bites of roast beef and potatoes au gratin, "was the best I've had since Paisanos in Taos, New Mexico."

Anne Moore laughed. "All you do is eat. I wonder why the Hardly boys put up with you."

"He's a big help," asserted Tom. "But now we'd better get cracking on our studies. Final exams are coming up soon."

The next day the boys paid close attention in school and concentrated on getting back into the academic routine.

After school they decided to check in with Chief Langly and find out what had been going on in Baymoor while they were away. Whit, Billy, and Tom were ushered in to Chief Langly's office by Officer Hunnicut. "Well, boys," said the Chief, "things were quiet in town over Thanksgiving weekend. How was your trip to the city?"

Tom told the Chief about the Black Widows' shopping sprees and sight-seeing tours. "Are you still looking for Sonny Stufflebean?"

"We keep an eye out for him and the others," said Chief Langly, "but we don't have the resources to stake out his home and business."

"We'd like to help," said Tom. "We can spend some time after school and on the weekends keeping a lookout for these crooks."

"We'll ask some of our chums at school to help. We'll tool around Baymoor on our motorcycles and in our boats to see what we can turn up," said Whit enthusiastically.

Fall had been mild so far and the boys decided to cruise around the bay and the Lockjaw River after school the next day. Marco, Marshall, and Whit took off up the Lockjaw in Marco's *Capri,* while Tom, Billy, and Izzy headed out into Welsley Bay in the *Flatfoot.*

All was quiet on the river as the boys motored slowly, keeping a sharp eye out for anything suspicious. Marco took the *Capri* all the way up to the dock at the old Burchfield Mansion, as Whit thought the gang might have returned there. "Maybe they consider this their headquarters," he suggested.

Marco tied up at the dock and the three friends walked up to the house for a closer look. The police had long since pulled their stakeout from the mansion and the boys walked around the grounds without encountering another person. They found all doors and windows locked, and saw no signs of activity in or around the place.

"It'll soon be dark," said Marco. "We should head back to the boathouse and meet up with the others."

The *Capri* pulled away from the dock and headed downriver, back to Baymoor.

As Marco increased his speed, a light, unseen by

the boys, came on in a third-story window of the abandoned mansion.

CHAPTER XVII

Finals Week

After putting their boats away, the boys agreed to continue their search after school the next day. In fact, they searched each day for a week, but found nothing of interest.

Whit, Billy, and Tom studied together each evening and were well prepared for the semester's final exams. All passed with flying colors and were excited about the upcoming Christmas break.

"We've got two weeks off," said Tom. "Let's get to work and solve this mystery."

DeVern Hardly had left Scranton after failing to turn up any clues to the whereabouts of the gang and headed to New York City where the Trafalgar sisters were still shopping.

Whit, Tom, and Billy were at the Hardly home eating one of Miss Jane's pecan pies and discussing their plan of action. "You know," Whit offered, "when Marco, Marshall, and I were at the old Burchfield Mansion, I had a strange feeling that someone was in the house."

"But you said you didn't see or hear anything," said Tom.

"I know. It was just a feeling, but I'd like to go back out there and see if I can turn up anything."

"Well, go ahead and see what you can find. Billy and I are going to those cabins on Richards Mountains and Jacks Peak before the winter snows hit."

The lads agreed to meet back at the Hardly home the next afternoon at three.

Tom and Billy took an aerial tour of the mountains early the next morning before trekking to the cabins on foot. From the air, they saw no activity around the hideouts on Richards Mountain or Jacks Peak. A closer search on foot produced no clues. Nobody had been around the cabins in weeks.

Tom and Billy got to their house in the afternoon, expecting to meet their chubby pal Whit at 3:00. By 3:30 Whit still had not shown, and he did not answer his cell phone.

"We'd better head up to the old Burchfield place," said Tom with a trace of concern in his voice.

They drove out to the mansion and parked their roadster a few hundred yards from the house, next to Whit's car.

"He's here all right," exclaimed Billy. "But where?"

The boys crept silently toward the dark mansion.

"Hey, over here," whispered Whit, who was crouched behind a large rhododendron bush.

"What's up?" asked Tom quietly. "Why didn't you answer your cell phone?"

"I had to turn it off. Someone's in the house and I didn't want him to know I'm here. I figured you'd come looking for me if I didn't show up at three."

"You could have put it on 'vibrate,'" complained Billy.

Whit blushed. "For once, you're ahead of me, techno-guy!"

Tom griped, "Keep your minds on the mystery. Who's in the mansion?"

"I don't know," Whit admitted. "I saw a man go in the side door. I couldn't tell who it was."

"We'd better call Chief Langly for backup right away," said Tom.

Billy got out his cell phone and headed back toward the parked cars, out of earshot from whoever was in the house. He reported to Chief Langly, who said he would join the boys as quickly as possible, and arrived a few minutes later with three other officers.

"OK, boys," said the Chief, "we're going in."

A policeman was stationed at each of the side doors and the back door. Chief Langly went to the front entrance and knocked. No response. He drew his pistol and then opened the door. He walked through the house, quickly but efficiently searching the basement and all three floors of the mansion. He found no one and saw no signs that anyone had been there. Puzzled, the Chief told his men to join him on the front porch of the deserted building.

Watching from the shelter of the rhododendron bush, the boys saw Chief Langly give the all-clear. They were about to head to the mansion when they heard a rustling in the nearby shrubbery. Moving stealthily toward the noise, they heard what sounded like a metal door being shut. As they came closer they saw a man raking leaves over a door set into the ground. As he turned to leave, the lads pounced on him and wrestled him to the ground.

"Chief!" yelled Tom. "We have him. Come

quickly!"

The Chief and his men were on the scene almost instantly, weapons drawn. As the Chief turned the man over, they all recognized Sonny Stufflebean.

"What are you doing here?" said the Chief, after reading him his rights.

"I ain't talkin'," muttered Stufflebean.

"We'll see about that," said the Chief. "Take him to the jail, men. I think I'll take another look around."

Chief Langly, the Hardly boys, and Whit opened the metal door that was set into the ground and headed down the dark stairs to a secret entrance in the basement.

Going up the stairs to the kitchen, the Chief mused, "So I guess he's been here off and on for quite a while."

"But why?" asked Tom. "Agent Steele removed all the computer equipment they had here."

"We must have missed something," the Chief replied. "We'd better look more closely. If there's one secret door, there may be another."

For the next hour, the Chief and the boys searched the entire house from top to bottom, but came up empty.

"Let's check the basement again," said Tom. "That's the most logical place for an escape route."

The four detectives pushed, prodded, and pounded the walls in the basement without finding any indication of a secret door. They were beginning to believe they were wrong when Whit Moore stumbled over a piece of wood. He fell heavily into the stack of firewood, which collapsed, revealing a single row of wood tied together

Hallmark
Shoebox

upright, in one piece. As Whit pulled himself to his feet, the last row of wood slid to one side, opening up a section of the wall.

With their flashlights on full beam, the group headed into a large room containing an array of communication equipment, a full kitchen and sleeping accommodations, and a few cartons scattered about.

But the biggest surprise was on a table in the far corner of the room. Standing on a protective Plexiglas pedestal sat the golden goblet encrusted with diamonds, rubies, sapphires, emeralds, and the occasional garnet.

CHAPTER XVIII

Water, Water, Everywhere

"Holy cow!" Whit exclaimed. "Look what we stumbled into."

"Good work, boys," said Chief Langly.

"I wonder if the goblet has been here the whole time?" mused Whit.

"You're forgetting that Custard and the Black Widows had the goblet down in Alabama," said Billy.

"You're right! So why is it here now?"

Billy shrugged. "I have no idea."

"Well," said Tom, slowly, "I don't know for sure, but I suspect Buttman thought that once we had searched the mansion and found the computer equipment in the attic we wouldn't come back. And we might not have if it hadn't been for Whit."

The Hardly boys' portly pal grinned. "I can't wait to tell my sister about this."

"Tom may well be right," said the Chief. "The important thing now is to get the goblet to a safe place and see if there are any clues to be found in this secret room.

"I'm going to call Agent Steele. I'm betting he'll want to send in an FBI forensic team. I'll get some of my men here to protect the scene until the FBI experts arrive."

"I'm glad we've found the goblet," said Billy. "But where are the weapons? And where is the deadly germ warfare agent?"

"We'll wait for the FBI, in case the weapons are here," said the Chief. "But I'll wager we won't find a single gun, or a single vial of germ warfare agent."

The Hardly boys and Whit began walking around the clandestine quarters, looking at the computer equipment.

"Don't disturb anything," cautioned the Chief. "The FBI will want to see everything just the way we found it."

While they waited for the FBI to arrive, the boys and the Chief found a corridor leading toward the Lockjaw and an underwater exit to the river.

"They probably used a mini-sub to come and go from this hideout," said the Chief. "This airlock system is very sophisticated. It must have cost a fortune."

"Money doesn't seem to be a problem for Buttman," said Tom.

When the FBI forensic team arrived, they went over the Burchfield Mansion very carefully. A residue of water in the airlock led them to conclude that the system had been used recently, maybe to transfer cargo from the storage room to some watercraft in the Lockjaw River. They found no weapons and no vials of germ warfare agent.

The next day, DeVern Hardly returned to Baymoor from New York City. The Trafalgar sisters had finished their New York shopping spree and taken Amtrak's high-speed Acela Express to D.C. Unfortunately, the sisters must have donned disguises sometime during the trip, because no one matching their description emerged

from the train in Union Station. The FBI was certain the
Black Widows were still in the capital, but they were
not registered at any hotel under their real names.

DeVern called a meeting in his home office on
Baker Street. The Baymoor police chief, his boys, and
Whit Moore were present. Also on hand was Robert
Fitts, an FBI agent who had come up from the District
of Columbia to confer with Mr. Hardly.

DeVern welcomed the Chief and the boys by
congratulating them on a job well done. "I'm
particularly proud of you, Whit, for your persistence at
the Burchfield place."

Whit Moore almost choked on a bite of cookie at
this praise from the world-famous detective. "Thank
you, Mr. Hardly," stammered Whit, brushing a crumb
from his shirt. "I got lucky, I guess. People say I
inherited Granddaddy Moore's lucky gene."

"Perhaps so, but you seized the moment when luck
proffered it," said DeVern with a slight bow in Whit's
direction.

"What do we do now?" asked Billy, voicing the
question on everyone's mind.

DeVern Hardly nodded at Agent Fitts. "Will you
describe the situation for us, Agent Fitts?"

Robert Fitts looked around at the small gathering.
"We believe the gang loaded cargo stored in the secret
room of the mansion onto a mini-sub then transferred
that cargo to some watercraft in the Lockjaw River. We
suspect that Buttman plans to sell the goods to a
terrorist group bent on destroying our country."

"Do you really think he would sell a biochemical agent to terrorists?"

"Buttman is utterly profligate, Billy," said DeVern Hardly. "And he has no love for this country. Yes, I believe he would sell not only guns but also biochemicals to the highest bidder. If that bidder were a terrorist organization, Buttman wouldn't blink an eye."

"We'll need all the help we can get to thwart this dastardly plot," declared the FBI agent. "I would like to have your assistance, Mr. Hardly. And that of your boys and Whit Moore since they were instrumental in getting us to this point."

"The boys and I stand ready to assist the FBI in whatever way we can. What is your plan?"

"As you know, the Trafalgar sisters left New York and went to D.C. Clive Custard was already there. And Buttman himself arrived in the capital last night. We know that he often takes a hands-on approach in his criminal business dealings. Our profiling experts believe he does so because he enjoys playing cat and mouse with the law—putting himself in the position of both cat and mouse. We suspect that the sale of the weapons and the biochemical agent will take place in the District."

"This devilish scheme must be stopped at all costs," said DeVern Hardly. "We'll do all we can."

"With your permission, sir, I want to arm Tom, Billy, and Whit with 9mm pistols for their protection."

DeVern Hardly pondered that idea for a few seconds. "Yes. I believe that is a necessary step."

"We've had Boy Scout training with our .22s," said

Tom, "but I've never handled a pistol."

"I'll call Chief Langly and arrange to get you qualified at the Baymoor police shooting range. You'll need to start training right away."

"Wow!" exclaimed Billy. "This is exciting! But...I hope we don't have to use the guns in action."

"I hope not, too," said DeVern Hardly, "but you must be prepared to do so. This is a risky assignment and Buttman and his cronies are dangerous people."

"Indeed they are," said Agent Fitts. "You will need to be extremely careful and keep your wits about you.

"I've arranged with the U.S. Coast Guard for you boys to travel with Lieutenant Shaeffer aboard the station's cutter."

"When do we leave?" asked Tom Hardly.

"Tomorrow. You'll go to the shooting range today, then head down to D.C. to try to intercept the Buttman gang before carry out their evil plan."

"You boys had better get cracking," said DeVern Hardly. "No time to waste."

"What if they aren't spotted on the water and we're not able to intercept their ship?" asked Billy with his hand on the doorknob. "What's our next move?"

"Lieutenant Shaeffer will head up the Potomac River and berth in D.C. Then," Agent Fitts said with a half smile at the Hardlys' corpulent pal, "we'll need a healthy dose of Whit's luck to catch these villains."

Then, just as they were about to exit, Tom looked back in concern. "What about our final exams, Dad? We might not be prepared..."

DeVern smiled proudly at his responsible son.

"Not to worry, Tom," he said. "I'll talk to your principal."

The boys headed for the police shooting range with great enthusiasm and resolve. The police instructor issued the 9mm pistols provided for the chums by the FBI. The training session was intense and the boys proved to be excellent students. After cleaning their weapons, the three friends headed home for a good night's sleep before setting forth at first light.

Miss Jane and Mrs. Hardly had prepared a picnic basket for the boys to take with them the next morning. "I'm sure they'll feed us on the Coast Guard cutter," said Tom laughingly.

"Maybe so," replied Whit, "but it won't hold a candle to these ladies' cooking."

The boys arrived at the Coast Guard station at 5:30 a.m. rarin' to go. Lieutenant Shaeffer had them taken to the berthing area and immediately got under way. The boys were invited to the bridge as the small ship headed south along the U.S. coastline. As they made their way down the Eastern Seaboard they encountered a number of ships, all of which were cleared by the Coast Guard. By nightfall the boys were tired and ready for sleep.

The next morning, the Coast Guard vessel had already started up the Potomac when the boys were awakened by the bosun's mate and led to the wardroom for chipped beef on toast points. By early afternoon the cutter was tied up in Washington, D.C., and the boys were taken to the Hay Adams Hotel, where they checked into their rooms.

"There are some great restaurants in this town," said Whit. He had picked up a tourist brochure at the concierge's desk and was sitting on one of the beds in the Hardly boys' room reading about various eateries. "Listen to this description of—"

"Stop worrying about your stomach," admonished Tom. "We've got work to do."

"But an army travels on its stomach," Whit retorted.

"Well, your stomach can already carry quite a big army," quipped Billy.

Later that day the boys went to FBI headquarters for a briefing and instructions on what their role should be. They were pleased to see Agent Fitts again. He introduced them to Peter Veitch, the agent in charge in the District of Columbia.

"Pleased to meet you," said Veitch. "We think the best thing for you boys to do is to pretend to be tourists. The Black Widows are probably still in town, and judging from their activities in New York City, we believe they will make the rounds of tourist attractions and expensive shops. We want you to visit museums and current Smithsonian exhibitions; take a tour of the White House and Ford's Theatre if you want; go to the Washington Monument and the Lincoln Memorial. Keep your eyes open at all times," instructed Veitch. "You know better than any of us what the Trafalgar sisters look like. But remember they may be in disguise. So look beyond the surface."

"We're going to need some of Whit Moore's

renowned luck in order to catch this gang," said Agent Fitts. "Do you boys have any questions?"

"I don't think so," said Tom, glancing at his brother and Whit. "We'll visit as many tourist sites as we can and keep our eyes peeled for any sign of the Black Widows, Clive Custard, or George W. Buttman."

"I just thought of a question," said Billy. "Who do we call if we spot any of the gang?"

The boys punched Veitch's and Fitts's cell phone numbers into their phones then headed for the Smithsonian.

The Hardly boys were eager to see the National Air and Space Museum. The story of man-made flight from the 1903 Wright brothers' plane to the *Spirit of St. Louis* to SpaceShipOne was an eye-opener for the lads. But they never forgot their primary purpose and kept a sharp lookout for any of the Buttman gang.

That night, Whit and the brothers dined at the 1789 Restaurant, where they all ate escargot for the first time. Whit had two orders of the snails before continuing with a rack of lamb with red candy onion, Yukon gold potatoes, and black mint, followed by a roast strawberry brownie sundae. Whit pronounced the meal the best he had had in Washington, D.C.

At FBI headquarters the next morning, the boys were brought up to date on efforts by various law enforcement agencies. "We've made no progress," said Robert Fitts. "The villains seem to have disappeared into thin air. We think you men should continue to explore the city. Keep your eyes open for anything that may lead us to a member of the gang. Generally, Buttman likes to flaunt his illegal doings in the face of law enforcement agencies. This circumspection augurs a new level of malevolence."

"We're enjoying seeing Washington," said Tom, "but Buttman and his crew are dangerous and may cause a great deal of property damage and loss of life. Are we doing enough?"

"We are leaving no stone unturned," Peter Veitch assured the boys. "You three are doing as much as anyone on this case. We are blanketing the area with as many pairs of eyes as possible. We need a small crack in the seam of their plan so we can pry it apart and stop Buttman from achieving his goal. Whatever that goal might be . . ."

The Hardlys and Whit took a tour of the White House, ate a bowl of navy bean soup at the Senate cafeteria, then headed for the Lincoln Memorial. The lads strolled along the tidal basin pool and walked up the stairs of the Lincoln Memorial.

As they stood looking up at the imposing figure of President Lincoln, a pair of tourists walking by caught Tom Hardly's eye. "Egad," he whispered. "It's the Trafalgar sisters!"

CHAPTER XIX

The Plot Sickens

The sisters had changed their appearance, but the boys recognized them immediately as they lit up their cigarettes when they left the monument. The trio followed the women at a safe distance, being careful not to be noticed. Billy phoned headquarters and reported that they were following the women on foot.

"Good work! I'll send backup immediately," said Agent Veitch.

"No, wait," said Billy. "They're getting into a limo."

"Stay with it," said Veitch. "We need to know what hotel the sisters are in."

Billy stayed on the line as Tom flagged a taxi and instructed the driver to follow the limousine. The boys continued their pursuit until the limo pulled up in front of the Willard Hotel and the sisters headed inside. Tom Hardly followed the women into the lobby and saw them enter the elevator. He headed to the front desk and identified himself to the desk clerk, showing him his FBI-issued credentials.

"Did you recognize the women who just got on the elevator?"

"Yes sir," said the young clerk, thrilled to be helping with an FBI investigation. "They're staying in Room 303."

"What are their names?"

The clerk checked his computer. "They are Jessa

Sheridan and Anne Moore from Baymoor, New Jersey."

"Are you *sure*?" said a stunned Tom Hardly.

"Yes, sir. I'm quite sure."

"Thank you," said Tom. He returned to the waiting taxi and reported the surprising news to Whit and Billy. Billy passed along the information to Agent Veitch.

"We'll be there in less than a minute," said the FBI man. "Walk to the corner of Fourteenth Street and wait for me there."

Tom paid the cab driver and the three lads walked the half a block to the corner of Pennsylvania Avenue and Fourteenth Street.

True to his word, Veitch arrived within a minute. He assigned agents to cover the hotel entrances and sent two more to watch the lobby. "This may well be the break we've been looking for," said Veitch. "Let's get back to HQ and get you all debriefed."

At FBI headquarters, a grim-faced DeVern Hardly was waiting for the group.

"Dad!" cried the Hardly boys in chorus.

"We found the Black Widows," said Tom. "And they're registered at the hotel as Jessa Sheridan and Anne Moore."

"So I heard."

"What's the matter, Dad?" asked Billy. "You don't look very happy about our finding the Trafalgar sisters."

"You boys have done a fine job, and I'm proud of you," said the famous detective. "But there's been a development."

The room full of FBI agents and other law enforcement officers grew quiet.

"We know," began Mr. Hardly, "that these criminals have in their possession deadly biochemical agents. We believe they are airborne agents."

He looked around the room. "I've been working for more than a year with various government entities, including many of you in this room, to bring this gang to justice. Each time we think we're getting close, Buttman twists out of our reach. He has been toying with us, leading us on wild goose chases and dragging red herrings across the trail. The trips to the West Coast, New Mexico, Vermont, New York, and Alabama were all meant to distract us from the truth."

"What *is* the truth, Dad?" asked Tom pensively.

"We thought Buttman was interested in selling these weapons to terrorists. Now we believe he *is* the terrorist."

No one spoke as the enormity of this revelation sank in.

"What next?" asked Billy Hardly.

"We must stop them at all costs," his father responded.

Agent Veitch stepped forward. "In three days," he said, "there's a special joint session of Congress. We believe that's their target. Both the president and the vice president will be in attendance."

"Can't you just have the session postponed?" asked Whit.

"That would cause widespread panic," said Veitch.

"And it would let Buttman know we're on to him. He would almost certainly shift his sights to another target. Our best hope is to catch the gang before they can put their evil plan into action."

"Not only must we nab the terrorists," said DeVern Hardly, "we must seize the biochemical agent. If it is released into the air near a crowd, many people will die. If they get it into the capitol building, hundreds will be killed.

"Agent Veitch will make assignments for the FBI; Chief of Detectives Anita Harlon will coordinate local police activities."

As the agents and police officers separated into two groups to receive their instructions, Mr. Hardly took Tom, Billy, and Whit aside. "This is a deadly game," he said solemnly, "and I want you boys to be extremely careful. The professional lawmen will be on the front lines of this undertaking, but the situation is so dire we must continue to do our part to bring this crisis to a successful conclusion."

"We'll do anything we can to help," said Tom Hardly.

"You bet," chorused Whit and Billy.

"You three lads have had more contact with Buttman and his gang than anyone else on this case. And you know them better than anyone else. Review what you know of Buttman's past actions, then put your heads together and try to outthink these villains."

"I think better on a full stomach," said Whit Moore. "Let's talk over lunch."

DeVern Hardly laughed. "That's a good idea. I

recommend the Krab Kettle. It's right on the river."

"Excellent," said Whit. "Let's go. I'll pay for lunch."

The boys got a table overlooking the Potomac. "What a view!" exclaimed Billy. "I wish we had the *Flatfoot* with us."

"That's an idea," said Tom. "We'll get a boat and cruise around on the river. You know Buttman's gang has often been on or under water."

Whit ordered the Kaptain's Platter, a selection of several kinds of fish and shellfish, along with french fries and coleslaw.

After lunch Tom called Agent Veitch and arranged to get a thirty-six-foot cabin cruiser for the rest of the day. The boys cruised around looking carefully at the boats, moored or moving, on both sides of the river.

"Let's head south," suggested Billy, "where the river traffic is thinner. Maybe we'll spot something of interest."

"That's a great idea," said Tom, "but it's a little late today. Let's start early tomorrow and head south past the Quantico marine base."

The boys phoned Agent Veitch and arranged for the use of the boat the next day. When they arrived back at FBI headquarters, they joined DeVern Hardly and Agent Veitch to discuss their plans. "If you run into anything suspicious," cautioned DeVern, "call for help right away. Don't take any chances."

"I'll inform the U.S. Marine base that you'll be in the area," said Veitch. "They're already on alert, as are all other branches of the armed services."

"The Trafalgar sisters spent the day shopping," said DeVern Hardly. "We're going to pick them up in the morning. We think that may stir up Custard and Buttman. Get some rest tonight, boys. Tomorrow will be a busy day."

"Well, Mr. Moore, my portly pal," said Tom Hardly, "what's for dinner?"

"Funny you should ask," responded Whit. "I've given it a lot of thought."

"What a surprise!" chimed in Billy.

"Did you see," said Whit, turning his back on Billy and directing his question to Tom, "that Moroccan restaurant near our hotel?"

"I did," said Tom. "What is Moroccan food?"

"I have no idea," admitted Whit, "but I'm willing to try anything called 'food,'"

The boys returned to their hotel for a change of clothes then walked to the Moroccan restaurant. They were seated on cushions on the floor and served an exotic array of North African cuisine.

"That was a delicious meal," said Billy. "I'm glad we tried it."

The boys slept well and were up before dawn the next day.

As the chums motored down the river, the FBI was preparing to arrest the Trafalgar sisters at their hotel. Peter Veitch, along with DeVern Hardly and several FBI agents, entered the sisters' suite at 9:00 a.m.

The room was empty.

CHAPTER XX

Together Again

"We have every exit and entrance covered; we have a man on the roof and men on every floor and in the lobby," said Veitch. "I don't know how they got past us."

"Nonetheless," said DeVern Hardly, "they did."

A search of the room revealed several disguises among the clothing that had been left behind. "They probably left one at a time," speculated Agent Veitch, "heavily disguised, and have gone to join the rest of the gang."

"Let's leave the experts to search for clues," suggested Mr. Hardly, "while we go back to headquarters and consider our next move."

Meanwhile the Hardly boys and Whit Moore were cruising down the Potomac past the Mason Neck Wildlife Refuge on their way toward Quantico. Arrangements had been made for the boys to have lunch during their search for the Buttman gang, and they were greeted warmly by the marines when they docked at Quantico.

The marines had been patrolling with boats, as well as with helicopters, for the last two days with no success. Marine Commander General Christopher Williams offered the boys a ride in one of his helicopters so they could get an overview of the search area.

They were thrilled at the offer. Tom Hardly phoned his dad to report on their plans for the day. DeVern told him about the Trafalgar sisters' escape and exhorted the lads to keep a sharp watch as they continued their search.

As the boys were boarding the helicopter, the pilot asked if any of them had ridden in a helicopter before.

"I have," said Whit. "Once."

"Military?"

"No sir. I'm not old enough to join the military."

"Not old enough—"

"It's sort of a long, complicated story," said Tom. "But we're not as old as we look. We haven't even graduated from high school yet."

"Haven't graduated from—" The major stopped in midsentence and shook his head. "Right. Whatever."

He motioned for the three chums to board the helicopter and directed Whit to sit in the back for proper weight distribution.

Keeping low, the pilot flew downriver all the way to Chesapeake Bay. The boys saw nothing unusual. But while they were surveying the area Tom had an idea. After they landed he called his dad with a proposal. "I'd like to go on down to Chesapeake Bay and anchor overnight before we head back to D.C.," Tom suggested.

"Not a bad idea," replied the elder Hardly. "Ask General Williams for supplies and extra fuel. And, son, be careful."

"Yes, sir," said Tom. "We'll keep you informed."

General Williams was happy to help. He had

someone gather enough supplies and provisions for the three chums, including charts of the bay. The Coast Guard was notified and the boys set forth in the cabin cruiser for Chesapeake Bay. The general had recommended a suitable mooring spot at Point Lookout State Park and promised that his pilots would keep an eye out for the boys as they continued to fly their search patterns.

As the lads moored for the night, Billy said, "This is a big piece of water."

"True," replied Tom. "But we'll stay here, near the mouth of the river. We should be able to spot any boat headed toward Washington."

Before dark, the boys had caught enough fish for a great dinner, and Whit was happy to cook the meal in the small galley. The boys took turns keeping watch throughout the night for any traffic headed upriver.

Billy Hardly was on watch about four in the morning as a large cabin cruiser passed close to shore. As he scanned the deck with the night vision binoculars provided by the marines, he saw three people on deck. Two women and a man were visible in the glow of the chart table lamp. The women were smoking cigarettes.

Billy began the process of getting under way, then woke Tom and Whit to report the sighting.

"It's worth tailing them," said Tom. "It may be not be the Black Widows. But if it is . . ."

"Right," agreed Billy. "We may be able to get a positive ID once it's light."

The boys motored slowly, about a mile behind the suspicious vessel, varying their speed and distance so they wouldn't call attention to themselves.

Day dawned with an overcast sky. It was near eight o'clock before the light revealed anything other than a dark shape ahead of them.

Only one person was on deck as the boys closed in for a quick look. It appeared to be a man clad in a heavy coat and a dark knit cap. No other features could be made out.   Tom called DeVern Hardly and reported their suspicions.

"We can't take any chances," said Mr. Hardly. "What's your position? I'll call the Coast Guard and have that boat stopped. I'll also call General Williams at Quantico for air support."

Within a few minutes a marine helicopter was overhead and minutes after that a Coast Guard cutter pulled alongside the dubious vessel. Some of the guardsmen boarded the boat. The Hardlys and Whit pulled their own boat alongside, as the man at the helm was brought to the stern and two women were brought on deck from the cabin. They did not know the man, but they immediately recognized the Trafalgar sisters.

A thorough search of the boat turned up nothing of interest. The two women waved and smiled at the boys as they were taken aboard the Coast Guard cutter and their vessel was taken under tow.

DeVern Hardly told the boys to return to D.C. but to keep an eye out for Buttman and Clive Custard on their way back. With Tom at the helm, the boys motored back toward Washington. As they passed Alexandria, Virginia, a large twin-engine speedboat traveling at high speed passed within a few feet of the Hardlys' craft.

"Look!" cried Whit. "The driver of that boat is Clive Custard!"

Billy Hardly called FBI headquarters to report the sighting. Custard's boat was going so fast it was out of sight before he hung up the phone.

The entire law enforcement team was notified. Helicopters went immediately aloft. Patrol cars rushed toward docking areas at the river's edge. The abandoned speedboat was found fifteen minutes later, the storage area open but empty.

A witness at the dock said a small white van had been waiting when the speedboat had arrived. Two men had rushed to the boat and moved several small wooden crates from deck to van. The two men in the boat also got into the van, which sped off toward downtown D.C. The witness had not gotten the license plate number.

The police immediately put out an all-points bulletin and monitored all roads leading to D.C. and the White House.

The Hardlys were instructed to head to the capitol. "Because you boys have been in contact with several of the gang members, you might recognize them before we would," said Agent Veitch. "But be extremely careful. These are desperate people. They will stop at nothing to achieve their ends."

As they headed toward Capitol Hill the boys discussed what kind of disguises they might expect the Buttman gang to use. "With all the LEOs on the prowl," said Tom Hardly, "the gang will have to be very clever to avoid capture. There are hundreds of—"

"What," asked Whit, "is a leo?"

"Law enforcement officer," said Billy.

"Oh. Thanks. Sorry, Tom. Go on."

"There are hundreds of LEOs on the lookout for the gang members," Tom continued. "Representatives from all branches of the military, Homeland Security, capitol police, city police, CIA, FBI, . . . you name it."

"But," Whit pointed out, "D.C. is filled with all sorts of weird characters. The LEOs can't check out everyone."

"Not only that," said Billy, "hundreds of tourists, government workers, congressional staff members, and lobbyists from all over the country, plus foreign dignitaries will be in attendance at tomorrow's joint session of Congress."

"It's an impossible task," Whit complained. "What could we ever do to stop Buttman from releasing the deadly biochemical?"

"We'll have to keep our eyes peeled and hope for the best," replied Tom.

"We could sure use a dose of Moore's luck right about now," said Billy, with a glance at his portly pal. "You wouldn't happen to know how to conjure up that luck on demand, would you?"

Whit shook his head. "I wish." And recalling the florist shop fiasco, he admitted, "It doesn't always serve me well."

"Maybe the luck will show up this time," Tom consoled. "Come on. Let's have a look around the capitol's service entrances. Food and other supplies will be brought in for tomorrow's special session, and there'll be the usual letters and packages from the U.S. post office, UPS, FedEx, and so on."

The boys were confronted many times by various law enforcement personnel as they poked around the capitol grounds, but the special security passes issued by the FBI allowed them access, wherever they needed to go.

The presidential motorcade was scheduled to arrive at noon the next day. If the gang had not been rounded up by 10:00 a.m., the joint session would be canceled and the capitol evacuated. The FBI and Homeland Security were hoping against hope not to have to resort to evacuation, knowing what chaos would result.

"We don't want to give in to these terrorists," FBI Agent Veitch had told the boys. "But if we don't nab this bunch by tomorrow morning, we'll have no alterative but to shut down Capitol Hill."

By late afternoon the boys had searched high and low, finding no sign of their quarry. Nor did they have any real idea just how the airborne germ warfare agent would be distributed.

They returned to FBI headquarters to meet with Agents Veitch and Fitts and plan their strategy for that evening and the next morning.

"We've got uniformed officers, plainclothesmen, and agents in disguise all around the city. Every security agency in D.C. has been brought in to help with this situation, and we have deputized hundreds of men and women," said Veitch. "You guys get some rest and join the search at daybreak tomorrow."

The Hardlys and their pudgy pal headed to the hotel, hoping for an idea that would lead to the capture of the Buttman gang. Tom called DeVern Hardly before turning in for the night.

"Get a good night's sleep and start fresh tomorrow," advised the elder Hardly. "I know you'll do your best. I'm proud of you."

The boys were asleep before 10:00 p.m.

At 4:33 a.m. Tom Hardly sat bolt upright in bed and woke Billy.

"I know," he exulted, "how they'll do it!"

CHAPTER XXI

The Last Detail

A sleepy Whit had joined the Hardlys in their room after Tom called him. He was now wide awake and listening to Tom's explanation.

"Distribution of the airborne virus is crucial," asserted Tom Hardly. "The ventilation systems are the obvious choice for disbursing the virus."

"No doubt," said Billy, "the LEOs have thought of this."

"Exactly," said Tom. "And that's why I believe Buttman will do something else. Something completely unexpected. Get dressed, boys. Lock and load. We have no time to lose."

By eight o'clock the boys had been busy for several hours. The day had dawned dark and cloudy, with the threat of a cold rain or even snow. The boys had met Agent Veitch at his office at five. The city engineer and his crew were at their D.C. headquarters when the Hardlys and Veitch arrived for a consultation.

"The theory is," said the FBI agent, "that the terrorists will use the sewer system from the capitol to distribute the deadly virus."

"But," said the city engineer Charles Clapsaddle, "the sewer system goes away from the building and we're in complete control of the water systems into the capitol as well as the rest of Washington."

"My theory," explained the older Hardly brother, "is that the terrorists will rig devices with compressed air to back flush the toilets of all the bathrooms in the capitol, which will release the deadly virus with a whoosh the likes of which you've never seen."

"There are hundreds of miles of pipes beneath the buildings and streets of D.C.," said Clapsaddle. "Where do we begin?"

"Start as close to the capitol as possible," said Agent Veitch, "and work away from the building. If we haven't found them by ten o'clock we'll have no choice but to evacuate the area. We'll put armed LEOs with each group of sanitation workers. There's no time to lose. Let's roll."

The boys left the city engineer's office and made their way to Pennsylvania Avenue. As they began walking west, they noted that every manhole leading to the sewer systems anywhere near the capitol had a crew working at fever pitch to inspect the underground pipes. By 9:30 that morning nothing had been found to support Tom Hardly's theory.

Tom was bitterly disappointed. "I was so sure I was right," he lamented.

"We've done all we can," Whit said dejectedly. "We might as well get a bite to eat. I'm starved."

The despondent trio walked into a coffee shop for a bagel.

A waitress brought menus to the table and asked if they wanted coffee. The plastic nametag pinned to her apron proclaimed that her name was Naomi.

"Just water for me," said Billy gloomily.

A morose Whit and Tom ordered Diet Cokes.

"Why the long faces, ducks?" asked the waitress,

in a British twang.

"It's a complicated story," replied Whit, automatically picking up the menu and perusing the breakfast specials.

"Right, dearie, my aunt Hattie says most people aren't happy unless they're complaining." Naomi scooped up the tip left by the last diners, straightened up the salt and pepper shakers and bottle of ketchup, and gave the table a swipe with a damp rag. "I can recommend the chocolate hazelnut banana oatmeal if the tummy's craving something a bit different, or the cheese, mushroom, onion, and ham omelet if you're really hungry." She gave the table one last swipe then stowed the rag in an apron pocket. "I'll get your drinks and be back in a jiff to take your orders."

A TV set was broadcasting the morning news. "At 10:30 this morning, a short time from now," intoned the newscaster, "the president will be meeting with key members of Congress in the Oval Office. This meeting is in prepara—"

"Not Capitol Hill!" said Tom nearly knocking over the chair in his haste to rise. "The White House!"

Naomi was setting drinks on the table as Whit and Billy stood up.

"Regretfully," said Whit, getting money from his wallet, "we cannot stay for breakfast."

"Right," said Billy as he made his way to the door. "Time's a'wastin'."

The waitress took the proffered money and tucked it into a pants pocket. "Good luck, ducks," she called to them as they hurried out the door.

Tom nodded.

"What do we do now?" asked Billy keeping his voice low.

"First, we find out how many of them are down here," whispered Tom. He reached out to touch the wall on his right. Then he took Billy's left hand and placed it on his own shoulder. They began to move ever so slowly in the direction of the voices.

"Hold that light still, Ivan! Fool!" Custard's voice echoed off the walls of the tunnel then died away.

"All right," replied the man called Ivan. "Just get on with it so we can get out of here."

The brothers continued their snail's-pace journey toward the light. When Billy's foot caught a piece of loose debris that skittered loudly across the floor, they froze, hardly daring to breath.

"What was that!" The Hardlys did not recognize this voice, which was sharp with tension.

"Rats!" said Ivan. "I hate rats!"

"I ain't signed on to deal with no rats," said the unknown voice. "Didn't nobody say nuthin' 'bout no rats!"

"Shut up! You'll finish this job or you'll be sorry," said Custard. "The boss doesn't take kindly to quitters. Now stop your bellyaching and hand me that wrench."

Moving forward again, the brothers soon realized that the tunnel made a sharp turn just ahead of them. Around the corner they could see the shadows of Custard and two other men dancing eerily against a wall in the light from an electric lantern.

Tom stopped and placed his mouth next to Billy's

ear. "I think there are only three of them." Billy
nodded. Tom then pulled out his gun and motioned for
Billy to do the same. With weapons drawn they moved
forward to confront Custard and his henchmen.

"Start the compressor," ordered Custard just as
Tom and Billy rounded the corner.

"Hands up!" shouted Tom over the roar of the
portable machine.

The three men turned quickly toward the Hardly
boys. The two ruffians with Custard put their hands in
the air.

"You too, Custard," ordered Billy. "It's the end of
the line for you and your cronies."

"Not yet, it's not!" sneered Custard. He made a
dive for the compressor and stabbed at the control
button that sent a rush of poisoned air up the sewer line
and into the White House.

Tom Hardly fired, hitting Custard in the arm. But it
was too late. The sound of the compressor changed as
air was pushed through the plumbing and up into the
Executive Mansion where the president was meeting
with the vice president and key members of Congress.

"Oh, no!" wailed Tom. "We're too late!"

Keeping his gun on the two sidekicks, Billy
reached over and turned off the compressor. In the
ensuing silence, Clive Custard's laughter rolled off the
walls of the tunnel and waves of despair engulfed the
Hardly boys.

"Come on," said Billy. "Let's turn these wretches
over to the FBI." He motioned toward the exit and
Custard and his cronies began walking. Custard

clutched a handkerchief to his arm to stanch the bleeding as the brothers herded the three culprits toward the opening. Tom suggested that he keep Custard and the other men covered while Billy climbed the ladder. Billy thought it would be better to have Custard go ahead of him.

"It'll be slow going for him with that bullet in his arm and I can be on the ground before he can run very far."

"Good idea," said Tom. "Get moving, Custard."

Custard made his way slowly up the ladder, muttering foul curses under his breath as he climbed. Billy tucked his gun into his waistband at the small of his back and scrambled up the ladder after him. Once outside he yelled back down to Tom, "Whit's here with Agent Veitch and some other officers. Come on up."

Back in the manhole Tom waved Ivan and his cohort toward the ladder. "You heard Billy. Head on up. We don't want to keep the FBI waiting." Agent Veitch and Agent Fitts, guns drawn, were waiting when Buttman's henchmen emerged, followed by Tom.

"Well done, gentlemen," said Veitch. "Well done."

"We were too late," said Tom, putting away his gun. "I'm so sorry."

"No!" crowed Whit. "We did it! You weren't too late!"

"What!" cried Tom and Billy in unison.

"We did it!" Whit exclaimed again. "We did it! The FBI evacuated the White House in time. The president is over in Blair House with the vice president and the members of Congress. Everyone is safe."

Tom and Billy looked from Whit to the FBI agents and back again. "He's right," said Agent Fitts with a smile. "We reached the White House in time to get everyone to safety. Having Whit call Veitch while you and Billy tackled Custard and company was a smart move, Tom."

"Talk about lucky," said Tom. He grinned at his brother. "I told you Moore's luck would show up when we needed it."

"Yeah, right," said Billy, slapping his brother on the back. "Moore's luck to the rescue." He high-fived Whit who couldn't stop smiling.

"I think there was more than luck involved," said Agent Veitch. "You boys did some fine detective work to figure out what Buttman's plan was—and then thwart it."

"We thought we were too late," said Tom. He lowered himself to the curb and rested his head on his knees. No one spoke for several seconds.

"It's OK, big brother," said Billy, reaching out a hand to console Tom. "All's well that ends well."

"Right," said Whit. "But, it's way past lunchtime. All would end better if we got something to eat."

The joint session of Congress went ahead without a hitch. The next day the Hardly Boys and their chum Whit headed back to Baymoor, tired but happy. DeVern Hardly stayed in Washington a few days for a debriefing with the FBI and other law enforcement agencies. He also met briefly with the president.

He returned to 223 Baker Street one evening just

before supper. Hazel and Miss Jane had cooked a special meal, complete with a cake decorated with the words Welcome Home. He took his boys aside before supper.

"Clive Custard, his henchmen, and the Trafalgar sisters are safely behind bars," said the renowned detective.

"What will happen to Sonny Stufflebean?" asked Billy.

"I don't understand how he ever get mixed up with the Buttman crowd," said Tom. "He seems more like a two-bit shyster than an international arms dealer."

"He knew about the underground cavern at Blackbeard's Island," said Mr. Hardly. "Custard recruited Stufflebean after he overheard him talking about the cavern to some of his cronies at the Thirsty Eye. The regrettable Mr. Stufflebean was indeed in way over his head."

"What will happen to him?" Billy asked again. "He may not be an international arms dealer, but he's a very unsavory character."

"I don't know, what will happen," replied Mr. Hardly. "He's going to turn state's evidence. But since he knew nothing about the weapons or the germ warfare agent I don't know how helpful his testimony will be."

He headed for the door of his study. "I'm proud of the part you boys played in this adventure. But our work is not finished. Captain Moses Folsom is still at large, as is the criminal mastermind George W. Buttman. I've been after Buttman for more than a year, and he has eluded me once again. I am still on the case and may need your help in apprehending this villain. He must be caught."

"We'll be ready, Dad!" the beaming lads cried in unison.

The two Hardly boys made their way toward the dining room where Hazel and Miss Jane waited to serve up the delectable repast they had prepared for their menfolk.

But, just before entering the dining chamber, Tom and Billy stopped short. Seated at the table were Jessa and Anne, eagerly awaiting them.

"Gads!" Tom whispered to his brother, grabbing him by the sleeve and pulling him back into the hall. "You know, it's been days since I gave any thought to the girls' invitation to spend a private weekend together."

Billy gulped. "Me, too," he admitted.

Tom shuffled uneasily. "Do you think there's something...wrong with us?" he asked.

Billy studied on this and then smiled. "Not necessarily," he said. "Maybe it's not so bad to be..."

"...50's guys, if you please ... Just 50's guys, we don't apologize..." they chorused.

Slapping each other on the back, they entered the dining room, Billy quipping to Tom, "Jinx, jinx, you owe me a Coke!"

Just before Christmas, Tom, Billy, and Whit, along with their friends and family, were invited to a ceremony at the White House. After receiving the thanks of the president on behalf of a grateful nation, the Hardly boys and Whit returned to Baymoor. Before long they would be deeply involved in their next caper, which would come to be known as *The Mystery of the Unfortunate Mouse*.

Do you have a story to tell?

CPSIA information can be obtained at www.ICGtesting.com
Printed in the USA
BVOW080341081112

304981BV00002B/1/P